A Little Bit Extra

For those that haven't found their "thing," it's never too late.

1
CASSIE

"Cassie Mitchell, I better not find you moping back there. Your shift hasn't even started." A familiar voice echoes through the kitchen of Dave's Diner.

With a groan, I lift my head from my hands. When I entered the diner, I made my way to the break room to clock in, avoiding everyone on my way through the restaurant.

I glare over to my left and see my best friend and roommate Lucy staring at me. She's standing with her left hand on her hip, the other holding her notepad and pen. For being at work a few hours before me, she's rather chipper. The opposite of how I'm feeling right now.

Working at a 24-7 diner was never part of my plan. The plan was simple: move to Los Angeles, join an acting group, be wary of distractions, and secure a lead role. But here I am five years later, having only checked off the first two items on my list. The last task I feel like doing right now is pretending to smile at customers and taking their orders. After a day of rehearsing lines, I'd rather be at home, in my pajamas, watching a movie, and devouring a pint of ice cream.

I shake my head and sigh. I've been at the diner for five minutes and I'm already wishing I could clock out. "Just exhausted. I spent, like, the last five hours rehearsing dialogue, and I still feel like a robot trying to run these damn romance lines."

I grab my apron from the hook, wrap it around my waist, and secure it with a bow.

"My offer still stands! I'd *gladly* stand in as your man."

I peer at Lucy and shake my head again. If I had a dollar for every time she offered to rehearse lines with me, I could hire someone with acting skills to monologue with. I wouldn't have to rely on myself, her, or anyone from my acting class. I needed someone in the industry that knew the best way to deliver a scene.

Too bad I swore off all industry guys. Frustrated by the repeated instances of betrayal and being objectified, I finally reached the breaking point and decided it wasn't worth the distraction. I won't subject myself to the ongoing accusations of receiving roles solely based on my personal connections with people involved in the film. I've been chasing this dream for too long to let others continue to ruin it.

"Thanks Luce, but you're not my type." I chuckle. "I know I'll be fine. I just need a little more time." And honestly, a bit of confidence.

"That's the attitude! Now come on, if we don't get out there, Dave's going to be yelling for us. Tonight's extra busy."

Lucy turns away from me, walking through the kitchen toward the front. I groan, rolling my head in a circle before following her.

"Why is it so busy tonight?" I ask as we reach the bar. I survey the dining room and realize there is a customer in nearly every seat. The diner is small, filled with a mix of booths and 4-top tables, enough to fit 100 people on a good night. Movie posters line the walls, paying homage to the history of the area. It's 9 p.m. on a Sunday night in early June, typically a slower shift. My preferred type of shift. It shouldn't be a full house. It takes everything in me to not roll my eyes and groan again at the sight of all the people.

"New movie!" Dave says as he appears to my right with a tray full of appetizers and drinks. "It films next week. Didn't you get my memo?"

Dave doesn't wait for me to respond before he shimmies past me and makes his way from behind the bar into the dining room. Of course I didn't read his memo. No one reads email anymore when our inboxes are full of daily ads from fast-fashion retailers. I only use my inbox to filter audition requests, of which lately I've had zero.

I should have known a new movie was starting up. Every few months a new one begins filming, bringing more customers into the diner like clockwork. Dave's Diner is located across the street from January Studios, which often means longer and additional shifts to accommodate the sudden influx of patrons.

"Yeah, Cassie, didn't you get his memo?" Lucy mocks.

I glance at her, my eyebrows scrunched. "Shut up. You didn't notice either."

With a smirk, Lucy shrugs and walks into the dining room, heading to her tables. She seamlessly transitions into refilling drinks and asking if anyone needs anything. I laugh at how quickly she can switch to her server voice, which is at least two pitches higher than her normal voice, as she moves from table to table.

"Cassie! I sat a couple for you in your section!" Madison, the host of the month, yells to me from halfway across the room. I respond with a slight nod and a thumbs up.

Same shift, different day. I glance at the couple before walking to greet them. They're both looking at their phones, sitting on opposite sides of the booth, and not saying a word to one another. Typical.

After working many, many nights, I've perfected my routine. Smile at the customer. Take their order. If I don't write it down, I will *absolutely* forget it. I fill my brain to the brim with monologues, leaving no space for anything else. It is beyond my capacity to remember whether someone wanted onions on their burger. Place the order. Refill drinks. Smile more, I need the tip money after all. Bring the check. Repeat.

This routine keeps me from needing to overindulge our customers in conversation and maintains the barrier between us. It wasn't always this way. At first, I figured working across the street from a studio would mean more opportunities for connections, right? *Wrong*. Nothing, zip, nada in all my night shifts. Just staff workers and tourists hoping to spot a celebrity.

I pat the front of my apron to make sure my notepad and pen are inside and head toward the table. Noticing my approach, the woman puts her phone down and meets my gaze with a smile. I immediately have two thoughts about her. My first thought is that her favorite color *has* to be purple. She has purple glasses on to match her purple shirt, and her hair is a light shade of pastel purple. My other thought is that I feel bad for her because this seems like a date, yet her partner on the other side of the booth remains face down, nose in his phone. His tousled, dark brown hair falls to conceal his forehead.

I take out my notepad and pen and flip to the first empty page. "Hi, my name is Cassie. I'll be your server this evening. Are you ready to order or do you need a few minutes? Our specials tonight are on the back of the menu."

"I'll just take a water for now, thanks." The girl softly smiles. She turns to face her partner, waiting for him to tell me what his preference of beverage is. After a few moments, I guess she kicks his foot under the table because he grumbles.

At last, he locks his phone and places it in his lap. Still not looking up, he peruses the menu, trying to find the specials I just mentioned. He flips it back and forth, once, twice, three times. I don't have patience for this. I lean over the table and point to where the specials are listed. He does the same, finally finding what he's looking for. Our fingers touch, and an electric jolt shoots up my arm, causing me to jerk away.

The man of mystery looks up at me, catching my gaze. I'm lost in his deep brown eyes, having a temporary moment of déjà vu. His lips curl up in a smirk, sending more jolts of something down my body. I have felt attracted to customers before, but this feels different.

Our staring contest breaks when the woman with him, his date, clears her throat.

"Right. Um." A soft shade of red rises on his cheeks as he glances back at his menu. "I'll just take water, too." His head lifts and his eyes meet mine once again. If he doesn't stop looking at me like that, I'll become a puddle from all of this tension.

"Great." I scribble two waters in my notepad to give my mind something to do instead of continuing to gawk over this woman's man. She's clearly irritated, and I need to get my shit together. I try to remember that part in my plan about no distractions. This is a distraction, and an off-limits one. "I'll give you two a few minutes to read over the menu, and I'll be right back with those waters." Clicking my pen shut, I shove that and my notepad back into my apron and turn on my heel to head back toward the bar.

I reach the bar and slide to the right, turning to face the computer. Clicking a few buttons, I open a tab and note the two waters. Out of the corner of my eye, Lucy is sleuthing her way around the corner.

"Yes?" I ask as she approaches before I slide to the other side of the bar to grab two cups to fill with water.

"Cassie, do you realize who you're serving right now?" Lucy whisper-yells in my left ear. I glance at her while she's smiling at a few patrons before grabbing two cups to occupy her hands.

"You know I don't," I whisper-yell back. "Just tell me so I can bring these waters to them."

A sigh escapes her lips. "Seriously?"

Based on her tone, it must be someone obvious. Unlike her, I don't remember the name of every person in this area that may come in. When I first moved, I memorized agents' and directors' faces, hoping to have them stop in for a cup of coffee and offer me an audition. I assumed someone would care enough to ask me about my dreams and find they could help me reach them. It took me a bit of time before I woke up and realized that if I wanted something, I would have to work my ass off to get it myself.

"We just watched his latest movie? The firefighter one?" Lucy is looking at me with raised eyebrows. She scoffs. "Emmett Davis?"

Emmett Davis. That explains the sense of familiarity when our eyes met, the reason I had an immediate pull toward him.

I pick up the two glasses of water and turn to Lucy, who is still standing there pretending to fill hers.

"Well, you see, celebrities come in here frequently, Luce. It's nothing new," I say as I push past her.

She follows me. "I know, I just wanted to—"

"Add some stress to my night?" I cut her off, turning my head to frown at her. "I need to go before they assume I've forgotten about them."

"No, I just think it's rare that actors are here, so it seems like fate they sat him in your section."

"Not this again," I mutter under my breath, rolling my eyes in her direction. Where Lucy believes in fate and that everything happens for a reason, I think the opposite.

Ignoring her reply, knowing she will corner me later anyway, I use my butt to push through the half-door that separates the bar and dining room. Turning in a 180, I stumble into someone. I curse, remembering I'm carrying glasses of water and fearing the worst. My fears are unfounded, though. Instead, two extremely capable hands grab the glasses as the tray slides in between us onto the floor.

"Oh my god, I'm so sor—" My head shifts to find Emmett standing in front of me. He's wearing a small smile, as if he's oblivious to my clumsy self. Turning to bend over, I reach between us to pick up the tray. When I stand up and glance back at Emmett's face, I find him staring at my ass.

His eyes meet mine, his cheeks tinted with red, knowing he was just caught checking me out. I bite the inside of my cheek, unsure what to say. This man is on a date, or something that resembles a date, and he's blatantly giving me more attention than the person he came here with.

"We can't have you getting wet while you're working, now can we?" Emmett winks at me, catching me off guard and suddenly causing me to forget the English language. He places both waters on my tray and walks away without saying another word. Pretending like he didn't just say an overly flirtatious line to someone he's never met.

My routine is all fucked up. I don't even have time to reflect on what just happened. I need to get their orders, place them, and give them the check. Emmett has become a blip in my system. Instead of yelling and throwing the tray, I smile the fakest grin to distract myself from letting thoughts about "you know who" invade my brain.

Following Emmett to the booth, I place the glasses in front of him and his date. I try my best to avoid eye contact, but I feel the weight of Emmett's stare. When my gaze finds his, a small smile appears on his face. Quickly, I look away, not wanting to blush. What is happening to me? Why am I feeling butterflies from our minor interactions?

I reach into my apron, grabbing my notepad and pen. I flip back to the page with their drink order. "Are you ready to order food, or do you need a few more minutes?"

Luckily, they're ready. I quickly scribble their food order and tell them it will be out in a few minutes. After I place the order at the bar, I check on my other tables. My feet are tired and I still have three hours left in my shift. I am not used to being this busy, but luckily most of my tables have their food, so I just need to refill drinks and make sure everyone has what they need.

I reach the bar for what feels like the 100th time this evening and am alerted that Emmett's food is ready. I pick it up and take not even one step toward their table to deliver it when my watch buzzes with a call. I glance behind me, to my right, to my left, trying to find someone to ask to take my tray. I spot Lucy at the register checking her phone discreetly. Perfect. I hand her my tray, thank her profusely, and push through the door to the kitchen, walking toward the break room. I pull my phone out of my back pocket and press accept on the call from an unknown number. I could have let it go to voicemail, but if someone is calling me about an audition, I don't want to miss it.

"Hello?" I say into my phone, taking a seat in the chair in front of the computer. I swivel to face away from the kitchen and toward the wall and cross my right leg over my left. This is probably my only chance to relax all evening, so I take advantage and sink even lower into the chair.

"Hi, Cassie Mitchell! This is Carla Green, from January Studios. Is now a good time?"

"Um, yes, now is good," I respond. Closing my eyes for a moment, I try to remember why January Studios would call me. Did I submit a tape for a movie? Or did they somehow find me?

"Wonderful. We received your application for the production assistant job, and I have to be honest, we need someone to start tomorrow and we don't have time to do interviews. I hoped that with your background in entertainment and your current experience in serving and dealing with lots of people, you'd be the perfect person for the job," Carla says.

Oh, fuck. I open my eyes and shift my body forward in the chair, my elbows finding their place on my knees, and my left hand instinctively moves to support my head. They don't want me for my acting. They want me to work there. It's all coming back to me now. Late night, movie marathon, sleepy, too many snacks, coming across a random job opening.

"Tomorrow?" Sitting back up in the chair, I massage my temple with my thumb and pointer finger, moving them in slow circles. Extra time is not something I have, but I've always wanted to work at a big-name studio. Even when I was a teenager and just acting for fun, I dreamed of working at one. When I found out Lucy lived down the street from January Studios, it felt like fate. Fate and I might not mix, but I know Lucy would tell me otherwise and that I should take this call as a sign. This is the first time in five years that they have had a job I was qualified for and would work with my schedule. It could lead to something more than working at this diner.

"Yes, tomorrow morning at nine. Can you be here?"

"I can, yes." I shift in the chair, crossing and uncrossing my legs. The weight of my schedule lays heavy in the pit of my stomach.

"Great. I'll send you an email with some details! See you tomorrow!"

After exchanging our goodbyes, we end the call with a final click. The urgency to return to my tables leaves little room for deep reflection on the matter.

When I reach the front, I notice Emmett hasn't left.

Lucy's voice comes from my left as she enters an order into the register. "I checked your tables for you."

I lean my back against the counter.

"Thanks, Luce."

"Mhm. Who called?" Lucy turns and mirrors my position on the opposing counter.

"Remember that time we came home late from work last week and felt it was a great idea to watch a movie until 2 a.m.?"

Lucy nods, her lips curving into a small, knowing smile.

"Well, you're looking at the newest production assistant at January Studios." With a shrug, I lift off of the counter, walking toward the half-door in the bar.

Lucy follows me, laughing at my impulsive self. "Goodness Cass, only you."

She's not wrong. I've made countless impulsive decisions. They don't always involve a new job. Sometimes they're ordering something we see on TV infomercials, giving into the ads, other times it's deciding to apply to foster a cat before remembering I'm allergic. And yes, these decisions happened after midnight when we were both too tired to think straight. I had a hard time remembering that actions led to consequences. That's what happened with the production assistant job. I thought it'd be fun to work there. Maybe I'd get to see a few films being made, maybe meet some people, make some more friends, who knows? I submitted the application and went immediately to sleep and didn't think about it again until tonight.

I glance around the dining room, prepared to go check on Emmett and his date, but he's sitting by himself. I stride over to him, notepad in hand, giving myself something to fidget with when I feel uncomfortable. He doesn't make me uncomfortable, it's the situation. The thoughts in my head telling me he's just smiling to be nice or the sudden feeling of how tight my shirt is in all the wrong places.

"How is everything?" I ask as I approach, choosing to stand next to the empty side of the booth. It's the farthest I can be away from him without looking strange.

Emmett glances up at me from his phone. As he smiles, a warm flutter washes over my chest. I remind myself he is off-limits because of his girlfriend, or date, or partner, or whomever was taking space in this booth a bit ago.

"You're back." He drops his mouth open and nervously chuckles. "I mean, the other server was great. Everything is great. The food is great."

Awkwardly laughing back, I say, "Great."

I stare at him for a moment too long and search his face to remember why I came over to his table. My body feels like a furnace. His eyes dance over me, and our gazes eventually meet, but not before I catch him biting his lip. Biting back something he wanted to say, perhaps?

As if the universe senses I need help, the sound of Lucy calling my name travels across the dining room, breaking the trance.

In a swift motion, I break our eye contact and look toward the bar, where Lucy's raised eyebrows meet my gaze. My eyes move to my notepad, where I had previously scribbled Emmett's order. Right. The last step of the routine, the check. Without shifting my focus, I ask the question. "Are you ready for the check?"

"Actually, would you like to join me?" His question prompts me to look up, and I find him gesturing toward the empty seat in front of him. The same seat his date had been sitting in.

I glance back and forth between him and the empty bench next to me. A million questions race through my mind. The main two: was he not on a date and is he actually flirting with me?

"Oh, Marcy left." That's all he says, as if I'm supposed to know who Marcy is and why she was at the diner with him. Nope, not going to ask. It's too early to take a break. I have too many tables to tend to. I can't succumb to the tempting chemistry between us tonight.

"I'm sorry," I mutter, feeling a mix of flattery and frustration. "I'm working right now, so I can't." I steal a quick look at the bar and then back at him, hoping he'll understand.

"Oh, right," he laughs. His eyes briefly flicker to his plate. "Well, I'll take the check then, Cassie. Thank you."

Biting back a smile, I sense a blush creeping up my cheeks, radiating heat. I quickly nod and pivot to walk to the bar.

Lucy corners me at the register as I'm closing out the tab.

"What was that about? You looked like you were going to pass out," Lucy says.

I give her my best side-eye and murmur, "It was nothing."

I continue to close Emmett's tab. When I raise my eyes to the dining room, I'm met with his intense stare, a surge of electricity rising between us. If my cheeks weren't red before, they sure are now. I turn around to grab the receipts out of the printer and feel Lucy at my side.

"That is not nothing." Lucy is back to whisper-yelling at me.

I turn to her. "Shush. I'll tell you at home."

I return to Emmett in the dining room and hand him the check.

My back straightens, trying to maintain a professional stature, as I smile and say, "Here's the check! Thank you for dining at Dave's."

Emmett casually hands me a crisp one-hundred-dollar bill, more than enough to cover the meals they ordered.

"I'll grab change," I say.

I take two steps before a grasp tightens on my left wrist.

With a quick pivot, I redirect my attention and cast my eyes downward, only to discover that the hand that had clasped on to me belongs to none other than Emmett.

"I don't need change," he replies.

My cheeks are now tingling and becoming increasingly hot. Wonderful.

I don't respond, but I also don't move. He shimmies out of the booth, still holding my wrist, finally letting go when he's inches from me. Standing next to him, my head would fit right in the nook of his chest.

A car flashes its lights on and off, the light radiating off the front windows and into the dining room. Emmett turns his head for a moment to look behind him at the door.

"That's my ride," Emmett explains, averting his gaze momentarily to the floor and then back to me. "I'll see you around, yeah?"

He most definitely will not see me again, but I nod anyway. It's the least I can do after it seemed as if we were feeling the same attraction to one another. Emmett stalls for a moment before nodding back and giving me a slight smile. He turns around and walks out the door, turning his head to look at me once more before finally exiting the building. For a moment, it felt as if none of this was real and he was about to run toward me and profess his love.

Except this is real, and I have to get back to work. It's rare for a celebrity to dine with us, especially when every American household knows their last name.

Tomorrow I will start a new job at the film studio, continue avoiding distractions, and land a major role. Those are my only goals for this year. I know it's June, and that's six months late for New Year's resolutions, but I can do it. One day at a time. Stick to the course, dedicate more time to acting, and don't fall for anyone who works in the industry. Yeah, I can do that. What's the worst that can happen?

2
CASSIE

January Studios is one of the best film studios on the west coast. It just so happens to sit across from Dave's Diner and right down the street from my apartment. It felt like fate when I first moved here, to live so close to a place that could be where I act in my debut film. Well, that was many years ago and now I'm questioning if I even want to be an actor.

Have you ever had a dream that you've been chasing for a while and nothing seems to happen with it? No matter how many times you wish for it or try to manifest it, it feels like the world is working against you? Well, that's how I feel. I've landed a few smaller parts and a few commercials, but I haven't found a role that fulfills me. A role I can look back on and feel grateful for because of all the opportunities that came from it. Instead, my resume contains low-budget films and my acting showcases.

This job at the studio may not lead to anything, but at least it will be something different. I love working with Lucy, but the late-night shifts at the diner are not my favorite.

I pull into the studio, drive to the employee lot, and park in the designated area for production. Carla included exceptionally detailed instructions in the email. I'm 30 minutes early. When I woke up this morning, a wave of anxiety washed over me, clouding my thoughts about my first day. I hoped arriving early would help ease some of that.

I get stopped by the doorman when I enter the building. I find out his name is also Dave. Dave the doorman. Cute. Although I already know where to go based on the email, I explain that I'm new and trying to find Carla, and I let Dave point to where I need to go for reassurance. He tells me I should pass through the door, head up the stairs on the right, and Carla's office is the first door on the right. If I continue going straight instead of up the stairs, it will eventually lead me to the set, he says.

I put on a fake grin and say thanks, trying to hide the fact that my chest is tight and my fingers won't stop fidgeting. I try to only focus on my excitement as I step into the studio.

I find the office easy enough. The door is wide open and there's a woman sitting at the desk at the back of the room.

Her mocha hair, curled to perfection, drapes over her shoulders as she leans over the desk. She's flipping through pages attached to a clipboard.

"Hi, Carla?" I ask. I don't want to assume that she's Carla, but she is the only person in the room, so it seems like a safe bet.

She looks up, eyes wide, mouth broken into a huge grin. She waves me over to sit.

"You must be Cassie! You find the office okay? I hope Dave didn't give you too much trouble down there."

"Oh, yes, easy enough. Thank you for the detailed email. It helped," I say as I take a seat across from her.

"Great, great. Okay." Carla flips through a few more pages on her clipboard before taking them off and handing them to me.

I look at the pages to find a schedule.

"That is the schedule for this week and next. Marcy will–" Carla says.

"Marcy will what?" A voice comes from behind us.

I turn around to find the same girl from the diner. Today she's wearing a purple dress to match her purple bob.

Marcy's eyes widen, and she points to me with a smile on her face. "Small world, eh?"

"Indeed," I say as I turn back around to Carla's desk, my thoughts wandering to how Marcy and Emmett know each other. Marcy takes a seat on the edge of the desk, avoiding the chair next to me.

Carla looks from Marcy to me with her eyebrows raised.

Marcy sees her confusion. "Oh, right, Cassie was my server at the diner last night."

Carla slowly nods. They both look down and I realize they both have clipboards. Are clipboards mandatory here? Do I need a clipboard for my three pages of paper? I make a mental note to order one online later.

Marcy gives me the rundown on what to expect for this job. I'll come into the studio a few times a week and do normal PA duties, such as deliver mail, ensure actors get to set on time, and occasionally run errands for the talent on off hours if their driver is unavailable.

Our days should stay pretty busy, but we have downtime to sit on set in case someone needs something. Marcy wants to give me a tour, so we tell Carla goodbye, and I smile before we head out the door and back down the stairs.

"Sorry, I didn't realize it was you last night." Marcy looks back at me.

"You couldn't have known, and I didn't know either. So not a problem. I'm just happy to be here," I reply.

Dave the doorman waves to us as we pass him and head down the long hallway. There are posters on either side from movies that were filmed at the studio, similar to the ones at the diner. There are also photos of staff and cast for some of them with autographs from the principal actors. I look at them and my arms prickle with goosebumps. I know that many movies are filmed in California, especially the classics, and most of them were filmed at January Studios.

I have to walk faster to catch up to Marcy, who veers to the right to follow another hallway. My gaze wanders from the bright lights on the ceiling to the staff standing around the corridor chatting with one another.

We say hello to other staff that pass by. Marcy calls everyone by name.

"How long have you worked here?" I ask. Watching how Marcy moves around the studio, recognizes everyone, and the confidence she exudes makes me think she's been here for a while.

"Um, three years?" She slows her pace to walk in line with me. "I started as a PA. Now, I'm an assistant director and manage logistics on set."

"Oh, that's awesome." I'm about to ask about Emmett, but we finally reach the set.

We walk through the door frame into a large room. To the left, there's a table lined with all sorts of food and drinks. There's also another double door, but I'm not sure where that goes. The rest of the room is full of different sets. There appears to be a police station, a café, and a living room.

Marcy leads me to the center of the room to a man sitting in a director's chair. His short gray hair matches his beard, which is trimmed short around his jaw and upper lip. He's wearing a black t-shirt and dark jeans with a white pair of Converse. He is the most stylish director I've seen.

The man smiles and stands to greet us.

"Marcy! Feels like we just ended the last film, right?" They hug. I shift from one foot to the other and glance around the room.

"Hi, Ed. Yes, it's hard to believe it's already been two months." Marcy turns somewhat to me and holds her hand out, gesturing in my direction. "This is Cassie, my new assistant."

Ed takes two steps toward me and extends his hand. I give it a shake.

"Nice to meet you, Cassie!" Ed beams.

"Likewise. What movie is being filmed right now?" I can't help but ask. I'm curious.

"You're looking at my next Academy Award winning movie." Ed chuckles. "It's about two detectives that try to solve a big crime happening around the holidays. We have a few office scenes and a café scene to film. I'm hoping for an easy first week!"

I nod and smile.

Ed turns to Marcy and asks her some questions about this week's schedule, making sure she has everything she needs. Once they align on the first few scenes for the day, Marcy lets Ed know she's going to continue showing me around.

I wave bye to Ed and follow Marcy through the double doors by the food table. It leads to the trailers outside where the actors hang out during the day when they aren't filming.

When I need to deliver script changes or check on an actor, this is likely where I will come, Marcy tells me. She points up to the mailboxes, which sit on the top of the stairs of every trailer by the main door. There are five trailers, A through E. Every mail item will have a trailer letter on it to make it super easy. So far, there aren't any tasks I don't feel like I can tackle. A lot of the job consists of checking on others, which I already do daily at the diner.

Once we pass the last trailer, there's another set of doors that leads back inside. Through these double doors is the cafeteria. Lined with large tables and chairs, the room is big enough to fit the entire crew if it needed to, but right now, there are only a handful of people since it's still early. I'm told most people don't arrive at the studio until a bit later, depending on when filming starts for the day.

"Marcy!" A tall man with gorgeous blond locks greets her.

Everyone we've run into so far has greeted Marcy with excitement, like it's been years since they've seen each other and they're reuniting. Here, it's only been a few months. From what I can tell, the people here are close, likely because it takes months on end to finish a movie.

"Hi, Tyler! Everything going okay for you?" Marcy asks.

Tyler directs his gaze at me before returning to Marcy. "Yeah, we're good. We have enough food for this week, and that's all that matters."

Tyler extends his hand to me and waits for me to grab it. "Hi, I'm Tyler."

I reach out to shake his hand. "Cassie."

"Oh, right." Marcy slaps her right palm to her forehead before taking it away. "Cassie, this is Tyler. He runs the catering here at the studios. Tyler, Cassie, is my new assistant. Don't give her shit." Marcy glares at him.

Tyler holds up both hands in defense. "Hey, it's too early for fighting."

"What's for breakfast this morning?" a voice behind us yells.

I turn around to find two other people walking toward us. They appear to be fighting about something because one of them has a clipboard and is pointing to something with extra oomph. The clipboard thing appears to stretch departments.

I'm still standing next to Marcy. I definitely feel like the newbie here, everyone seems to be such great friends.

Marcy ignores their question and turns to me. "That is Max." She points to a red-headed man wearing jeans and a white t-shirt who's easily over six feet tall. He waves. "And that is Lane." The person walking with Max is a few inches shorter, with a shadow of a beard that matches his dark brown hair. He's wearing black everything; shirt, pants, and shoes. He smiles and dips his head. "They lead casting at the studios."

I smile and say hello to the both of them, trying to contain the bundle of nerves that want to burst out like confetti. First impressions are everything, and I want to be sure that I leave a great one in case they end up hiring me for a job one day.

I don't have a lot of friends in Los Angeles. I hang out with Lucy, but she's my roommate, so I don't have a choice but to see her. I've made a few friends at my acting class, but they aren't the type of friends that prioritize seeing you. Our friendship remains mostly at surface level. There is no grabbing coffee together or hanging out outside of mandatory class activities.

Besides class and the diner, I don't have a lot of energy to give to find new friends. I would have to give up something if I wanted to pursue more friendships. Many people don't understand the hustle of trying to become an actress in such a saturated market. It's easier to spend time alone.

Marcy and I eat a little snack with everyone before heading back to set. She wants me to watch Ed film the first scene of the day. I'm familiar with small commercials filmed in dusty conference rooms or low-budget short films shot outside or in people's houses, but this is my first time being on a more formal movie set.

We move to stand by Ed and prepare for him to yell action. They're filming a scene that takes place in an office setting where the main character enters through the door and appears to be arguing with someone on his cell phone. A brief scene that will then cut to follow him in a close up by a desk.

Marcy pulls up two chairs for us to sit in.

Ed yells, "Action!"

The door flings open on the opposite side of the set and in walks one of the main characters of the movie. A tall man, dressed in a full suit, with shaggy brown hair. He's on his cellphone, like the script states, yelling about some lead that is no longer a lead.

He's walking toward a desk when his eyes catch mine.

Shit.

"Cut!" Ed yells. "Emmett, eyes toward the desk when you're walking."

Emmett nods quickly and apologizes. He glances at me for half a second, his eyes wide and his head tilted. Mocking me from last night.

I bite my lip to stifle a laugh.

They only need to run the scene one more time before it's perfect and Ed is content.

Emmett walks over to us after the scene and smiles. It's the kind of smile that is contagious, not quite reaching his eyes, but enough to cause me to need to catch my breath.

"Way to already suck on your first day on set," Marcy says, not even looking at Emmett. She's busy flipping through her clipboard and reading the schedule for the day.

"Yeah, Emmett, what Marcy said," Ed chimes in.

I stay quiet.

"Hi, Cassie." Emmett looks directly at me this time, not shying away from the fact that we have indeed met before.

Ed looks at Emmett with a cocked eyebrow. Emmett basically just admitted why he lost focus on set, and it wasn't because he forgot his lines. To be fair, I wasn't expecting to see him so soon, either.

I thought after leaving the diner last night, I would never see him again. And if I did, it would be on a TV screen when I'm on the couch watching him act in his latest movie. For whatever reason, the thought did not cross my mind that he would work out of the studio. It makes sense now, since Lucy told me there was a new movie being filmed, but when I saw Emmett last night, I couldn't think about anything other than the way he was looking at me.

A while later after filming a few more scenes, Emmett walks off the set with Marcy and me. We're heading back to the cafeteria for lunch.

"You want to join us?" Marcy asks. Emmett is walking to her left. I'm on her right.

He nods. "Yeah, I have a little bit of time."

Instead of sitting next to Marcy, Emmett sits next to me, and they talk about what they did during their time off. Emmett stayed here in his apartment, preparing for the next role since he committed to doing back-to-back movies. "Pretty uneventful," were his words. Marcy went to visit her family in southern California.

Emmett turns to me. "So, Cassie, didn't expect to see me so soon, huh?" He smirks.

I know Marcy is staring, but I avoid looking at her. Instead, I continue to stare at my salad and put a forkful of lettuce in my mouth. I give him a side-eye glare, which he must find funny because he knocks my leg with his and releases a small chuckle.

After we finish our food, Marcy asks Emmett if he can give me a tour of the inside of his trailer, just in case I'm ever tasked with running any errands for any of the actors. She was going to show me with one of the empty trailers, but she needs to go meet Ed.

I tell Marcy I'll come find her when I'm done. My heart races at the fact that I'll be alone with Emmett. I take a deep breath and tell myself that he's only being nice because it's my first day, hoping that helps to calm the butterflies in my stomach.

"After you." Emmett gestures to the inside of his trailer. He holds the door open as I pass by him and move inside.

It's bigger than I expect.

Emmett walks past me and takes a few steps to the right. He shows me the living room, which has a single couch big enough to fit a few people on it. On the opposite wall, there is a mounted TV. Emmett mentions that his gaming system sees a lot of use when he has company over in the middle of the day.

He walks past me again, this time walking to the kitchen. He shows me where he keeps his snacks and such, although it can vary from trailer to trailer.

He points out the bathroom, and that's pretty much everything. There isn't much else to it. Just two rooms and a bathroom, enough to keep the actors content during the day.

Some actors live in hotel rooms, but Emmett tells me he has an apartment nearby that he's owned for the past few years.

He looks at me. We're standing in the kitchen, and I'm about ready to head out to find Marcy.

"Want to stay for a few minutes?" he asks.

I shouldn't, but I nod. "Just a few minutes," I say.

He smiles and gestures to the couch.

I don't know what it is, but I'm nervous. My stomach feels like a swarm of butterflies has invaded and they keep fluttering from one side to the other.

I sit on the couch and take a deep breath. I know I should have left, but I figure it's good to get to know who I'm working with. Right? Yeah, that's it. It's research. Smart Cassie is taking the seat now and will have none of Emmett's looks distract her.

That is, until Emmett sits close enough to me on the couch that our knees bump. He's facing me, and his right arm is sitting on the back of the couch, bent so his head can rest on his hand.

I look over at him. He's just staring at me, not looking anywhere but my face.

"What—" I start.

"So—" He interrupts.

We speak at the same time. He nods at me to talk first.

"What do you typically do during your breaks during the day?"

"It depends. Sometimes I only have enough time to go to the cafeteria to eat. Max, Lane, and Tyler come over if I have more time to kill. Why? Want to spend more time with me, Cassie?" he asks, flirting with me.

I didn't prepare for this. Smart Cassie would think with her brain and respond with something like, 'I would love to get to know you on a professional level', but that's boring.

"Wouldn't you like to know?" I say and immediately regret it because Emmett suddenly gets up from the couch and wanders into the kitchen.

He chuckles to himself while he's perusing in the fridge. He grabs two sparkling waters, handing one to me when he comes to sit next to me again.

"I think you and I are going to have some fun," Emmett says.

I'm still too nervous to ask him what his definition of fun is. So, instead, I settle on responding with a nod.

"So, tell me about yourself." Emmett smiles.

"That's like asking me how the weather is," I quip.

"So, you're a little sassy. Got it." He winks and it's taking everything in me to not fidget, to remain still, as my stomach fills with little zaps of movement.

"I'm not sassy," I retort. Emmett dips his chin and raises his eyebrows in question. "Okay, fine." I give in. "But would you rather I be dull, Emmett Davis?"

"No, that'd be awfully boring." Emmett responds, lightly shoving my shoulder. "But seriously, humor me."

My eyes roll involuntarily, but I oblige. "Let's start with the basics. Moved here five years ago from Indiana to pursue acting. One younger sister, Annie. I normally work whenever I'm not rehearsing." I pause, taking a sip of my drink.

"Boyfriend?"

"Why? Interested?"

"Do you want me to be?" Emmett asks, his lips turning up in a smirk.

"Is this how you get a lady's attention?" I tilt my head.

"First time trying. Is it working?" Emmett shifts in his seat. He turns more toward me, his gaze never wavering from mine.

"It's not *not* working." I'm honest.

"Mhm, good." His lips curl inward and his gaze drops momentarily, then a small smile makes its appearance.

"Tell me about yourself. Always wanted to be an actor?" I ask.

"Acting is all I've ever done. My dad had me signed up for gigs as soon as I muttered my first word. But no, it's not what I've always wanted to do."

"What did you want to do?"

"Stick around, Cassie, and I'm sure I'll spill my secrets to you soon enough."

Why do I want that? I shouldn't crave more from Emmett, I hardly know him. Yet, for some reason, I'm drawn to him. More than I should, and part of me thinks he feels the same.

"Emmett." A voice echoes from the kitchen.

"My radio." Emmett looks toward the kitchen and sighs before standing up from the couch to make his way over to where the voice originated.

"Go for Emmett."

"Can you send Cassie to Carla's office? I'm assuming you're done showing her your trailer." Marcy's voice echoes from the speaker. She doesn't ask why it was taking so long to show me the 300 square foot trailer.

If she asked, what would I even say? Oh, yeah, *sorry*, I'm too busy trying to convince myself to not stare too long at this gorgeous man in front of me.

"On it," Emmett responds and sets the radio back on the counter.

He walks over to me and extends his hand toward me. I grab it, and that's when I realize that I am definitely attracted to this man.

He pulls me up too fast and I stumble forward into his chest. I'd like to say I'm surprised that he catches me, but I'm not.

"Um, s-sorry," I say and move to take a step back, but I forget the couch is right behind me.

I teeter backwards and Emmett's hands instinctively reach for my waist, pulling me back into his embrace.

"Falling for me already?" Emmett asks.

My gaze meets his, his arms still wrapped around me. Neither of us move. One step from either of us would bring our chests together. I picture myself tipping my jaw up, Emmett doing the opposite, and leaning down to press his lips against mine. My cheeks fill red from the thought. I bite my lip, which isn't smart because Emmett's eyes track my every movement.

"I should go," I force myself to say out loud.

He nods and releases his hold on me. Similar to last night, I immediately want to be wrapped up in him again.

I head back into the studio to find Marcy and find my thoughts replaying the last hour with Emmett. I don't understand how he's left such an impact to invade my every thought. I've known him for less than 24 hours, yet I find myself wanting to spend more time with him. He wasn't wrong. I want to see him more.

I've already faltered in my goal of avoiding any complications. If I looked up "Complications for Cassie" in a dictionary, Emmett would be number one, bold and underlined. I need to stay focused on my plan.

Time to put up a barrier against Emmett and keep things professional.

3
EMMETT

CASSIE JUST LEFT MY trailer and I've already received a strongly worded text from Marcy reminding me she is off limits. I text back to remind her that nothing in my contract states I can't be friends with staff. She doesn't need to know that I want to spend more time with Cassie.

I'm not looking for anything serious, though, which is exactly what I told Marcy when she asked me last night at the diner after she caught me staring at Cassie one too many times. I couldn't help myself. I was in a trance with the way her brown waves fell right below her shoulder, bouncing and swaying with every step she took.

Honestly, after last night when she rejected me, I didn't know if I was going to see her again unless it was at the diner. My friends like to go there occasionally, but I don't get out much other than that.

During filming, I try to stay home as much as possible. I only have a few key people I hang out with. Everyone else I've tried to develop relationships with just ended up using me in the end and got frustrated when I wouldn't take selfies for their Instagram page.

I like Cassie though. As friends, maybe. She's easy to talk to, and I enjoy saying things that cause her cheeks to turn the prettiest shade of red. It would be easier to ignore her, or at least calm my flirting, but I can't help it. When I'm near her, my heart strings tug to be closer, to touch her.

It'll pass. This feeling of infatuation and attraction is nothing more than a fleeting feeling because she's new and not someone I've known for a while. Our relationship stands free from the pollution of my deep-seated trust issues from childhood.

There's a knock on my trailer door before it swings open. I'm grateful to have a distraction from my thoughts.

Tyler walks up the stairs, waves, and takes a seat on the couch. He reaches for the remote and turns on the TV. I grab my drink from the counter in the kitchen and join him.

"Did you have someone in here?" Tyler asks.

"Why?" I ask, turning my head to face him.

Momentarily breaking his gaze from the TV, he looks at me. "You just have this look on your face."

"I don't have a look on my face." I look the same as I always do. Sure, I have Cassie on my mind, but that doesn't have any effect on my facial expressions.

"You're making that face again," Tyler says.

I sigh and decide to change the subject.

"First day going okay?"

He nods. "Yep, already met with Marcy and her new assistant. Have you met her? She's—"

"Mine," I interrupt, quickly shaking my head. I'm digging myself into a hole.

Tyler's eyes widen. "Cassie and you? Already? How?"

"Not like that." Great, now I need to explain. "I met her at the diner last night. She was here right before you came over." Tyler's eyes grow wider with every word. "Ugh, not like that. Get your mind out of the gutter. Marcy asked me to give her a tour of the trailer."

He turns back to face the TV, crossing his right ankle over his left knee. "Hm, okay. We can talk more about this later."

Not the outcome I wanted from that conversation, but at least it's tabled for later. Tyler knows I don't see women often, if at all. I stay to myself. My parents aren't the best around new people in my life, so I've closed myself off from forming any new relationships.

Growing up, they only supported relationships that helped the Davis name. My dad would make sure I wasn't friends with anyone that wouldn't strengthen our reputation in Hollywood, even when I was little. It wasn't enough to just be kind or fun to be around, they also had to be famous or have a lot of money. He argued it would "help my image." My image doesn't need help. I do just fine by myself. I tried to hide my friends at first, but that didn't work. The older I got, the more my "friends" wanted to exploit me and use me for my last name. I suppose that's what my dad was trying to avoid, but it didn't help me find genuine friendships until I started working at January Studios.

I met Tyler first but ignored him in the beginning. Trying to keep things professional, I wouldn't talk to anyone about anything other than work. One day, there was a knock on my door and Tyler was standing on the other side of it with a bag full of food leftover from that day. He said he heard I had an Xbox and he had dinner if I wanted to hang out. That was the start of our friendship. He introduced me to Max and Lane. For the past year, it's been the five of us, including Marcy. Best friends. Something I never thought I needed until I had it.

They all come over most days, even if I'm not here. It's the best place for us to get together on set. Tyler has an office but no couch. Max and Lane don't work out of anywhere... At least, I never see them in an office. They're either on set, in the wardrobe department, or in my trailer. Come to think of it, they might work out of my trailer the most.

I turn my head back to Tyler. "Are Max and Lane coming over?"

He shrugs. Extremely helpful.

I take my phone out of my pocket. I have an urge to text Cassie, even though I know she's still on set with Marcy. Since she's the new production assistant, they included her number in this week's memo with the schedule.

What would I even text her? I just saw her an hour ago. Would it be too soon to ask her to spend time together? This is always the time I wish I wasn't me but someone with the freedom to do things like grab coffee with a pretty girl. If I go anywhere, I'm mobbed by photographers or bombarded by people asking for selfies every five minutes. It's why I stay home often and only go out in controlled environments, like the diner, where they don't allow photographers to camp out.

I turn to face Tyler again. "What would you say about coming over tonight?"

He sighs heavily. He hates when I interrupt his show. I can see him roll his eyes before he presses pause on the remote and turns his head to me. "I would say we always fucking come to your apartment. Why are you being weird? Is this because you want to invite Cassie to hang out but you don't want it to seem like a date?"

Tyler takes the opportunity of our conversation to stand up and walk into the kitchen to grab another snack and a drink.

"Want one?" he asks, lifting the sparkling water in his hand. I nod. He walks back to the couch, hands me the drink, and sits back down. He's waiting to play the show until I answer him, not wanting to be interrupted again.

"And yes, it's because of Cassie. She's just *everywhere*. All I want is another chance to talk with her, preferably in a non-work environment. Asking her to come to my trailer during a workday doesn't seem like a good idea. I don't want to invite her over without others being present because of what happened when we were alone today…" I shake my head, blinking slowly. "I just want her to be comfortable and say yes."

"Hold up, what happened when you were alone?"

"Nothing."

Tyler raises his eyebrows, not believing me in the slightest. "Okay, we can talk about it later with the guys. I'll text Max and Lane. Now, shut up and let me watch my show." He takes his phone out of his pocket to send a message before pressing play on the remote.

I don't know how to describe the feeling I had when I was alone with Cassie. It was a mixture of *what the fuck am I doing* and *holy shit, I want this girl*. I enjoyed watching her squirm. I didn't know it at first, but I chase the red overflow on her cheeks. Observing her response to me is enthralling. It's different.

I'm used to women and fans throwing themselves at me. They don't respect my boundaries. Every time I leave my apartment and go somewhere normal, I'm always given some girl's number or asked to take a photo with them. At first I liked it. I felt wanted. That feeling is fleeting though, more than this feeling for Cassie might be.

With others, I didn't want to get to know them. I most definitely didn't want to invite them over to my apartment. The last thing I need is some girl selling my underwear on the internet and an article being written about me.

I'm going to text Cassie and see if she wants to come over. Actually... I look at my phone to check the time. She might still be here. I'm going to go find her and ask her in person. It might be harder for her to say no.

I expected it would take me a while to locate her, but I find her grabbing a blueberry muffin from the snack table. The infamous muffins, a famous pastry for all actors and staff here at the studio. Something about the blueberry to crumble ratio. It's so good.

I walk up next to her to grab one. A breath escapes from her as I lean across her, lightly brushing her chest with my arm.

"Excuse me," I say, slanting my head to look at her reaction.

She's glaring at me. I'm off to a good start.

I clear my throat and bite my lip. Why am I nervous? Get it together.

She gives me a small smile and moves away.

"Wait," I say to her back.

She turns around. Bringing the muffin to her mouth, she looks me in the eye as she takes a bite. Damn, those lips.

"Are you going to just stare at me?" she asks. She places her right hand on her hip, shifting her weight to that side.

I'm still looking at her lips. I trail my eyes up her face until I meet her gaze.

"Come over to my apartment tonight." I say it remarkably fast.

"Why—" She starts to speak, but I interrupt her.

"My friends, Max, Tyler, and Lane will be over. Um, we can eat pizza." The words spill out.

"Okay."

"Okay?" I want to make sure I heard her right.

She nods. "Okay."

Huh. I don't know why I thought she was going to say no.

"Okay." She laughs because at this point I'm just repeating her. I run my right hand through my hair and look at the floor. This is embarrassing.

I peer up to find her looking at me, biting her lip. Again, those *damn lips*. What I would do to feel my lips against hers.

Shit. I'm staring again.

"Um, I'll text you my address," I blurt.

Her brows draw together and her head tilts to the side. Right, she hasn't explicitly given me her number yet.

"Your number was kind of included in the memo for this week."

She grimaces and raises and lowers her head in an exaggerated nod.

"Alright, Hotshot. I'll wait for your text, then," she says with a wink. A *fucking wink*. I'm struggling to find the right words. It's as if they've disappeared into thin air. She smiles at me one last time before turning around and walking back to Marcy and Ed, her hips swaying from one side to the other. I can't take my eyes off of her.

Someone clears their throat behind me.

I whip around to find Max getting a muffin.

"Whatcha' doing?" He takes a bite, savoring the flavors, and lets out a contented moan. He takes another bite, shoving half of the muffin in his mouth.

"Me?" I point to my chest and look around to see if anyone else is standing by us. Nope, of course not. He just caught me staring at Cassie.

He nods.

"Why are you here and not at my trailer?" I try to change the subject.

Max raises his eyebrows. He moves around me to throw the muffin liner in the trash. We walk together toward the doors to the outside.

"I was on my way and saw you chatting with Cassie. Figured I'd eavesdrop," he says with a shrug. He's honest. I'll give him that.

I give him a pointed look as I hold open the door for him. "I just invited her over tonight and she said yes. Didn't Tyler text you about our plans?"

"Yeah, he did. I'm curious about you and Cassie, though, but we can save this discussion until we get to the trailer. Lane is also texting our group chat about it. So, you have some explaining to do."

We reach the stairs to the trailer and I see Lane walking over from the cafeteria. Perfect timing.

"Well, you all are going to be disappointed because there isn't much to explain," I say.

"Did you ask him?" Lane asks Max.

Max nods.

We all step into the trailer to find Tyler where I left him, on the couch, watching some vampire show.

"What did she say?" Tyler asks, eyes remaining on the TV.

I shake my head and sigh. "You all are going to be the death of me, I swear."

Tyler pauses his show, now giving us his full attention. I swear that guy would stay in my trailer all day and get no work done if he could. "So she said...?" He directs his gaze to me, waiting for an answer.

"She said yes, okay? Damn." I walk into the kitchen, grab a snack, and prepare myself for more questions.

"Sooooo," Lane says. "Cassie is nice."

I glare at him.

"I hope you weren't this grumpy when you were with her earlier," Max says.

"Don't you all have anything better to do?" I ask. I make my way over to the couch and sit next to Tyler. Max and Lane are sitting at the barstools in the kitchen, facing toward the living room.

"Nope," they say unanimously. And because of that, they start laughing. All I can do is laugh with them before I explain what happened.

"I met Cassie last night. I went with Marcy to the diner and Cassie was working there. She was our server."

Tyler starts to interrupt, but I glare in his direction as I talk over him. "No, I didn't know they hired her. I saw her today while I was on set. I had to film a scene twice because she distracted me." Those damn beautiful blue eyes.

"Anyway," I continue, "Marcy had me give her a tour of my trailer. She ended up staying over for an hour, and that's it. You all better not be weird tonight." I look around the room and make eye contact with each of them.

"Shit, Em. I think this is the only time you've been obsessed with a girl," Lane says.

"*And* you've only known her for a day!" Max says.

"Less than a day!" Tyler chimes in.

They all nod and laugh. Why are these guys my friends again?

"I hate you all." I join in on their laughter. "But for real, I just want to hang out with her tonight and you're all just there as buffers. Okay?"

"We met her earlier. She's cool," Max says. "We ate a snack together. Her, Marce, Lane, Tyler, and myself."

I wonder if her meeting them earlier and me letting her know they will be at the apartment later added to the reasons she said yes. Does she feel the pull between us like I do? Lane is right. I never obsess over a girl. It's always the other way around.

I'm not concerned about settling down yet. I'm only 29. I still have time to figure my shit out. When the right girl comes along, that's when I'll face my demons. Maybe I'll have the strength to stand up to my parents, especially my dad. What I wouldn't give to tell him I don't want to act anymore and follow in his footsteps. This was never a dream I wanted to chase. I never *wanted* this.

For now, I'm content. It's enough. I have a few loyal friends. I have a job that earns me money. It's a privilege to have even that, and I'm grateful. There's just a small part of me that wonders what it would be like to wake up in the morning and have someone next to me. To have that person you text when you have exciting news or when you have something dreadful happen to you. Another person who adds to your strength and multiplies it, giving you the confidence to do whatever you want to do. Maybe then I'd have the courage to chase my dream.

4
CASSIE

Somehow the day is over, and I've made it back to the car. Marcy had me running between the set, wardrobe, and offices upstairs. It was all a blur. I've never walked so much in my life. My legs are heavy, and I know they're going to be sore tomorrow.

I allow myself to sink into the driver's seat. I'm exhausted. I need to figure out my sleep schedule if I'm going to survive. I need time to reflect on the day, from working with Marcy to the surprise that is Emmett.

I thought I wouldn't see Emmett again, that he was too big of a celebrity to notice me more than once. It just wouldn't happen. I'm normal me, a simple server working at a diner. A girl with too much on my plate and hair that never lays the way I want it to. In the diner, I assumed him asking me to sit with him was him being nice? Or maybe he was lonely? Hard to say.

I'm taken out of my thoughts by my phone ringing through my car's speakers. It's Annie.

"Hello?" I answer.

"You didn't call me yesterday!" she says.

Oh, shit. I call Annie, my only sibling, most days before my shift at the diner. We're five years apart, and she still lives with our mom back in Indiana.

Annie is currently a senior in high school. She's planning to move out here to attend UCLA in the fall, but she hasn't told anyone yet. Definitely not our mom. When I left, our mom didn't take it the best. While aware of my love for acting, she thought my dream was unattainable, so she tried to talk me out of moving here. She bluntly informed me that because I wasn't from here, my aspirations of becoming an actress were trivial.

Aren't parents supposed to support and root for you? Aren't they supposed to tell you that you can do whatever you put your mind to?

Well, not my mom. If it weren't for Annie, I wouldn't have moved out here. Little Annie encouraged me and, even though she was only 13, I believed every word she said.

I wanted to achieve my dream so she knew it was possible, that you can do hard things. Failing is just a part of life's journey. You fall; you get back up. Discover the people that will support you and encourage you. You choose the people you have in your life and you hold them tight.

Yeah, it'd be nice for your family to want to know what you're up to, to ask questions, and to support you, but that's not the case for everyone. That's not the case for me. It's why

I don't talk to my mom a lot. Maybe once a year when I come to visit to see Annie for the holidays.

"Sorry Anns. It's been a busy day. Well, busy two days. I, um, got a new job?"

"You got a new job? What new job? What about the diner?"

"Still at the diner. It's a long story and my drive home is short, so to summarize: I forgot I applied for a job, and I ended up getting it. I started today as a production assistant at January Studios."

She gasps. "The studio Emmett Davis films at?"

"How do you know that?" I ask.

"His Instagram, sis. And the online forums. Seriously? You don't know what's going on at the studio closest to your apartment?"

That's what Lucy said to me as well.

"I hardly have time to think about what's going on in my life. So, no, I don't follow what's going on in other random people's lives."

"Well, then yes, Emmett Davis is filming his new movie there. Did you see him? Is he as dreamy in person as he is in photos? Ugh, have you seen his smile? I just melt whenever I see him," Annie says, practically swooning over the phone. She's definitely laying in bed, daydreaming about Emmett. This is great, everything is great. My sister is obsessed with the guy that I am hanging out with tonight. *Shit*. I just remembered I'm hanging out with him tonight.

Emmett. Emmett "Hotshot" Davis. One of Hollywood's most famous young actors. His smug smirks, dark brown eyes, shaggy mocha hair. Long enough to run your fingers through...

"You there?" Annie pulls me from my thoughts once again.

"Yep, sorry. Just distracted. Um, can I call you tomorrow or later this week? I just pulled into my apartment and I need to eat. I'm starving."

"Yeah, that's fine. I'll want to hear about your day though, and know if you ran into the hottest actor ever!" she yells into the phone.

"Yeah, yeah. Next time. Love you, okay? Keep me updated on your college plans too. Don't think I forgot about that."

Her sigh and groan are loud enough to come through the phone. "Deal. Love you! Bye!"

I press end on the call. I sit in the car for a moment now that I'm parked and gather my thoughts.

Okay. I have a few hours to decompress and rest before I have to head over to Emmett's. At least others will be there tonight, otherwise I wouldn't have said yes. I don't know why I agreed in the first place. I used to think that if I encountered a Hollywood actor, I would become even more anxious and withdrawn. Instead, Emmett pulls out the sassy side of me. I winked at him, for crying out loud. I don't wink! Ever.

God, I hope it didn't look weird. What if it looked weird and not sexy? Wait, I don't want to go for sexy either.

Emmett is off-limits. Someone I can be friends with, but that's it. That's where the line gets drawn. I am mentally putting up a tall barrier as we speak. A barrier that will be impossible for either of us to break.

A knock on my window breaks me from my thoughts. I slam a hand to my chest. What is up with people today?

"Hey!" A muffled yell comes from the other side of my window. Peering to the left, I recognize that it's just Lucy.

I grab my bag and open the door.

"Couldn't have tapped the window any softer?" I ask.

"That wouldn't have been as fun," she fusses. "First day go okay?"

We walk in step to our apartment doors. Lucy is wearing her art overalls, which are all covered in various colors of paint, so I'm assuming she just came from the studio.

I nod. "Yeah, um, Emmett kind of asked me to hang out tonight?" I grimace and look over at Lucy in time to see her jaw drop. "Is that weird?"

She holds the door for me as we go in.

"What do you mean he kind of asked you to hang out?" she inquires.

I look back at her and shrug. I don't want to see her facial expression when I tell her about my day with Emmett, so I turn back around and lead the way to our apartment.

"So, he's kind of working there? You know that new movie?"

"Yeah..."

"Well, that's kind of his movie. And um, he gave me a tour of his trailer and we got a little close and then he cornered me by the food table on set. They have fantastic blueberry muffins. Do you want to hear about those? I think they are the—"

"I don't want to hear about the muffins," Lucy interjects.

"Right, well um, so yeah where was I?" We get to our apartment, and I unlock the door to let us both in. I throw my stuff on the bench by the door and move to take a seat at the island.

"He cornered you by the food." Lucy helps me remember.

"Right, so he cornered me with the blueberry muffins and just asked me to come over tonight. With his friends, not just him. And then I winked and—" I groan and throw my head on my hands. I lift my head up and glance at Lucy. "He didn't seem repulsed by that. In fact, he was quite stunned."

I place my hands on my lap to stop myself from fidgeting. Noticing Lucy's eyes locked on me, I can only assume she's thinking of what to say. Bless her. Here I was, talking away, while she patiently listened.

One of my favorite things about Lucy is her attentiveness when someone else is talking. She's the *best* listener. Since moving in with her, I've had my fair share of tales to share. Lots of failed auditions, bad dates, and many stories to fill her in on the drama with my mom. She also gives great advice, blunt advice, granted, but it's ordinarily what I need. Everyone needs a friend like Lucy.

"So, let me get this straight," Lucy finally speaks. I sit there and nod, trying my hardest not to interrupt her. Where she's good at listening, I'm not. I'm quite the opposite. I mean, I *listen*, but I also want to talk. My brain competes with wanting to keep quiet and wanting to "help" by inserting my commentary.

Lucy leans on the counter, passing a drink my way. I don't even remember her grabbing it. I think I got sidetracked while trying to tell her about my day with Emmett.

"Emmett came into the diner last night. He asks you to eat with him, you say no—"

"Because I was working." Damn it. She's glaring at me for interrupting. I bite my lips. I touch my pointer finger to my thumb and drag them across my lips like I'm zipping them closed. This gets a chuckle out of Lucy.

"Mhm. And then you find out he's working at the studio, which anyone who's anyone would have been able to tell you. You flirt with each other alone?" she asks with a raised eyebrow. I nod in confirmation. "Alone. Then he asks you to hang out. Sounds like he just wants to spend time with you? That's not weird. He's hot, Cass. You could have some fun, ya know, you deserve a break." She walks around the counter, grabs a granola bar from a bowl, and sits next to me.

A sigh of relief escapes me. I could use a break, but then I'd feel like I was slacking on everything else. If I take time for myself to "have fun" like Lucy is saying, that means less time dedicated to acting. It also means less time to read my lines for upcoming auditions.

"I can see your mind thinking through everything," Lucy says. I peer over at her.

"You know I've been chasing this dream, Luce. I can't let up now. Even taking this job at the studio is hard because I don't know if it's going to pay off," I tell her.

"Why did you say yes to tonight?"

"I don't know, honestly. Normally, I wouldn't have said yes to hanging out with someone I barely know... *especially* someone like Emmett."

"You're just saying that because he's an actor."

She's right. I am. If it were anyone else, I wouldn't feel so off about my decision. The chances I've taken with guys in the past typically ended with me being taken advantage of, or I ended up being with guys who thought acting was just a hobby.

The last guy I was with ruined my trust in men. I know it's the same story as everyone else, but it's true. It wasn't even a genuine relationship, just someone who promised they wouldn't be like everyone else and ended up tossing me aside for some other girl one step above me. I wasn't good enough.

That was about a year ago and I haven't been with anyone since, not even for one night. It was the wake-up call I needed. I ended up taking more shifts at the diner, reading more, watching more movies, and immersing myself in the local acting scene. Nothing has happened yet, but I'm a more confident actor than I was a year ago. If I were to get an opportunity, I'd be ready for it.

"You're right, but do you blame me? Honestly? You know what I've been through," I say.

"Yes, *but*," Lucy draws out, "Emmett seems harmless."

I roll my eyes. "You're just saying that because Emmett is hot, and he was nice to you at the diner."

She shrugs and her lips curl inward. She gets up from the stool and stands next to me. "Maybe I am, or maybe I just want you to have some fun. You've been working so hard, Cass. All the past can do is hold you back. Don't overthink it. Just be friends with the man. What's the worst that can happen?"

Best-case scenario, we become friends and it makes my job fun. Worst-case scenario, I fall in love with him. There is no middle ground. I don't think I'd be able to do casual with him. There's too much of an attraction between us, and I know myself. My feelings would make an appearance.

I only spent one hour alone with the man and made a fool of myself. Smart Cassie would have said no and reminded herself that it will only be a distraction. Hanging out with Emmett will only lead to confusion and complications because of his position and status in the industry.

I smile to myself.

For once, I don't want to be Smart Cassie. I want to be *reckless, impulsive,* and *fearless.*

I'm so tired of keeping myself guarded. Lucy is right. I deserve to have fun. I'm allowed to have more friends. Just because I choose to go hang out with Emmett tonight doesn't mean anything will come of it. We'll be friends, just friends. It'd be nice to know someone in the industry that isn't a complete asshole.

"You're right. I am overthinking it. It's scary sometimes how well you know me." I laugh.

"Mhm, I know. Okay, well, I'm going to head into my room to watch a little something and rest. I have to go to the diner soon. Have fun tonight and be safe, okay? Text me if you need me and I'll come save you."

I smirk. "I'll be fine. Thanks Luce."

She walks past me, giving my shoulder a squeeze on her way to her room.

My phone buzzes on the table. I reach out to slide it over to where I can view the screen to see who texted me. It's from Emmett. He's sent me his address. He said to come over whenever, but I have nothing else to do. My stomach is already in knots, and I can't stop my fingers from fidgeting with everything in sight, so I react to his text with a thumbs up. It's enough to let him know I saw it without me sitting here for the next hour trying to think up a response to him that doesn't seem too eager.

When I get nervous, my extroverted side comes out at full force. It's why I winked earlier. I would end up texting him 10 exclamation marks and a heap of emojis.

Emmett's apartment is surprisingly just down the road from me. It only takes me 10 minutes to get there. I park in the garage like he told me. The guard at the entrance just waved me through when I told him who I was here to see, which makes me wonder if women arriving for Emmett are a regular occurrence.

On the elevator ride up to his apartment, I can't help but think about how tonight will go. I pace the length of the elevator while I wait for it to open on his floor. His friends will be there, so it will be good. I'll just talk to them all and it will be fine, yep. I don't even have to worry about being alone with Emmett.

The elevator stops and I get out on his floor. His apartment is the last one at the end of the hall. I barely get a third knock on the door before it swings open.

Emmett stands in front of me with one hand on the door and the other in his jean pocket. He's wearing a brown v-neck, matching the color of his eyes.

Emmett's gaze drifts down and back up my body. When his eyes reach mine, he smiles. "Hi."

"Hi. You going to invite me inside?" I ask.

His eyes go wide and he steps back, opening up the door wider for me to enter.

"Thanks." I bump his shoulder with mine. I suppose I'm flirting early tonight.

"Hi, Cassie!" I look up to see Tyler waving from the kitchen. I walk over to the island. "Hi." I smile.

Max and Lane wave from where they're sitting on the couch. Emmett comes next to me, leaning his elbows on the island.

I turn my head to the right to find him looking at me. "So, Cassie, can I get you something to drink?" he asks.

I nod. He pushes off the counter, which looks sexier than it should, and walks over to the fridge. He calls out some options they have stocked, and I decide on a non-alcoholic drink. Something fruity.

He hands me the can and then walks into the living room area. I follow him.

The front room is open-concept, decorated minimally with a few art prints on the wall. My seating options are either a spot on the large sectional couch or the oversized chair. I decide on the chair because it'll be easier to have conversations with others in the room.

I thought Emmett might join the rest of the guys on the couch, but he comes and sits on the flat arm of the chair. When he sits, he doesn't even look at me. He just continues to talk to the guys like it's not a big deal that I'm here.

I don't like it.

I want him to talk to me. I should be grateful that we have other people here, diffusing the tension between us, except Emmett is sitting so close to me that all I want to do is reach out and touch him. Anywhere. I want to pull him to sit next to me and snuggle up under his arm.

Emmett says my name.

"Hm?" I ask, looking up at him.

"You okay?" he asks, studying my reaction.

I nod. "Promise."

"So, Cassie, what brought you to the City of Angels?" Max asks.

Emmett leans back, catching his body with the back of the chair. He snakes his arm along the cushion, resting his hand close to my shoulder. If I shifted two inches to the left, I'd touch him. When he turns his head to look at me, waiting to hear my answer even though he already knows, I also realize that a mere foot separates his mouth from mine.

"Well," I return my gaze to Max, "I arrived with a single suitcase and a dream. I figured if I wanted to become an actress, there were limited places to do so, so I decided to move somewhere I hoped would bring me the most opportunities."

"And? Has it?" Lane asks.

I turn to him and say, "Has it what?"

"Brought you opportunities."

"Um," I hesitate, not wanting to dump all my problems on this group of friends. Emmett's hand comes in contact with my shoulder and he gives it a light squeeze. All eyes are on his hand touching me. Claiming me.

"I've been in a few things, but I'm determined to land something larger." I smile softly, also remembering that Max and Lane could one day hire me.

"Sometimes it takes a while. It took Max and I a few years to get our company off the ground, then when Tyler started working at the studio, he brought us on," Lane says.

"And the rest is history," Max chimes in.

"Have you all been friends for long?" I ask, looking around the room to each of them.

"We have been," Tyler says, gesturing at Max and Lane. "Emmett is the newest addition to our crew."

Emmett leans toward me, his mouth inches from my ear, and whispers, "They forced me to be friends."

I bite my lip to stifle a laugh as the guys talk about some memories from working together at the studio.

They try to tell me embarrassing stories of Emmett, but that gets shot down. All it takes is a glare from Emmett and their lips zip shut.

I'm having so much fun that I don't realize it's past midnight. Max and Lane left an hour ago, so it's just Tyler, Emmett, and me.

"I think I'm going to head out. You two going to be okay?" Tyler asks with raised eyebrows.

I look at Emmett. Emmett looks at me.

I look back at Tyler. "Yeah, we'll be okay." I smile.

Tyler winks at Emmett. Goodness. You'd think we were high schoolers being left alone for the first time. It feels like that a bit. This little crush that I'm trying hard to push down is slowly making its way to the surface.

It doesn't take much for my stomach to flutter. The entire night Emmett has been doing things that make it hard to ignore him. Every glance and small touch is enough to drive me insane.

With Tyler gone, we both just stand facing the front door. I suddenly realize he may want me to leave soon also, since it's getting late.

"Do you want me to leave?" I turn to face him to try to read his expression.

His eyes are soft. His lips curl into a smirk, the kind of smirk that makes my stomach do flips.

"No, I don't want you to leave, Cassie. Do you want to leave?" He poses the question as he walks past me into the kitchen.

I turn around and follow him.

"I should leave, but no."

Emmett glances over his shoulder and smiles in my direction.

It seems neither of us have a clue what's going on. I know I should have left already. There's no reason I need to be here this late, but I can't bring myself to say goodbye. The pull between Emmett and me is... something else. It's clouding my judgment. It's making me want to be pinned against the counter and have his lips pressed against mine.

We move to sit on the couch, plopping next to each other. The brush of his leg meeting mine, enough to feel his warmth.

We spend the next little while just talking. I'm learning a lot about Emmett.

He opens up about his childhood and tells me about his parents. I always thought they depicted a picture-perfect family. I only saw the pictures online, of course, but they just looked happy. He tells me how he likes to write, but when I ask about it, he says it's just a hobby right now. Him opening up to me is a sign that he trusts me. Even just a little.

I tell him about Annie and how she wants to move out here this fall. I also tell him about my mom. That's a hard subject, but I feel comfortable around him. I only talk about my family to Lucy, but she knows everything about me. If I ever meet someone new, they don't get to know me like this. They get the public-facing version of myself and not my inner demons.

The Emmett I'm getting to know is different from how I thought he would be. I didn't think he'd have such a soft interior.

His arm is on the back of the couch, and his fingers lightly caress my shoulder. I let him. It's comforting. He's not trying to make a move or push any boundaries. His affection is subtle, yet endearing and intentional.

I don't know what I'm going to do about Emmett, but I hope we get to have more nights like this.

5
EMMETT

THE SUN PEEKS THROUGH my curtains, blinding me as I squint and find myself not in my bed. I'm still on the couch. I try to move my left hand, but it's trapped. *What the...*Oh. Right. Cassie.

We talked into the early hours of this morning. She asked for a blanket at one point and eventually asked me to move over so she could lie down. Her head started next to me, but during the night, she shifted it to rest on my lap.

I free my hand without her stirring and trace the pattern of freckles on her arm. She slowly blinks awake. Her eyes go wide as her gaze meets mine.

"Ah!" she yells and rolls backward, landing on the floor at my feet.

I lean over, place a hand under her arm, and help her back onto the couch. She pulls both of her legs up, sinks her elbows on either leg, and places her head in her hands.

Cassie turns her head to the right, enough to peek at me. She's blushing. "Well, I guess we fell asleep, huh?"

"Seems that way." I smile at her.

Standing up from the couch, I make my way to the kitchen. "Coffee?"

"Please," she replies, throwing her head back on the couch with an exhausted sigh.

I make a pot of coffee, clicking the 'bold' button to brew it extra strong. I don't remember what time it was when we eventually fell asleep, but it was late.

"How do you take your coffee?" I look over my shoulder to ask her.

"Black is fine," she answers.

This morning I'm immensely grateful for a coffee machine that only takes a few minutes to make a half pot. I walk back with a cup in either hand. She takes one from me and brings the mug to her nose and inhales deeply. With her eyes closed, a small smile plays upon her lips.

"How do you take yours?" She opens her eyes to look at me.

"Black with two sugars," I reply, sitting back in the same spot on the couch.

"Hm. I'll have to try that next time we hang out," she says and immediately looks at me. "I mean…"

"Next time." I smile and bring my mug up to my lips to take a sip.

She nods.

We take a few moments to sit in the silence. I enjoy having her here. It's similar to when we were alone in the trailer and last night, but this feels sacred. No one knows she's here. It's a secret between the two of us.

"I want to see you again." Cassie looks up at me. "Alone, preferably," she adds.

"I'm sure we could arrange that."

She's got a smug look on her face, and I want to wipe it off with my lips.

Cassie's phone buzzes. She groans, sets the coffee on the table in front of us, and starts typing furiously. After she sends the message, she sighs and leans back.

Her head rolls back to the right to look at me. "My roommate, Lucy, she, uh, knows I was here last night and sent me a text to make sure we were... safe." She bites her lower lip, but doesn't look away.

I laugh, which earns me a glare and a light punch in the arm.

"I should probably go, though. We have to be at work in a little while," she says.

"Maybe you could come back over tonight?" I ask, knowing it's a long shot. After hesitating to invite her over yesterday, I don't know if asking her to come back tonight is too soon. What I do know is I don't want to go to work. The thought of staying here and holding her close, maybe with her on my lap, is much more enticing. I want to trace every curve of her body with more than just my fingertips, feel the warmth beneath my touch. I want to hear the little noises she makes when I find the spots that give her pleasure.

I want her to want me.

I have never wanted someone like this. It's baffling to be obsessed with someone's thoughts and opinions shortly after meeting them, but that's how I feel. It's quite terrifying, actually.

Cassie stands up from the couch and offers me her hand, which I accept. She pulls me up, and I find myself mere inches away from her. I'm not sure what she wants me to do. I want nothing more than to press my lips against hers and find out if our kiss is as electrifying as I'm predicting it will be.

She surprises me by taking a step forward toward me. She wraps her arms around my waist and pulls me into a hug. I take a deep breath and realize that it's been a long time since I've hugged someone. Genuinely hugged someone. Not a side hug or a quick goodbye hug to my mom. Hugging Cassie feels like I've taken a blanket fresh from the dryer and wrapped it around myself, losing myself to the warmth.

She lets go of me, and naturally I do the same. She still hasn't answered my question and I've yet to speak. My patience is hanging on by a thread. I'm aching to know what she's going to say. I realize that makes me sound like a teenage boy that just found out girls don't *actually* have cooties.

Cassie walks over to the front door, slips on her sandals, and grabs her bag. She turns around to face me and that's when I realize a light pink has crept onto her cheeks and she's staring at me with soft eyes. "What time?" she asks.

"What time?" I'm entranced by her staring at me. I somehow forgot what we were discussing. Her touch has a way of drawing my attention away from everything else, and I find myself missing it.

Cassie places a hand on her hip and rolls her eyes. "You're going to have to keep up with me, Hotshot."

The way she calls me 'Hotshot' fuels the fire in my gut. The nickname is a tribute to a past role of mine, and the way she says it makes me want to slam her against the door and claim her as mine.

"6 p.m. Don't be late," I respond.

"Or else?" She wiggles her eyebrows.

I groan, which causes her to laugh. Our emotions feed one another.

"See you at work, Emmett." She smiles and exits my apartment, glancing back at me one last time before shutting the door.

That girl.

I slump back on the couch and take a few minutes before I have to get ready to leave for the studio. I already know Cassie is going to be a distraction for me today, but I don't mind. In fact, I welcome it. After we spent all night talking, I'm excited for the day to go by quickly so I can be with her again tonight.

Talking to her was easy. I wanted to tell her things, to open up about my life. I even told her I wrote stories, but I haven't told her I would love to chase that dream and pursue it full time.

The timing was never right. When I was younger, my dad found a script I wrote and yelled at me to explain myself. He called me childish to think I could do anything without his backing and said he wouldn't support me doing anything other than acting. To him, the Davis name would disappear if I didn't follow in his shadow.

I tell myself that one day I can do something for myself. I'm content for now. In fact, I should feel pride in the work that I've done as an actor after hearing that Cassie has been trying to land something ever since she moved here.

I only glimpsed her past and know she's had bad luck with men in this industry. She even made me pinky swear (yes, clasp our pinkies together and all) that I would not bring this up to anyone and would not use my position as an already successful actor to help her.

Normally, it would have thrilled me to have someone open their heart up and not expect anything in return. With Cassie, I would have called any contact I had and gotten her auditions the next day. Even though I won't do that, I did secretly cross my fingers behind my back in case I decide to break that promise at a later date for a good reason. I can't promise something to her if there's a possibility I won't have the chance to keep it.

For now, though, I let her have the satisfaction of knowing I won't do anything to help her succeed. She's prideful and wants to achieve something herself. It's hot. She's full of ambition, and I thank the world for throwing her in my path.

I get to the studio just before 10 a.m. and find Marcy leaning against the railing of the stairs that lead up to the door of my trailer sandwiching her clipboard under one arm. She's busy staring at her phone.

"Hey Marce," I say as I walk over to her.

She looks up from her phone to meet my gaze but doesn't smile.

"What?" I say.

She shakes her head and sighs. I move past her on the stairs, opening the door and walking into my trailer. She follows me and shuts the door behind us.

"Don't *what* me. You know what," she retorts.

I do. She's talking about Cassie and the fact that she came over yesterday. She doesn't know she stayed over by accident. No one knows that. Well, besides Lucy, but she's an exception.

I walk into the kitchen and lean into the fridge to grab a glass bottle of cold brew.

"I'm sorry we didn't invite you, but you could have come over, anyway," I say as I twist the lid off the bottle and take a sip, not breaking eye contact.

Marcy is like a little sister to me. For that reason, she's a little blunt and a pain in my ass.

"Emmett, you know that's not what I mean."

I nod. "What do you want me to say?"

I walk past her and sit on the couch. I still have a few minutes until I have to be on set, but I like to get here early to rehearse lines and make sure I'm prepared for my scenes.

She sighs heavily and moves to sit on the arm of the couch.

"I don't need you to say anything, Emmett, just be careful. You know you're not allowed to see anyone that works here. It's a conflict of interest."

"I'm not seeing her Marce, it was a friendly hang out. Didn't the guys tell you that?" I fire back. I'm seeing her, but not how Marcy is insinuating. We are two people enjoying each other's company.

"Mhm." She drops her head and shakes it back and forth a few times. "You couldn't just leave her alone, huh? I knew after I saw she was the girl from the diner that this was going to be trouble."

She stands up and moves to the trailer door. She rests her hand on the handle, turning back around to face me. "You know I love you and I'm just looking out for you, right?"

"Love you too, Marce. I got it handled, don't worry." I give her a fake smile.

With that, she dips her head and leaves the trailer. My phone buzzes on the counter a few minutes later. I reach over to grab it, thinking it's just one of the guys texting me to warn me about Marcy bombarding me or something about last night.

Instead, it's a text from Cassie. I laugh.

Cassie

> Marcy has this look in her eye. Should I be worried?

Emmett

> She may have yelled at me for us hanging out last night, but no need to be worried.

Sounds like we will need to keep us hanging out a secret?

It sounds like it. I text her back and let her know I'm excited for tonight. I make a mental note to add Cassie to my list of approved people for my garage so she doesn't have to talk to anyone on her way in. It'll be easier that way for her to get to my apartment with the lowest risk. Photographers like to camp outside at random times and I'd like to avoid an article and photo with her in it.

I groan just thinking about it. I don't want to explain her to my dad. There isn't even anything to explain, and I don't even know if whatever *this* is will last longer than a week. We might hang out tonight and decide that's it. I highly doubt it, but I have to think about all the possible outcomes.

My radio beeps and Ed's voice comes through the speaker. I'm needed on set.

The rest of the day is a blur. Ed has me staying busy, helping with others and giving advice to newer actors. The more I'm busy, the less I look for Cassie. I think she's avoiding the set, though, because I've seen Marcy plenty of times. I don't know if it's Cassie's doing or Marcy's. Marcy has her way of weaving herself into my life, which I would typically welcome because she's one of my best friends, but I'm annoyed at the moment. She has nothing to worry about because Cassie and I are just friends.

Anyway, I'm home now and waiting for Cassie. I check the time on my phone for the tenth time before the display finally turns to 6 p.m. I already have dinner ready to go to the table. It's not much, but I thought Cassie might enjoy it. It's a simple summer salad full of greens, various vegetables, and topped with grilled chicken. The dressing is a light vinaigrette I'm obsessed with. I also have a variety of non-alcoholic beverages in my fridge, since I know she chooses not to drink most days.

There's a light tap on the door, which I can only assume is Cassie.

I open the door and somehow forget how to speak. Cassie is wearing a mid-length floral dress. It's a mix of light purples and pinks and blues. My gaze tracks from her collarbones, down the front of her dress, and back up to meet her eyes. She has the cutest smile. It's radiating joy, yet subtle, like a soft rainfall.

"Want to come in?" I ask playfully.

She rolls her eyes. With her right hand, she pushes on my chest to move me out of her way and walks into my apartment.

I close the door and turn around to find her staring at me.

"What?" I ask.

"This isn't a date," she says.

A challenge that I accept.

"This isn't *not* a date," I respond.

Cassie glares at me, but it's cute when she does it. She thinks she comes across as mean and grumpy, but I can see behind the mask she's wearing. She's not angry. She wouldn't have come over here tonight if she didn't want to spend time with me, so to me, this is a date. Maybe not the perfect first date, since it's in my apartment, but it has everything a date should be. Two people, dinner, and... yeah, that's it.

"Come on. Let's eat and you can tell me about your day," I say.

We walk over to the table, and I pull out her chair to let her sit. This gets a small chuckle and smile out of her.

We spend dinner talking about our day. Once again, it's just *easy*. I don't have to impress her with any stories from my past. The conversation just flows. It's not forced and I feel that the most.

I've never had a first date like this. I always feel put in the spotlight. There's this persona that I embody, and if I deviate from it, the date always ends badly. The girl would always try to bring it back around because they just wanted to go home with me. I was a consolation prize to them, something they could go back to their friends and gossip about.

"Tell me more about your writing," Cassie says as she sticks a forkful of lettuce in her mouth. We both agreed this is the best salad we've ever had.

"What do you want to know?" I ask, leaning back in my chair.

She pushes a strand of hair behind her ear. "Why is it only a hobby? I can tell you love it."

"Do I talk about it that much?" I ask. She nods and giggles. "Well, it was never an option. My dad, um, he never gave me the option to be anything other than an actor."

"And your mom?"

"She just follows the lead of my dad. We don't have much of a relationship."

"Oh." There's sadness in her voice. If anyone knows what it's like to have a dream that feels so close, yet so far away, it's Cassie. Her dream of acting has been at her fingertips, but out of grasp.

"It's okay though. I enjoy acting, I do." I try to sound convincing, but the way she's looking at me, I know she sees through my lie. "Do you, um, want to read some of my writing?"

She nods so enthusiastically that I worry she's going to fall out of her chair.

"Okay, okay, don't get too excited." I laugh with her. "I don't show many people this, only my core group of friends. This means you're included in that, so if you want to read this, promise not to sell my secrets to the media." I glance at her over my shoulder as I make my way down the hallway.

She takes her hand and pretends to draw an 'x' over her heart. "Promise."

6

CASSIE

EMMETT GUIDES ME DOWN the hallway to his office. I'm shocked at how quickly our friendship has developed. I still won't go past that line with him, but that doesn't mean I don't want to.

It helps that he is nothing like any other actor I've ever met. Sure, he's proud of his successes, but he doesn't weave his awards and movies into every conversation. That happened most of the time on dates with other actors. It was like they were always trying to one-up me.

Instead, Emmett has dreams like I do. It shouldn't be surprising, but it's hard to not be jealous of someone who has what I want. Who doesn't have to *work* for what I want. I would say that some people are born lucky in life, but there's always something you don't know.

Emmett feels like he can't chase his dream. He feels stuck, and he's having to live up to his family's expectations, even though he doesn't even seem to like them that much.

I get it though. I rarely talk to my mom now that I've moved here. It's not that we don't like each other, she just doesn't support me, and it's hard to love someone when they aren't rooting for you.

"Here." Emmett hands me a stack of papers held together by a paperclip. "You can read this. It's one of my favorite short stories."

I stand in the doorway and look around to find a place to sit. This is my first time seeing this room. When I was here yesterday, I only came down the hallway to use the bathroom.

Bookshelves line the left wall, and they are *overflowing*. There are books on every shelf, in front of the books on the shelves, and in piles on the floor. There is a desk against the far wall. While his bookshelf is messy, his desk is pristine. A laptop sits in the middle with a notebook and single pen to its right. That's it. To my right is a couch. I walk over and have a seat.

Emmett's still standing by the door.

"I'm going to make us some tea. It's going to take you a moment to read through that," he says.

"Okay, that sounds great."

I grab a blanket off the back of the couch, drape it over my legs, and begin reading.

A few minutes later, Emmett brings me a mug of tea and sets it on the end table next to me. Smells of cinnamon, ginger, and nutmeg fill the room. Chai, my favorite. It's the same tea he made me last night.

I take a sip and watch Emmett walk over to the bookshelf. He stares for a moment at the shelves, looking around like he can't find what he's searching for. I take the small time I have to appreciate the view. His hair appears effortless, falling perfectly around his face. He's dressed casually tonight, just a simple shirt and jeans, yet it accentuates all the right places and it's hard to tear my eyes away.

When he finds what he was looking for, he turns back around and sits next to me on the couch. His gaze meets mine and his lips turn up in a soft smile.

"Let me know when you're done. I'm curious to hear your thoughts."

I let him know I will, but I'm not sure I'll know how to put my thoughts into words.

I take the next 30 minutes to read through his short story. The narrative tells the story of a man who was forced to move every year. He'd make friends and then say goodbye to them. Some years he tried to maintain a long-distance friendship, but it was never reciprocated. Over time, he stopped trying. Until one day, someone took a chance on him. The story ends with the man saying yes to hang out with someone new. It was about friendship, both lost and found, and it was beautiful.

I look up from the pages when I'm done to find Emmett staring at me. He has his elbow on the back of the couch, propping up his head on his hand.

"I hope your silence means you liked it," he says. I can see he's trying to be confident but is fearful to hear my thoughts.

"I did." I add a pause for dramatic flair. Emmett knows it. He's fidgeting with the tea packet while waiting for me to respond. "I thought it was a beautiful story, and I can see you in it. I get why you act, but I could picture you writing full time if you wanted to. This story was heart-wrenching but in the best way. I felt for the characters, and I liked that although there was a loss of friendship, the main character found themselves by the end. I even liked the small cliffhanger, where you think they made a new friend, but you're not sure. It was wonderful, Emmett. Thank you for sharing it with me. I know it's difficult."

His eyes are glossy. I place a hand on his right thigh and give a light squeeze.

"I don't mean to get emotional." He laughs and wipes a tear from his eye. "I don't share this with many people but for some reason, I *wanted* to share it with you. I felt like I *needed* to share it with you. And you just got it without me having to explain anything."

He brings his left hand to clasp mine and gives it a squeeze. I want to tell him I get him, that I understand him because it's what I'm going through as well. But, I want him to have this moment.

Have you ever met someone that you just *know* will be in your life forever? You just click instantly and blend so well together. I thought what I felt for Emmett at the diner was just lust and attraction, but now I wonder if we knew each other in a past life.

We sit there for a moment, maybe too long, but we enjoy the silence together. It's a moment of silence for our dreams that feel unachievable and far away.

My phone buzzing breaks the moment. Emmett removes his hand from mine and stands up. He rakes a hand through his hair, looking at the floor with a small smile on his face. A slight tint of pink appears on his cheeks.

I reach into the pocket of my skirt and take my phone out. The notification was a text from my acting class teacher, reminding me about the reading we have tomorrow. Shit.

"Everything okay?" Emmett asks.

I look up to meet his gaze and nod. "I'm in this acting class and I forgot I have to rehearse something before tomorrow. It's been a little hectic with the new job and..." I pause and give a slight nod to show that Emmett is a recent addition to my normal mix of activities.

I stand up from the couch and hand him his story.

"Anything I can help with? I've been told I'm a great rehearsal partner."

I wouldn't doubt that. I've seen him on set. He exudes confidence with every line he delivers. He not only films perfectly almost every time, but he also helps everyone around him. If someone is struggling with a line, he's right there to help them rehearse it until they feel like they've got it. Or, if they're filming and there's a lull, he improvs. It's impressive, but I can't rehearse with him.

Trust me, I want to. It's not every day you have an A-list actor offer to run lines with you, but I don't want his judgment. I like to think I'm a decent actor, maybe not the best, since I can't even land a job, but I know I'm good. I mostly like dramas, anything that I can bring extra sass and flare to. That's what I *normally* showcase. This time, my teacher thought it'd be fun to go out of our comfort zones. She could have stuck me with horror, or action... Instead, she stuck me with romance.

Out of all genres, she chose romance. The one script that ends in a happily ever after. I stopped believing in happily ever afters a long time ago. You can only be so hopeful when your mom stops believing in you and any love interest slowly fades. So, acting with Emmett? It sounds like a dream and I'd very much like to explore that side of our relationship, what it'd be like to pretend to be other people, but I can't.

Because of that, I shake my head. "I appreciate the offer, I do, but I'm okay. Thank you, though." I smile. "I should go home, otherwise I'll be even more stressed about this tomorrow."

"I'll see you tomorrow though, right? I'm not sure when you work at the studio."

He walks out of the room, and I follow him.

"I'll see you tomorrow, yes. I think Marcy's going to have me come in most days during the week. Why? Can't go a day without seeing me?" I look over my shoulder as I walk to the front door to gather my things. I know I'm flirting, but I can't help it. Emmett just has a way of bringing it out of me.

"I'd survive." I catch him wink before I turn back around to slip on my shoes. "But I'm happy to see you tomorrow, too."

"I know." I smile smugly.

"Text me when you get home?"

"I'll do whatever helps you sleep at night, Emmett." I say the first answer that comes to my mind, which apparently has sexual undertones. Emmett opens his mouth, but immediately closes it.

I expect him to make a joke or comment on what I just said, but he doesn't. Why does he have to be so frustratingly nice? Why can't he be like every other person in this industry that I've tried to befriend? Instead, I just want to be around him *more*. I'm glad I have acting class tomorrow and a shift at the diner the day after because I'm getting attached to Emmett more than I want to.

"I'll text you," I finally say, mentally pretending I never made a sexual joke in the first place.

"I had fun tonight, Cass," he says. He's standing to the right of the door, waiting for me to leave. He has one hand in his pocket, but he brings the other to his face. He drags his pointer finger down one side, his thumb down the other, meeting them at the bottom of his chin. He does that a few times, as if moments from tonight are replaying in his head and he wants to savor them.

I take one step. Two steps. Three steps. I walk until I'm inches from Emmett. I lean forward, wrapping my arms around his waist. He takes the hint and mimics me, wrapping his arms around my shoulders.

"Thank you for sharing your writing with me," I say into his chest.

He takes a deep breath. It's the kind of breath that makes me wonder if he's been holding it in ever since handing me those pages with his most treasured words. The relief he must feel to not only hear my thanks for sharing something so close to him, but also to not be mixed with judgment or mockery for the one hobby he loves with his whole heart.

"I'd share anything with you. You only have to ask," he says. I feel the truth in those words.

It's at this moment I know we are both feeling similarly about whatever is going on between us. He knows I don't date. I know he has a past of people using him. It's kind of funny that we appeared in each other's lives and two days later seem to be inseparable. It feels like I'm in high school and I just found out a girl in my class also loves Harry Styles and reading romance novels and we become best friends instantly.

Except I'm 24 and I've fallen into a quick friendship with a 29-year-old actor that half of America loves. Most people would hear this story and wonder if we've slept together yet, especially if they hear I'm a nobody from the Midwest. They would look at us and think it's just a moment in time and I'll be forgotten by next week. Except I don't think that will happen. At least, I hope it doesn't, because I'm getting awfully used to Emmett in my life.

After I get home, I text Emmett that I've made it, to which he responds with a smiley face emoji.

I grab the stack of papers with random scenes for tomorrow's class and spend the next hour sitting in bed, reading through lines. I don't have to rehearse them a ton. Tomorrow is just a group reading. It's practice, anyway. I just like to be a bit more prepared than I would for a typical weekly class.

I've attended these acting classes since I moved to LA. On my first morning here, I walked to a coffee shop at the corner closest to our apartment and they had a flier on the bulletin board. It was one of those papers with a "take one!" written on the top and the most vague description of a local acting group. The bottom of the paper was cut into strips, just a phone number on each one. I might have been a little too trusting because of my Midwest upbringing. I took one, called the number, showed up at a random office building up the road, and the rest is history. It ended up being legit, although Lucy scolded me, telling me not to trust so openly over here and yada yada yada.

My phone is buzzing somewhere. I look under and above my sheets, under papers, and even under my legs, trying to find it. Finally, I locate it next to my pillow. Of course, the one place that's most obvious and I look there last.

"Whatcha' smiling at?" Lucy appears at my doorway.

I look to meet her gaze with raised eyebrows. "I don't know what you're talking about." I place my phone on the wireless phone charger on the nightstand.

"Hm, yeah, okay," Lucy walks past the threshold into my room.

My phone buzzes again. Lucy takes two giant strides and practically throws herself toward my nightstand. "CASSIE!" She gasps. Both of her hands hit the nightstand to stop her from falling forward. I clutch the phone to my chest.

"You're texting Emmett, aren't you?" she asks.

"Maybe." I wince.

"I thought you two weren't supposed to be all friendly and such?" Now that Lucy has caught her breath, she walks to the edge of my bed and has a seat.

I sit up a bit and take a peek at my phone. The message wasn't even from Emmett; it was from Annie. I set my phone in my lap and look up at Lucy.

I give her an *"are you kidding me?"* look because she is the only person who knows I spent the night at Emmett's apartment. Of course we're being friendly. The fact that we're texting has nothing to do with the fact that we spent the last 48 hours in each other's company. I count the time at the studio, even if I barely saw him there. We were in the same building. It counts.

"You know what I mean. Don't get me wrong, I am thrilled for you to add another friend to your roster besides me." Lucy brings a hand to her heart and dips her head. "I'm just here to remind you that *you,* "she points in my direction, "wanted me to remind you to not catch feelings."

"Luce, I've known him for two days." I don't like him like that, right? I mean, it *has* only been two days. 48 hours. It's the attraction between us, that's all. I'm a straight woman and I'd be *foolish* to not find him attractive. In fact, I bet there's a fan club for plenty of people who find Emmett attractive and haven't even had a conversation with him. Based on that logic, I think I'm handling all of this just fine. Plus, I won't see him outside of work for the rest of the week. Separation will be good, not that I need it, but to help calm whatever tension is rising whenever we're around each other.

Lucy furrows her eyebrows. "Okay, fine. I'm just doing my job as your best friend to remind you of these things. Now, tell me more about your job. I didn't hear enough yesterday." She pulls her legs under her and throws one of my many blankets over them.

We spend the next hour talking about January Studios. She asks me questions about what my tasks are, to which I respond with it depends. It depends on what Marcy is doing, who is filming that day, scene location, if some other department is having an issue, or if some actor needs something on set. We talk about the movie posters in the hallway, which is one of my favorite areas in the studio. We rabbit hole down a few of the movies filmed there, so I tell her I'll take a photo of the signed posters when I go back in tomorrow. She asks me about Emmett's friends too, but I don't have a lot to tell her on that front.

"They all work at the studio. Lane and Max work in casting, Tyler works in catering. The three of them were friends first, and then Tyler befriended Emmett a year ago when he was filming his last movie. Maybe you can come the next time I hang out with them all?" I ask, not even thinking about the words as they come out of my mouth. I don't know if there will be a next time. Lucy doesn't question my wording, thankfully.

"Yeah, that'd be fun. As long as I'm not at the studio or the diner, I can probably make it."

"How are your paintings coming along?" I ask. Lucy has a huge showcase this fall. It's only June, but she has to finish three connected paintings by October. The winner of the showcase gets a year-long permanent feature in the art gallery Lucy has been trying to get into as long as I've known her.

She sighs and leans to the left, catching her head with her hand and resting her elbow on the bed. "It's fine. I know I'll think of something. Every time I think I have something, it never turns out the way I want to once I paint. The first one is always great, sometimes even the second, but once I paint the third..." She groans and rolls over onto her back. She presses both palms to her forehead. "They don't connect. I keep trying, but every time I fail." She turns her head to look at me, placing both of her hands on her stomach. "I think it's the pressure, but you know what it's like, to be so close to having something you want for it to still feel so far away." She turns her head back to the ceiling.

I know what it feels like, except I had what I wanted before someone took it from me.

I landed a role. The most perfect role. It was a supporting role in a limited series, a small-town drama. I would have played the best friend to the main female character. I had a script, plenty of lines to pour myself into, the possibility for the limited series to turn into an ongoing series depending on viewer support.

I had the role, verbally, for a whole day. When I walked into the studio to sign the contract, I found out they cut my character. They found it a conflict of interest because they somehow found out I slept with a writer of the show. Once. I tried to tell them I didn't know he was a writer for the show before I auditioned, but they didn't believe me. Why would they? I was a *nobody*. I had no resume, no references, nothing to brag about. So, I took whatever dignity I had and left. That's why I don't date anyone in this industry. It's too easy to get burned.

"You'll figure it out, Luce. You always do." I try to reassure her. She gives me a small smile.

We only talk for a little longer before I kick her out of my room so I can go to sleep. It's getting a bit late and I'm drained from the past few days. My legs are sore from all the walking. I never understood why it could take a day or two for physical activity to set in, but I'm *feeling* it now and I'm very thankful to be laying in bed.

After setting my papers for class tomorrow on my night-stand, I place my phone back on the charger. Then I pull the chain on the lamp and snuggle back into bed, pull the sheets to my chest, and sink into them with a vast sigh. I may be friends with Emmett, but that doesn't mean I want to be anything more. I just hope he's on the same page.

7
CASSIE

I WALK INTO CARLA'S office to find Marcy sitting at her desk frantically searching through papers, grunting with every page she picks up, and throwing them on the floor.

"Everything okay?" I ask. She looks to acknowledge me, shrugs, and directs her eyes back to her stack of papers. I decide to take a seat and wait for her to find whatever she's looking for.

The phone on the desk rings. Marcy side-eyes it, but doesn't move to answer. It continues to ring.

"Ugh." Marcy picks up the phone. "What?" She keeps her tone short, not even offering a greeting. Just a demand to whomever is on the other side of the line. "You have to be fucking kidding me. What are we supposed to do, Lane?" A pause. An eye roll. "You're the one running casting. You're supposed to have a list of people for these kinds of things. Where can we find someone at the last minute?" Another pause. Longer this time. She now looks at me and widens her eyes. "Wait, Lane, Cassie will do it." She can't mean what I think she means. No. She wouldn't. It's still my first week. Marcy just smiles and nods a few times at whatever Lane is saying on the phone. "You're fucking lucky. You better have a list of people on speed dial in case this happens again. Carla not being here today is one thing. Having to deal with your casting fuckups is another. I don't have time for it."

Wait, *casting fuckup*? She volunteered me for something. She can't mean, no, there is no way she just said I would fill in for someone.

Marcy hangs up and stands from the desk. Walking past me, she heads toward the front of the room, toward the door. "Cassie, you coming?"

Oh. "Yes. Um, what am I doing, exactly?" I stand from the chair, throwing my bag back over my shoulder and rushing to meet her by the door.

She looks over her shoulder as we descend the stairs. "Oh, I need an extra today for a café scene. Lane reminded me you have acting experience." Shit. Shit. *Shit*. He must have remembered from when we hung out the other night. Just because I have acting experience doesn't mean I want to play an extra in this movie. On short notice.

"You don't need me to do anything else?" I ask, secretly hoping she needs me to do something way more important than be an extra. I'm sure someone else can do it. Literally *anyone* else.

"Nope, this is more important. Plus, you have a line or two to deliver and I don't know anyone else that works here that can confidently do that," Marcy says.

We reach the set and find Ed sitting in his director's chair, one leg crossed over the other. He's holding his clipboard with his left hand and flipping through pages with his right. His glasses are slowly falling down his nose, but he doesn't push them back. He's studying whatever's in front of him with great intent.

He finally looks to see us walking his way. "Ah, ladies! To what do I owe the pleasure?"

I smile and offer a small wave.

"Cassie here is going to fill in as your café extra today," Marcy says, glancing at me with a smile. I wonder if this is some sort of revenge for hanging out with Emmett the other night. I know they're close.

Ed's eyes widen. He slams his clipboard on his lap, followed by both hands on top of it. "That's incredible news! Cassie, my dear, have you been briefed about your lines?"

I look at Marcy, who seems to be too busy with something on her phone to even care about the conversation.

I shake my head. "No, but I'm a quick learner," I say. I'm good at learning lines quickly. You kind of have to be when you move out here. Auditions happen on such short notice sometimes. It's an excellent skill to have. Memorizing one line is one thing, becoming the character is another.

Ed briefs me on the role. I'll be playing a barista for a coffee shop, Cooper's Coffee. It's a minor scene. I have to stand at the register, take an order, and smile. In that order. Should be easy enough, considering I take orders at the diner regularly. I just need to think of this as a warmup for my acting class tonight. Ed sends me off to the wardrobe department, where I receive a tan ball cap with 'Cooper's Coffee' in red embroidery and an apron to match. I realize I didn't ask who I'm filming with. I look down at the sheet of paper with my lines. *Michael.* I don't know who's playing Michael. I shake my head. It's too late to back out now. Plus, they don't have anyone else, I'm already here for work, and I can use the extra money.

A costume designer directs me back to the set to wait for filming to begin. I had all of 20 minutes to memorize my lines and pray to the acting gods to please let me remember them. I'd like to look like I know what I'm doing since this is for a movie. Oh, my god. I'm going to be in a movie. My palms start sweating, my heart beats a million times a minute, and I suddenly feel like I can run a marathon with all of this nervous energy. This doesn't check off the "land a leading role" item on my life plan, but it's a fun experience so far.

I look around the set to take my mind off filming. It's a small coffee shop. There are a handful of tables full of other extras acting as patrons. I'm behind a coffee bar at the back of the set, with another extra who is the one "making" the drinks. I don't remember his name, but he's been working as an extra at January Studios for a few years now. He gave me a few pointers. A lot of things don't apply to me, like speaking to the crew and not making any noise when I'm not supposed to. He also said to not speak to any of the principal actors, to which I just have to smile and nod.

He doesn't need to know I'm friends with the same principal actor walking toward the set right now. Since I'm wearing a baseball cap, I don't expect Emmett to meet my gaze. He stops by Ed on the edge of the set, so he hasn't even looked in my direction yet.

The music in the café plays, and the extras sitting in chairs start talking. I quickly shake any remaining nerves off at the same time Ed yells 'action.'

I'm looking at the register when Emmett approaches. He has the first line, so I'm just pretending to clean the counter while I wait for him to speak.

"Hi there," Emmett says.

I meet his gaze. He smiles and tilts his head in confusion, but still seems happy to see me. I smile back.

"Hi, welcome to Cooper's Coffee. What can I get started for you today?" I am holding a cup in my left hand, a marker in my right, getting ready to write his order on the cup.

"Black coffee, large. Two sugars."

"And your name?" I ask.

"Michael."

"Michael," I repeat, while writing the name on the cup. I pretend to ring the order into the register. "That will be $3.50."

Emmett reaches for his wallet in his jacket pocket and pulls out $20. He hands me the bill, our hands touching a little longer than necessary, before he pulls away. "Keep the change." He winks and walks to the end of the bar.

I'm not sure if the wink was part of the script or just for me. I put the money in the register, pull out the change that was already set aside, and dump it into the tip jar. When I shift my attention to the end of the bar, Emmett's piercing stare captivates me, his eyes reflecting a subtle shimmer. This brief encounter is bound to come up in conversation later.

Emmett gets his coffee from my fake co-worker, looks at me one last time, then turns toward the edge of the set and walks out the fake door. Ed calls "cut."

We're told we don't need to film again, which I'm grateful for. This opportunity surprised me a bit with Emmett being the principal actor on set, but it was...*easy*? When he offered to rehearse with me yesterday and I said no, I never could have imagined acting together so soon. As soon as my gaze met his, I knew I'd have no trouble remembering my lines. They were at the tip of my tongue, ready to spill out. The café faded away, and it was just him and me. It should scare me how that made me feel, but I feel quite the opposite. Intrigued, maybe even wanting to do it again.

I exit Cooper's Coffee and make my way back to Ed to make sure I'm okay to leave the set. Emmett is standing to his right, peering over his clipboard to look at something Ed is pointing to.

"Cassie! You did great!" Ed holds up his hand, asking for a high-five.

I slap my hand into his. "Thanks, Ed. All of those years of acting prepared me for this moment," I say with sarcasm and a smile.

That gets a chuckle out of him. "Well, you can tell. You and Emmett are natural when acting together! I would have never guessed you've only known each other for a few days," Ed says.

I glance at Emmett at the same time he looks at me, which adds to the flush in my cheeks. I quickly look back at Ed.

"I'm glad you could fill in today. It would have been a disaster if you couldn't. If you didn't start working here this week, we would have had to delay shooting just because of how much trouble we've had with extras! It's normally not a big deal. But this movie has to do well, which means we have to cast extras with experience." Ed nods, like he was saying it more to himself than to me, but I nod back.

"I'm happy to help, Ed. I should probably go find Marcy, though, see if she wants me to help with any post-lunch tasks."

Ed mumbles something before he's back to looking at his clipboard. I give a small smile to Emmett and turn to walk off set, hoping to find Marcy somewhere around the upstairs offices. Just as I start walking, someone grabs my wrist and pulls me back. I fall into a firm chest, instinctively grabbing onto it with my free hand to regain my balance. My heart races as another hand snags around my waist, anchoring me to the person I was about to crash into.

My breathing is strained after the suddenness of almost falling. I look up to see a pair of familiar brown eyes staring at me, our faces inches from one another. All it would take is a slight lean forward from him and me stretching on my toes, and our lips would be on the verge of a kiss.

He releases his grasp, and I take a step back. His right hand moves through his hair, a gesture of nervous energy that matches the unease in his eyes. I look around to see if anyone saw, but I don't see anyone looking in our direction. Explaining to Ed or Marcy that Emmett and I are simply friends, not romantically involved, is something I'd rather avoid.

"Goodness, Emmett. You could have just called my name to stop me. It would have been just as effective," I say, placing my right hand on my hip and shifting my weight to my right side.

"I was *trying* to be secretive," he says, dipping his head and looking to the left and then to the right before returning his eyes to me. "I don't like how you left without saying bye."

"Oh, um, I smiled at you?" I shrug.

"Not good enough, Sass." Emmett crosses his arms, mocking me. How does he manage to look sexy instead of intimidating when he does it?

"I'll remember for next time. Bye, Emmett." It's my turn to wink at him before I turn back around to leave the set. He doesn't stop me this time.

I don't see Emmett for the rest of the day.

Marcy has me cleaning and organizing random offices I didn't even know existed. She's handling all the set duties for today. I don't know if she thinks I want to be away from the set since I was an extra this morning, or if she's wanting to keep me away from Emmett. Either way, I'm kind of grateful. I get to sit in the same room, with music in my ears, instead of walking around the set from one side to the other, over and over. My legs are thankful for the break.

I've been texting Emmett anyway, so it doesn't matter that I haven't seen him. He's been filling me in on everything happening on the other side of the studio: if filming is on schedule, what snacks are out on the table, Ed's moods after filming a scene. You know, the usual. Although nothing eventful happens, my stomach still flutters with every text I receive.

I text Annie too, helping her plan her move to LA this fall. We also talk about how to tell our mother, who still thinks Annie's going to be attending Indiana University, which is just a short drive from her house. Annie is a lot closer to my mom than I am. Even before she told me I wouldn't make it in Los Angeles, my mom and I never got along. She was always working, or hanging out with her friends, or doing something she didn't invite us to. For as long as I could remember, I was the one in charge, watching Annie, making sure she got to school on time. I was the big sister, yet Annie was more my responsibility than our mom's.

When I found acting, it was like I found what I was meant to be doing with my life. Even as a teenager, I knew I had to make this my career. I remember saving tips from the diner I was working at and being so proud when I finally had enough saved to take a small trip out west. I went to ask my mom, thinking she would *smile* and *hug me* and *say she's proud*, but that didn't happen. She sighed deeply, asked if I thought I could be better than everyone else, scoffed, and said, "You're going to do what you want anyway," and walked away. I packed my bags and left the next week.

Annie understands, but she also wants our mom to understand. So, her coming out this fall is a big deal. I know Annie has this big idea of us making up; her being happy for Annie, encouraging Annie, helping Annie move, but I don't see it happening.

I send her a text to let her know I'll call her later to talk about it. I have to finish up in this room and head to my acting class in a little while.

After a few more hours of cleaning and organizing, I tell Marcy I'll see her tomorrow.

I get to my acting class a few minutes early and find a seat. It takes place in a back room of a coffee shop by our apartment, the same one I originally found the paper to join in. We moved here shortly after since it was closer to where most of us lived, and being able to get coffee at any point during class is always a plus.

I call it class, but I could also call it a club. A group of people who all want to be actors. Some are from here, most are transplants. We all have side jobs in various industries: retail worker, construction site manager, bartender, bus driver. The amount of acting experience each person has also varies. One guy only joined the club because he was bored and his girlfriend was in the class. I think he's a better actor than she is, but that's my secret. There is another person who has been acting for 20 years. They typically take on extra roles or small independent films, and they always have the best advice when I try to improv.

My favorite part about the group is that everyone is honest and is there to find people that love acting as much as they do.

We have small performances with each other throughout the year, but we only do one big showcase a year. That's the one coming up at the end of July.

We start every class with a warmup. Typically, we start with a call and response game called "Big Booty," which is also Tom Hiddlestons' favorite way to warm up. We sit in a circle and designate one person to be Big Booty, aka the leader of the game. We designate a number to other players. A player will respond when their number is called and call out another player, or Big Booty. The player you choose doesn't matter, as long as you keep the 4/4 rhythm. It might sound ridiculous, but it's a lot of fun and gets us laughing, which can be important after a long day of dealing with our daily lives and problems.

After warming up, there are a few things we might do. Trust exercises or improv might be on the agenda. We might perform a monologue if we receive scripts ahead of time. As a group, we typically collaborate to plan out the next few sessions. To prepare for the showcase, we're practicing short monologues and reading scripts.

It's not my favorite. In fact, part of me wishes I could escape to the back of the room and just watch. When I was told I had to do romance for my scene, I thought I was being pranked. Honestly, I thought the teacher wouldn't give me a romance script. I knew I had to do a different genre, but *romance?* I like to read and watch romance, but romantic acting is not my cup of tea.

But that's the point, right? To get me out of my comfort zone? Make me a better actor? After acting this morning with Emmett, I'm wondering if saying no to him as a rehearsal partner was a bad idea. Maybe he could help me? It felt natural... and had the chemistry I *wish* I had with someone else in my class. No matter who I practice lines with, it always feels forced, and I can't seem to move past it. But I don't think I'm at the point where I need to look desperate for help. I'll be fine. I've been alone for this long, I can certainly navigate my way through this.

8
EMMETT

THE *KNOCK, KNOCK, KNOCK* on my front door wakes me up before my eyes open. I blink a few times, letting the sunlight bring life into my groggy body. I roll over onto my left side and reach onto my nightstand. I search through the mess, a chapstick and my water bottle topple over, until I finally uncover my phone. I look at the screen to check the time. It's seven in the morning. There is only one person who shows up unannounced this early.

For that reason, I take my time getting out of bed. I swing my legs around, step into the pair of shorts on the floor, then walk to my closet and grab the first shirt I find, a very worn Foo Fighters shirt that has a faded logo and frayed edges. I stop in the bathroom to look in the mirror. To wake myself up, I turn on the water and splash cold water on my face.

The *knock, knock, knock* echoes through my apartment again.

"Coming!" I yell from the bathroom. I look back in the mirror one last time, taking a deep breath before I turn off the light and walk toward the front door.

I turn the lock, twist the knob, and open the door. On the other side, there's a man dressed in a full three-piece suit, holding a briefcase in his right hand and a cellphone in his left.

"Hi, Dad. How wonderful it is to see you on this bright and early morning. Please, do come in," I say with added sass and wave my hand toward the living room.

He doesn't even look at me. Typical. He strides into the room, his fingers furiously tapping on his phone as he sends off a final text before acknowledging my presence.

By the time he completes his task, I've already closed the door and begun my journey to the kitchen, my mind set on making a fresh cup of coffee. I'm going to need my largest mug filled to the brim to get through whatever he came here to talk to me about.

"Don't you have someone clean this place?"

Of course that's the first question he asks. I look behind my shoulder to see him snooping and looking around the living room.

"Why do I need someone when I'm the only one living here? I can clean just fine," I mutter as I pour my coffee.

He scoffs, clearly unimpressed.

"What are you doing here, Dad?" I ask. Taking a sip from my mug, I lean against the counter, my gaze fixed in his direction.

He walks toward me now, setting his briefcase down at one of the island chairs.

"What? A father can't stop by and check in on his son?" he asks. Passing by me, he grabs a mug, fills it with coffee, and turns back around at the island, facing me.

"I haven't seen you in months, so sorry if I seem taken aback by the sudden drop in," I respond. I don't mean to be so short with my dad, but it's hard to argue against the truth. The only form of communication we have had lately is through random texts, and it has been a while since I last saw him. He hasn't checked in.

For most of my childhood, I was close with my dad. I wanted to be just like him. He would come home after a job and tell me about his day. He'd tell me about the scenes he filmed, the people he met, and anything else that went on. I looked forward to it. Then, before bed, he'd act out my bedtime stories and do a voice for every character.

Everything changed when I got older. My dad wanted me to act, which I was excited to do at first. I looked up to him. Why wouldn't I want to follow in his footsteps? My first job in a movie was a minor role. I played a little boy in a family on a summer road trip. It was a comedy and so much fun. Acting for that was great and all, but I fell in love with the script. I wanted to know who could write something so funny and intriguing. I was only 13, but I asked the director if I could see the writers' room. He took me; I met the writers, and just like that, I had a new dream.

That dream was stifled when my dad found my first script shortly after. I don't know if you could even call it a script. It was just some words on a paper that barely morphed into a story. It was more a shell of something that could have been a script. My dad told me to be *realistic* and *pragmatic* and *sensible* and all the synonyms to describe his disapproval.

That's why I stopped talking to him when I got old enough. Once I turned 18, I moved out. I only saw my parents on holidays and sent texts on birthdays. Eventually holidays turned into once a year and that's where we're at now. Sometimes I see them more, depending on if my mom asks to see me. They only live to the west, in Malibu, but I do a good job to stay busy or just avoid them.

"What are you doing here, Dad?" I ask again. It's too early to try to be nice and have a semi-friendly conversation.

"I thought we might get breakfast," he says, like it's a normal outing for us.

I suppress a groan. "Today?" Maybe he meant with my mom, on a different day, on a day that we plan ahead of time.

"Do you have any other plans for breakfast?" he asks.

"No."

"Great. Go change. We're going to Amore Bakery. I'll meet you in the car."

I offer a thin lipped smile and a slight nod.

He walks to the door, but before leaving, says, "Don't take too long," then slams the door.

Of course he shows up, unannounced, just to eat breakfast. I'm sure he wants to ask me questions about my next movie, which I haven't signed a contract for yet. I don't even know if I want to keep acting. Ever since meeting Cassie, I'm doubting it.

I find his car in the garage, open the back door, and slide into the seat. For once, he doesn't say anything. Instead, he's on his phone typing away and sighing every five minutes.

On our way, we hit traffic on I-5. I groan and slide down in the seat, knowing I'll be stuck with him for a little while.

I decide to text Cassie because I've been scrolling and my mind is still distracted from thoughts about her. Her hands on her hips as she scolds me, her eyes always finding mine, and her mouth responding to my banter like we have been doing it for ages.

Emmett

Help. I have an emergency.

Cassie

What is this *emergency* you speak of?

Emmett

I'm being kidnapped.

Cassie

And this kidnapper didn't take your phone?

Emmett

He's not very smart, I have to admit, but I'm here against my will.

Cassie

And here is...

The sound of my dad clearing his throat catches my attention, so I shift my gaze from my phone to him.

"We're here," he mutters.

Sure enough, I look out the window to see the bakery. Busy as ever on a weekday morning, and it doesn't bother my dad in the slightest. He would rather a place be busy with opportunities for press than to be empty. I'd rather have the latter. While I don't mind conversing with a few people who recognize me, being constantly interrupted to take photos while eating prevents me from enjoying myself. My body stiffens when I think of the added attention, and my mind remains on edge.

I exit the car and follow my dad inside. The soft lights of the inside compliment the soft music playing in the background. We're directed to a table by the window, Dad's signature table. Anyone can see him sitting here while they walk by, and he can see anyone who enters the restaurant.

We place our order, eggs benedict for him and an egg sandwich for me, and I'm thankful to have some food in my stomach before the interrogation begins.

"So, Emmett." I look up from eating to find my dad staring at me, a mug full to the brim with coffee in his right hand. "How is the movie going? How long is your current contract, again?" He leans back in his chair, crossing one leg over the other.

"It's going well, still early in the schedule. It's a few months long." Like any other movie.

"And after?"

"After what?" I raise an eyebrow in challenge, daring him to make a scene in the restaurant.

"You know what I mean," he deadpans.

"I have a few options, haven't signed anything yet." Not sure if I will.

"If you need more options, or advice, let me know. You might have capacity to take on two movies in parallel if you didn't hangout with those guys."

"Those guys are my friends, Dad. You've met them plenty of times," I say, rolling my eyes. Every time we talk about my career, he has to throw my friends under a rug, as if they aren't important to me.

He doesn't respond, just nods and waves the waiter over for the bill. We don't talk much for the remainder of our time together, except for our exchange when he drops me off at the studio for work.

The rest of the day goes by smoothly enough. I rarely see Cassie, glimpsing her once or twice on opposite sides of the studio. Marcy likely has her occupied with various tasks that don't include me. I believe it's revenge for spending time with her. That's okay though, because we find ways to talk to each other all day long.

I want to get to know Cassie. I want to know what her favorite color is, even though I could bet that it's blue. She's always wearing blue. I want to know what her favorite food is, whether she prefers scrambled or sunny-side-up eggs in the morning, or what her go-to activity is when she's stuck inside all day. I want to know Cassie better than I've ever wanted to know anyone, and the thought sends shivers down my spine.

Cassie has taken to calling me Hotshot, so I've started calling her Sass, as her sassy remarks seem to be never-ending. I like it. It's a nice change of pace from always hanging out with the guys.

Finally, the day is over and I'm able to head home to my apartment. It's Friday, so thankfully I don't have to be at the studio tomorrow. I get the next two days to relax and prepare for my scenes for next week.

When I finally get home, I collapse onto the couch, drained. I pull out my phone to text Cassie back, but at the last minute decide to call her.

"Hello?" Cassie answers.

"Hi, Sass. This okay?" I ask.

She chuckles. "Yes, it's okay, Emmett. What's up?"

"I just wanted to see what you thought about your first week."

"Oh, um, it was good. Exhausting. Is it always like this?" she asks.

"Yep, the first week of the job is always the worst."

The first week is typically full of stress and anxiety, but ever since I started considering quitting acting, it has been a relief. I'm still ensuring I do the best job, but I no longer feel the overwhelming need to constantly be "on" around others. I'm there to act and that's it. I know I should worry about what's next for me, but I think for a little while I'm going to pretend that nothing is.

"Well, I'm tired and not looking forward to working tonight. What are you doing tonight? Are you going to spend any time writing?" Cassie says.

"Maybe. I'll likely open my computer, stare at a blank document for an hour, and close it without typing a word."

"That's still considered writing, you know. Do you want to talk about it?"

"Yeah, I know. I'm just starting to think I don't love acting as much as I thought I did. I thought I would be an actor for life. I thought that if I did it for long enough, I would learn to love it. Or at least, resent it less."

"Does anyone else know that you write?" *Does anyone else besides her know?*

I lean back on the couch, sigh into my phone, then say, "Tyler, Max, and Lane know. But they think it's just a hobby, not something I'd actually want to pursue."

"And do you?"

"Want to pursue it?" I clarify.

"Yes. If you were given two pills; red for acting, blue for writing... which one would you take?"

"Okay, Morpheus, I'll play your game." I laugh. "I'd take the blue pill, assuming I would still have the experience from acting, but be able to pursue what I love."

"That's what I thought." I can hear her practically grinning through the phone.

"You know me so well already, Sass. I wish you were here." The words are out of my mouth before I have time to second guess them.

"If I didn't have to work, I'd be over in a heartbeat," she admits, and it does something to my chest.

"I know."

After a few minutes, we end our call because she has to go to the diner. I decide to try and sit at my computer, but it's hopeless. It only took a moment for imposter syndrome to rear its ugly head and infiltrate my thoughts. Just like that, I close the Microsoft Word document I was writing in and forget about it. Writing didn't seem like something I could actually transition into.

Not only was I feeling like a fraud in my life, I thought maybe it was too late for me. I turn 30 in a few weeks. Shouldn't I have my life figured out by now?

I know it sounds ridiculous, but you get into a routine as you get older. You go to your job that makes you money and provides a decent living, hang out with friends when you have the mental energy to be with others, and keep your living space clean. Thinking about transitioning to do something else is mentally exhausting. It's uncomfortable. But, that's what they say right—you only grow when you're uncomfortable? Well, no one ever said growing was easy.

The rest of the weekend goes by faster than it should. Each day begins with a run, then I dedicate a few hours to practicing lines, and finish by relaxing in front of the television at night. I open my computer, intending to write, but I find myself lost in old stories; the cursor blinking patiently on the empty page. I still consider it progress since I haven't opened those documents in months.

When I get to my trailer on Monday morning, I find Marcy standing outside my trailer again. It's like déjà vu.

"Hi, Marce. Have a good weekend?" I say to her as I walk up the road to my door.

Marcy looks up from her phone and smiles. I walk past her on the stairs and unlock my trailer door, open it and walk through. Marcy follows me like last time and closes the door behind her.

"Hi. Yep, it was fine. I didn't do much. What about you?" she says, stopping to stand next to the island. I move into the kitchen to make myself a coffee before I go onto set. I could get coffee from the cafeteria, but it's never as strong as I need.

I grab a mug, position it under my coffee machine, press the bold button, the 12 oz button, and brew. I direct my attention toward Marcy as the machine brews my coffee.

"Same, uneventful. I think I'm still recovering from seeing my dad on Friday." The coffee machine signals it's done with a series of beeps. I turn toward the counter, stir in two scoops of sugar into my mug, and carefully slurp a sip.

Marcy rolls her eyes and sighs. "I forgot Mr. Davis stopped by."

"Mhm." I nod and take another sip. I forgot I had just brewed the coffee and ended up burning my tongue. Under my breath, I let out a curse, and then set the mug down with a sigh. "It was a great time, let me tell ya."

She laughs at that. "As much as I'd love to chat about your daddy issues, I wanted to let you know Ed has asked me to work on a side project since I have Cassie as my assistant."

"Side project?"

Her lips move into a thin line and she nods. "Yup," she says, drawing out the 'p' with a hint of sarcasm, and releases a long, dramatic sigh. "Not exactly the best timing, but Ed volunteered me to help with an independent film. It's offsite, which is why Cassie will take over my daily tasks. I know you have a..." She pauses, which I can only assume she's trying to think of how to put what she's thinking into words. "*friendship*." She winces.

"C'mon Marce, can't share me with another female?" I tease.

She groans.

"Don't worry, I'll be on my *best* behavior." I wink at her.

"I don't know why I deal with you sometimes," she says, heading toward the door. "Just don't do anything stupid while I'm not here, okay? You know you're not allowed to date *anyone* that works at the studio. She's not an exception."

I just nod in response. She doesn't need to know how excited I am for more time at work with Cassie, even if it is just seeing her more often. Her schedule is so busy this week with acting classes and working at the diner, I was already annoyed that I wouldn't see her at work. Marcy always has her doing some dumb activity on the other side of the studio, or being on set when I'm not.

Now, she can't do anything about it. I have no intention of taking things with Cassie beyond friendship. I just want to talk with her and hang out with her like I do with everyone else. Of course, all of that is subject to change. I don't have a hard rule on no dating or anything, I've just avoided it.

I wanted someone with whom I could be myself around, and that never happened. It was always Emmett, the actor, that they wanted. They didn't want Emmett, the writer who had a soft spot for romance movies, the guy who always chose a cozy night in over a night out.

When I was at the diner with Marcy last week and I saw Cassie, I felt this pull between us when our eyes met for the first time. I had just had a string of bad first dates and didn't know why I was feeling different about Cassie when I didn't even know her name. I know she knew who I was because I saw her talking with her friend. They kept whispering to each other and looking in my direction. I barely even knew her, and I asked her to sit and eat with me.

When I saw her the next day, I took it as another sign to talk to her. She's never tried to keep me in the box that I live in everyday, and I think that's what I like most about her.

Every time we talk, she sees me. She doesn't see the mask I put on for everyone else, and maybe that's because I've let her be close enough to me already to see that side of me. It's why I've already shown her my writing. Whenever I see her, my heart races and my feet automatically gravitate toward her. I get *nervous*. I don't get nervous about anything.

Maybe seeing her more will be bad. Or, maybe, just maybe, it'll curb this infatuation. Only time will tell.

9
CASSIE

THE NEXT FEW WEEKS are a blur. I have a few auditions for smaller supporting roles, but no callbacks. I have another today after work, and I'm trying not to lose hope, but it's hard when I can't get past the first audition to save my life.

Plus, between working days at the studio, picking up a few shifts each week at the diner, and acting class once a week, I've hardly seen Emmett. Alone, that is. Marcy is still off-site and I'm stuck at the studio. I help Ed make sure the principal actors are on set on time, assist Tyler when he needs an extra hand with inventory, and deliver mail to the trailers for Carla.

I stop by Emmett's trailer sometimes and stay for a few minutes, but in my defense, it's the only time I'm able to talk to him. When I have a free moment outside of work and acting class, I'm hanging out with Lucy or talking to Annie on the phone. I know I should do less, but I can't. Keeping myself busy is the only way I'm able to keep my mind off Emmett.

The less I'm able to be alone with him, the more focus I have. My romance scenes are giving me a hard time, but I still have a few weeks to perfect them before the showcase. I just have to practice more than normal. I *have* to do well at that showcase. If we're lucky, a few directors and scouts may be in the audience. It's my chance to prove my talent and show them they can cast me in something worth watching.

It's not even eight in the morning when my phone buzzes. I'm sitting at the island, drinking a cup of coffee. While scrolling on my phone, Emmett's name pops up.

Emmett

> Think you could stop and get me coffee on your way in? I have a question to ask you.

Not knowing how to respond, I leave him on read. We have been texting a bit, but I can't think of what he'd want to ask me. Could it be to go out on a date? An actual date? That's not likely, since the studio forbids us from seeing each other. What else could it be? Do they need someone to be an extra again? Does he want me to read more of his writing?

I should just text and ask, but I thought maybe not knowing would be better than knowing. Who knows if he would even tell me if I asked.

I stand up from the stool and push it under the island. I text Lucy to let her know I'm leaving for the day. We're planning to eat dinner together when we get home from work later. I walk to the front door and grab my bag off of the rack, slinging it over my shoulder before heading out.

From the apartment to the coffee shop and from the coffee shop to the studio, I cannot silence the thoughts in my mind. Sure, Emmett and I are friends now, I suppose, but I don't know what he could want to ask me. Also, he's already been asking me a ton of random questions over text. He's asked questions like what my favorite color is (blue), how I best like my eggs (scrambled), and which romance movie is my favorite (The Holiday). What could he possibly want to ask me that he couldn't text? Is it that secretive that he needs to do it in person?

Apparently.

When I reach Emmett's trailer, it's as if I step into an alternate version of myself, one who is cautious and on edge, more than I typically am around him. It's been a few days since our last moment alone in his trailer. I haven't been to his apartment since we shared a fleeting moment of intimacy. It was in that moment of blurred judgment that I realized I could have kissed him without any hesitation. But right now? I'm doing what I do best, building a 10-foot tall wall around myself to hopefully protect myself from Emmett being, well, Emmett.

He must have been expecting my arrival because the door to his trailer swings open just as I approach the stairs.

"Hi, Sass." He winks and the 10-foot wall I tried to build up cracks enough that my cheeks get warm. I would blame it on the sun, except it's awfully cloudy this morning.

"Here's your coffee." I shove the coffee cup and a bag that has a bagel in it in his direction.

His smile reaches his eyes. "Thought about me enough to get me breakfast too?"

"Don't overthink it." I glare as I move past him into his trailer.

I've been here enough times that I could close my eyes and still find my way around. It helps that the trailer is small and there isn't much to it besides the main sitting room and the kitchen. Even so, it's familiar.

We spend the next few moments in silence and eat our breakfast. I steal a glance or two, but it's hard to steal glances when he's already looking at me.

"What?" I demand. He won't stop staring.

"I, um..." He's nervous. He leans forward abruptly and adjusts his position to face me more directly. It's as if doing that makes him feel more confident. "I want to ask you something."

Taking a sip of my coffee, I watch him anxiously shifting before I reply. "Go ahead."

"Right." He nods and gets up from the couch. "Be right back."

Emmett moves to the kitchen to set his coffee on the counter and throws his now-empty bag in the trash. He opens the pantry, stares into it for a moment, and shuts it. He opens and shuts drawers in the kitchen. Grumblings follow and a curse under his breath, before finally an "AHA!"

He walks back over toward me, holding an envelope. I tilt my head in confusion.

"Here." Emmett hands me the envelope. "Open it."

"Now?"

"Please." He takes a seat next to me. His presence feels considerably closer than it was a few minutes prior.

I take the envelope from him. The front of it is blank, not addressed to anyone. I flip it over, put my pointer finger under the corner of the flap, and rip it open. I pull out a thick piece of cardstock. It's black with letters in gold foil that read, "You're invited to Emmett's 30th birthday party." I have to move my hand to my mouth to stop myself from laughing.

"What?" It's his turn to demand.

I remove my hand from my mouth, thinking I'd be okay except what comes out of me is louder than a small chuckle. I'm full-on laughing. Here I was, worrying Emmett might ask me on a date and I'd have to figure out how to tell him no. Instead, he wants me to go to his birthday party.

"Nothing, I just thought that you were going to ask me something different."

Emmett just stares at me, his eyes fixed on mine, as if silently urging me to provide more details.

"I thought you were..." I pause. Part of me feels vulnerable by revealing this to him. He will know that I was thinking of him like that, except that I wasn't. Not really, anyway. "...*goi ngtoaskmeonadate.*" My words come out jumbled and quick.

Emmett puts his elbow on the back of the couch, resting his head on his hand. He's just sitting there, staring at me, and it's currently having the opposite effect on me than it should. I should be able to withstand Emmett. That's the reason I built this metaphorical 10-foot wall around my feelings. Instead,

I'm internally swooning because all it takes is a slight dip in his head and his gaze on me and I'm *melting*.

"Cassie, if I was going to ask you on a date, you'd know." I open my mouth to say something in response, but he beats me to it. "But that's not happening right now. I simply want you to come to my party on Friday."

I look back at the card. The party is at the Moonlight Club down the street. It's known for being the place where all celebrities host events and parties.

"I didn't know it was your birthday."

He smirks. "Saturday is my birthday."

"And you're, um, turning 30?" I ask.

Emmett points to the card that I'm still holding in my hand. "That's what they tell me. Tyler, Lane, and Max are hosting."

I nod and I'm not sure what else to say. I haven't made enough friends out here to be invited to a birthday party. Whenever it's mine or Lucy's birthday, we just stay home, order in some Indian food, and watch a movie. It's typically uneventful. The opposite of what I can assume Emmett's party will be.

"So, will you come?" Emmett asks.

I nod again and look up to meet his gaze. How could I miss his party? I'm as close with Emmett most days as I am with Lucy, and I've only known him for a few weeks. I don't know if this is technically allowed or if Marcy will be there, but I'll worry about that later.

He smiles, anticipating my answer.

I can't help but roll my eyes, which he must find funny. "I suppose I could cancel the plans I had and attend your party." My plans included me sitting on the couch, eating snacks, and catching up on one of the latest movies on Netflix. "Do you mind if I bring my friend, Lucy?"

Emmett shakes his head. "Tyler would *love* it if your friend came."

I groan and slump into the couch. I turn my head to the left to look at Emmett. "Really?"

"Mhm." He nods. "You'll find that I'm always serious, Cass."

I roll my eyes. Again. "He doesn't even know her. *You* don't even know her," I retort.

"You forget I met her once already, but, for real, she is more than welcome. I'm sure there will be room in the club for one more person."

"If you say so, birthday boy." I smile.

It's Emmett's turn to groan and roll his eyes. He gives my shoulder a playful shove, almost spilling my coffee.

"Hey!" I try to sound stern, but I do a terrible job because I just end up laughing.

"Sorry." He bites his lip. My eyes quickly shift to track his movements, returning to his gaze. For someone I'm trying awfully hard to remain professional with, I'm doing quite the opposite. If someone were to walk into the trailer, they'd see us sitting a little too close to one another. Emmett turned toward me, still leaning on his hand, looking almost longingly into my eyes. I'm still slumped, my face angled toward him, our eyes locked.

I bring my coffee up to my lips and take a small sip. I keep getting stuck in quiet moments like this with Emmett. It's not awkward or intentional silence, it's just...comfortable. I try to think of a time when I felt like this and I'm having a hard time remembering when I felt so safe and at home with someone else. I mean, aside from Lucy and Annie, of course. Besides them, I've never hung around anyone else long enough to develop a deeper relationship.

Luckily, I love them, but I'm stuck with them for obvious reasons. Emmett is different. I could easily ignore him and choose to treat knowing him as part of the job. But that would mean saying no to a lot of things I want to do. I wouldn't be able to text him and answer his silly questions about my favorite things. He wouldn't wink at me in passing, something I've come to look forward to. I would have had to say no to his party.

But, I am making the irresponsible choice. I haven't quite figured out why I'm choosing to let thoughts of Emmett invade my brain when I'm busy trying to land an acting gig. You know, the whole reason I moved to Los Angeles five years ago. I've tried for so long. I'm not giving up, but just trying to live my life for once? Letting myself be selfish? I shouldn't have to give myself reasons to do something outside of improving my acting, yet I need to rationalize it. If I don't, then it feels like I'm already on the road to forgetting my why.

"I should go," I say. Neither of us have moved from our spots, but I know if I don't leave, I'll make a poor decision and kiss him or something.

"You're busy tonight?"

I nod a few times in response. "I have an audition. And tomorrow I have acting class."

"Sounds like we'll need to make up for a lot of lost time on Friday," Emmett says with a sly smirk.

His response is different from that of most people I've tried to be friends with. I'm normally rather busy with various jobs and acting classes, so I have little time to hang out with someone. It wasn't something I prioritized. Acting *always* comes first. It was easier when I started to hang out with people in the industry, but they were always just as busy or they wanted the same jobs I wanted. It was easier to not try for new friends.

I wasn't even looking for Emmett, he just kind of happened and now look where we are.

I stand up from the couch and walk into the kitchen to throw away the trash from my breakfast. When I turn around, Emmett is standing by the trailer door, waiting for me.

I walk up to him, stopping a few feet away. I look up to meet his gaze.

"What?" I ask, momentarily getting lost in his big, brown eyes.

He shakes his head like he wants to say something, but I won't push him. It's possible he wanted to hug me, but I won't comment on it. The very idea of laying a hand on him fills me with such anticipation that it feels as though my entire being would collapse, succumbing to an overwhelming desire.

It's not a good idea considering I still have work to do. Also, we are friends. Friends, friends, friends. Maybe if I keep saying it, my brain will eventually process it and instruct my body to stop reacting to Emmett. It's not helping.

Emmett's gentle touch lingers on my skin as he leans to the left, making my thoughts scatter. I tense and the heat rises in my cheeks. I will need to be a bit more stern with my "Emmett is only a friend" talk to myself.

Emmett swings the door open, peeking his head out and looking to the left and right before bringing it back inside and glancing toward me.

"You're clear," he says.

Right. Our friendship is *mostly* a secret. I make a mental note to text him later about how I should act at the party, because I don't know who all will be there. Should I pretend I don't know him? Has he even thought about this? Why does he even want me there? Okay, I'm overthinking and it's barely the beginning of the workday. I have all day to spiral. I don't need to start now.

"I'll text you later," I say as I walk out of his trailer and toward the doors that lead into the set.

By the end of the day, I'm exhausted. I didn't know Marcy did this much stuff, but I suppose it's why I'm here to help with most of it. I was helping Ed one moment, Carla the next, and some other random department would need me. It was chaotic and I'm ready to eat Indian food and veg out on the couch.

But first, I have to stop by a casting office for my audition.

After signing in and letting the receptionist know I've arrived, I sit in the waiting room until someone calls me in.

My phone buzzes with a text from Emmett wishing me luck. I need it.

"Cassie."

I look up to see an associate standing by a now-open door to the auditioning room. I smile softly, raising a hand to let them know I'm here, and proceed to gather all of my items.

Once we're in the room, I stand on the mark and wait for their cue to start. They say "rolling," and I start performing my scene. A few short lines as the best friend to the main character of the film.

They seem happy enough with the first take that they don't ask for me to run the lines again. Excitement bubbles up inside me, knowing I gave it my all. So, with a smile, I thank them for their time, sign out, leave, and hope this is the one.

When I get home, Lucy is already there with the island full of containers of food. I could smell the garlic, cumin, and onions down the hallway, and my mouth was watering before I even opened the apartment door.

"I'm home," I yell into the apartment. I slip off my shoes and hang my bag up on one of the empty hooks to the right of the front door.

"Finally," Lucy says. She emerges from her room wearing a face mask. It's all green and literally all over her face. She looks like a beautiful Shrek. Before I have the chance to laugh or say something about it, she holds up a hand. "Don't you start."

I hold up both of my hands. "Caught me." I laugh. "You think I'd be used to seeing your various face masks by now." For real. She has a different face mask for every night. Sometimes it's green, like now, other times it's blue, or white, or it has sparkles. Her skin is flawless though, so instead of keeping track of the various colors, I should probably try one sometime.

"You think, huh? Busy day?" Lucy walks past me and into the kitchen. She takes a piece of naan bread and dips it into a vegetable curry. "This is literally the best food to ever grace this earth." She moans, taking another bite. She doesn't even bother to dish out a serving for herself, but it's a typical dinner for us. The fewer dishes, the better. She holds up the bag full of naan.

"Thank you," I say, taking a piece and dipping it into the curry. "It was a busy day, yes. I didn't realize how much Marcy did while she was sending me off to the other side of the set." If I looked at my watch, I bet I would see that I walked 10k today. "Gosh, you're right. If someone stranded me on an island, this—" I shake the naan, "is the only food I'd want."

Lucy's eyebrows narrow, showing hints of skepticism. "Last week it was Chinese."

"And next week it'll likely be pizza." I smile and shove the rest of the naan into my mouth.

"I'll make sure to provide a buffet if I ever throw you a surprise party. With how often you change your mind on your favorite food, I'd never be able to predict what your favorite for that week would be."

"True." I pick up a samosa and take a bite. "Speaking of parties... are you busy Friday?"

Lucy narrows her eyebrows again. "What's Friday?"

"Well, Emmett may have asked me to go to his birthday party, and I need you to come with me."

"What if I have to work?"

"You'd get someone to cover your shift and keep me company, obviously," I say with confidence.

"Well, lucky you, I *do* have to work but I am done by eight. I might just have to drive separately, that okay?" Lucy asks while also eating a samosa.

I nod.

"How did the audition go today?" Lucy asks.

"I think it went as well as the others." I shrug, knowing that none of my auditions have led to anything.

"You'll land something this year, I can feel it." Lucy grins.

"Thanks, Luce."

Changing the subject, I fill her in on what I've been up to the last few weeks at the studio. I haven't worked at the diner a lot, so I haven't seen her. We're at the stage in our lives where we're working opposite shifts and catching each other at the door or in the parking lot. While I'm at the studio or acting class, she's busy painting or working at the diner.

It's been nice to have one person to talk to about Emmett. I haven't told Annie yet, so Lucy is the only one I can vent to about things. I'm trying hard to keep the wall built up, but it's getting hacked piece by piece. Emmett isn't even in full flirt mode, either. It's the small interactions: the little shoulder touches, the random winks, the text messages to tell me good morning. It somehow makes it even more special to hide this relationship, however platonic it might be, from others.

I weighed the pros and cons, and even though it might not be the best decision, I'm still excited about going to the party on Friday. Although, nothing good can come from a dimly lit club where it'll be tempting to dance with Emmett. What am I getting myself into?

10
EMMETT

"TODAY IS THE DAY, birthday boy!" Tyler greets me as I walk into the cafeteria for lunch. He walks up to me, pumping his fist into the air. He's a fool, but I love him. When he came over to hang out for the first time and only wanted to play video games, I thought he was kidding. He knew who I was, right? And he *doesn't* want to go out? I remember standing next to the couch as he turned on the TV and tried handing me a controller.

I didn't take it at first and he yelled at me to stop being weird and sit. Okay, he didn't actually yell, but if you've heard Tyler in person, he says everything with enthusiasm and a *very* loud tone. Any bystander would think I'm being yelled at, but nope, that's just Tyler.

I groan and roll my eyes once I get within a few feet of him, making sure he sees the fake agony.

"Need me to help with anything?" I ask, although I already know the answer because he, Max, and Lane have been texting me updates nonstop.

Like I predict, Tyler shakes his head and glances my way. "Don't you trust us?"

"No," I reply. I receive a shove for that. "Kidding."

"What's the update on your girl?"

"Not my girl." I glare at him. Do I even want her to be my girl? It's been a while since I've had a friend to talk to like I do with Cassie. It's a more intimate relationship than I have with Marcy. But I know Cassie doesn't want to date anyone right now. She's made that statement more than once. Instead of pushing her and flirting more, I just keep showing up and being the friend she needs right now.

"So, she's coming? And bringing that friend?" Tyler wiggles his eyebrows.

"I'll introduce you, don't worry. Anyway, I need to grab a quick bite before going on set. See you later?"

"Duh. Have someone to drive you tonight?" Tyler asks.

Shit. "I don't, um, I'll ask..." I look around to make sure no one is around. "You know who."

Tyler just smirks and gives me a nod of understanding. "Bye, *lover-boy*."

I give him a shove for that as he walks away. He just laughs and shakes his head. *Asshole.*

"What are you bitter about?" A familiar voice greets my ears from behind.

I spin around to find Cassie with her arms crossed and a clipboard in her left hand.

"Just the person I want to see." I smile.

Her eyebrows narrow. "I don't understand how you go from broody to cheerful in seconds."

"That's simple," I say with a shrug.

Her eyebrows raise in question.

"You've graced my presence, Sass." I wink and that earns me my first eye roll of the day.

"And what can I help you with? Hm? You're supposed to be on set—" Cassie pauses to look at her clipboard, her finger trailing left to right to bottom to left again on the page. "Now." A groan escapes her mouth. "Emmett," Cassie drawls, a hint of a smirk blooming on her lips.

"Walk with me?" I ask, grabbing a granola bar.

"Oh, I suppose. It's not like I have a million other things to do and other principal actors to track down or anything," Cassie replies, glancing my way as we exit the cafeteria.

I gasp and slam my right hand to my chest. "You mean to tell me I'm not your one and only?"

"In your dreams, Hotshot." Cassie winks and starts walking a little faster to get ahead of me.

I walk faster to reach her. "What would you say if I asked you for a ride to my party tonight?" I ask and hold the door for her. My radio goes off as Ed tries to get ahold of me, but I ignore it now that we've arrived.

I almost think Cassie is going to walk away. It's possible she didn't hear me over the noise coming from the set. Instead, she turns to face me and lowers her clipboard to her thighs.

"I can do that."

"Great. I'll—" I get cut off by a staff member coming up to Cassie to ask her questions. I catch her eyes and mouth "text you" which she must understand because she smiles, nods, and walks away with the staff member.

For the rest of the day, I stay busy. Ed has me alternating between filming and helping other actors during their scenes. Normally, I would get irritated and do everything possible to go back to my trailer during my downtime, but I didn't feel that way today. I *wanted* the day to go by fast. The faster it went, the sooner I would get to my party.

Except, I didn't want to go to my party to celebrate myself. Truthfully, I don't like celebrating my birthday, but the guys insisted I have a party. I think they wanted a reason to stay out late on a Friday night, which is not something we typically do. I would rather stay in, watch a movie, eat some pizza, you know, our usual Friday night routine. Even growing up, I wasn't a fan of birthdays.

My parents *always* took me out to a fancy restaurant with a menu full of unfamiliar dishes, just the three of us. I should be grateful for my parents taking me out to dinner on my birthday, but I can't help complaining. Growing up, I never had the opportunity to enjoy birthday parties that were meant for children. I've never hosted a party at a roller rink or park, and I've never had friends to invite, even if I did. I thought it wasn't a big deal until Lane asked me what I was doing for my birthday this year.

When I told him nothing, he thought I was kidding. I didn't realize how significant turning 30 would be until Tyler and Max stepped in to help Lane with everything. Without it, I wouldn't have another excuse to hang out with Cassie in public.

We haven't had a moment alone in over a week, and all I can think about is grinding with her like two horny teenagers at their first prom.

Ridiculous, I know, but it's the truth. I thought about it every time I saw her today and I *could not* get the image out of my head. I had to turn away from her before she saw my cheeks flush. Embarrassing.

Asking Cassie to take me to my party may have been selfish on my part. I could have asked a driver, but I wanted another excuse to have alone time with Cassie.

I asked her to come up to my apartment when she arrives. For no specific reason except to see her. A few knocks come from the front door as I'm finishing getting ready.

I give myself a final once-over in the mirror. For tonight, I've worn one of my favorite outfit combinations: a pair of jeans, a white shirt, and a navy corduroy button down. I thought going with the outfit I'm most comfortable in tonight will help my confidence around Cassie.

I open the door, and Cassie greets me a small smile and a hello. Her hair is pinned half back, allowing loose curls to cascade from the lower sections. From head to toe, she's clad in black—a black corset, black straight jeans, and black strappy sandals. She is *breathtaking*.

Cassie looks at the floor, rocks back on her heels, and glances back at me. "I, um, hope I'm dressed okay. I wasn't quite sure what to wear. It's been a while since I've gone out." She moves her right hand and rubs her left arm up and down.

"You look great, Cass," I say. "Beautiful. I'm sure you'll be the best-looking person in the club."

She rolls her eyes and the first thought that comes to my mind is *"there's my girl."* Nope. Not tonight. I am shoving all "my girl" thoughts to the very back corner of my brain and shutting that door with a padlock. Friends. We are *friends*.

"You good?" Cassie's words take me out of my thoughts.

"I am now that you're here. Let's go."

It only takes us 10 minutes to drive from my apartment to the Moonlight Club. When we arrive, I spot a group of photographers waiting outside the venue to get the perfect shots for their articles.

We kept the guest list small to avoid the press, but I'm not surprised to see a few cameras. This club hosts a lot of private events, so they might not even know about my birthday party. If I dodge photographers and prevent an article from being run with a misleading story, I would avoid any scrutiny from my dad.

I ask Cassie to drive around back so we can go through the back door and avoid the cameras. I slump down in the seat and put my arm over my head, trying to hide my face from people peering into the car windows to see who's pulling up.

Cassie doesn't ask, but she glances my way when I shrink to hide myself.

Unlike my dad, I stay away from places where people are eager to capture every moment on camera. I despise the forced smiles and obligatory small talk, especially with those who twist my words if I slip up or have a slightly off tone. Tyler, Lane, and Max understand that. It's how I know they are genuine friends.

In the past, I've had so many "friends" want to go out, even when I tried to get us to stay in. They'd always promise we'd go somewhere secluded, but it always ended up in a story the next morning with some quote that was not approved by me. All they wanted was the association to a Davis. They wanted everyone to know we were hanging out. They thought it helped their career to be friends with a family that is known in the industry. As if I'd ever give a recommendation to someone like that—only using me for their own gain.

If anyone but Cassie were driving, they would've pushed back at my request to go to the back. They would have given the car to valet and walked right through the middle of the crowd.

I got so used to shielding myself from new relationships that I forgot what it feels like for someone to value me as a person rather than an asset. *Fuck.* I don't know what's worse, family or friends that try to use you for their own personal gain. That's another reason why I'm so grateful for the people I have in my inner circle.

Marcy and the guys helped heal the trauma induced by my *loving* father and abandoned friendships. The small group I had around me made me content. I felt like I had enough. What more did I need if I already had people to talk and laugh with?

I was missing *Cassie*.

I found something new in her smile, laugh, and ability to see through my bullshit. I hardly know her, but I'd like to know every inch of her. Do you know how incredible it feels to find someone that you can be your *complete* self around?

I was so against developing new relationships that I could have missed having Cassie in my life. At least, in my life for the time being. Nothing is permanent, but I sure hope she's in my life for a while.

"Okay. What now?" Cassie turns to me. She places both hands on her lap, glances toward the club, and then looks back at me. "Do we need to wear sweatshirts with hoods up or something to enter?"

I tilt my head to the left and bite my cheeks to hold back a laugh.

Cassie looks back at the club. "Or I can go first to distract anyone and you can sneak in?"

My teeth struggle to contain my cheeks as I burst into a wide grin. Trying to stifle a laugh, I bring my hand to my mouth and muffle the sound.

"What?" Cassie glares. She lifts her hands from her lap and crosses her arms.

I shake my head. "You're cute, you know that? We don't have to sneak in. I don't think there are any cameras back here, anyway."

"Mhm, okay, Emmett. Well, if you end up on the front cover of some gossip site, you better not blame me."

"I'll be sure to tell my dad when he calls that I almost covered myself in a hood, but thought it wasn't necessary," I tease.

Cassie rolls her eyes and playfully hits me in the arm. "I don't know how this works. Don't make fun of me." Her eyebrows narrow and she tucks her top lip under her bottom in a pout.

"I'll make it up to you later." I wink. "Let's go inside."

"I'll hold you to that."

We exit the car, meet in the middle, and stand face to face.

Our hands accidentally brush, but she responds by intertwining mine in hers. I give her hand a gentle squeeze, the warmth of her skin brushing against mine, and steal a quick glance in her direction, unable to hide my smile. She returns a smile, her cheeks glowing under the street lights.

I guide us to the door, opening it and letting Cassie go in first. She gives my hand a squeeze this time and then lets go. As soon as we enter the club, people swarm us, making it impossible for me to grab her hand back and hold her.

People from past jobs, current jobs, and random others I don't know come up to wish me a happy birthday. In the swarm of it all, I lose Cassie and try to look around to find her.

The Moonlight Club greets visitors with a dark ambiance, enhanced by the soft glow of low lights along the exits. Red lights illuminate different spots throughout the venue, where groups of people gather. Positioned to my right is the music and dance floor, and I have every intention of taking Cassie there later.

My gaze finds Tyler and a cluster of people huddled around a collection of tables. I wave. Finally, I spot Cassie on my left. She's sitting at the bar, sipping a drink. When we make eye contact, she smiles and raises her glass a few inches like she's toasting to me.

I start to move toward her, but more people swarm around me. Luckily, I can see Tyler headed toward her to make conversation. I've asked the guys to keep her company and help her feel welcomed if I find myself occupied at various points of the night. I'm glad I did, because there are way more people here than I expected. I thought it would be fun to throw a party and catch up with everyone, but I'm already tired of having the same conversation over and over. I pull out my phone to check the time. I've only been here for 20 minutes, but it feels like hours.

It's like going to a family reunion and having to repeat the same answers over and over. Everyone asks about what you're up to, how things are going, what's next, *blah blah blah*. I don't even think that's the worst of it. It's the smiling. The fake smiles and nods from people who pretend to care about what you're doing. When truthfully they just came for the free drinks and publicity.

I guarantee most people are here to post that they attended my party. Hence why I'm not friends with a lot of them and I let Lane, Tyler, and Max be in charge of the guest list. I didn't care who came. I thought I would spend the night sitting at the bar or in a booth with my core circle of friends and I would have a great time. Honestly.

Then, my priorities shifted. I now want to sit next to Cassie at the goddamn bar, but I can't get away from these people.

Ah. I have an idea.

I bring my phone up to my ear and mouth, "Sorry, I need to get this" to some guy I was talking to, and he nods, smiles, and turns to walk away. Success.

Keeping the phone at my ear, I walk toward the bar to find Cassie. Except Cassie isn't there anymore. Hm.

This place isn't that large. Maybe Tyler coerced her to join him somewhere.

I survey the room.

She's not at the booths. Or at a table. She's on the dance floor. With every step, her hips effortlessly move in a seductive rhythm, tempting me to ask her to dance. She's with my group of friends, and her laughter floats through the air to assure me she's having a great time.

I move through the crowd, offering smiles to those who approach, but I don't let them distract me. I'm going to ask Cassie to dance with me and no one is stopping me.

11
CASSIE

"HI, I HOPE YOU'RE having fun," a familiar voice whispers in my ear. Little bumps rise on my arms as a chill runs down my spine, making my heart beat a tiny bit faster.

Glancing over my shoulder, I catch sight of Emmett grinning at me. He's standing a few inches behind me, and the warmth of his presence brushes against my back, leaving me wishing he were closer.

As if the universe heard my thoughts, Emmett's body bumps into mine and his hands find my waist. His head whips behind him, glaring at whoever just bumped into him. With so many people on the dance floor, it was bound to happen. There isn't much room between the clumps of people.

"Sorry," he murmurs in my ear, but he doesn't let go of my waist.

"Hey, man!" Tyler yells over the music. He walks across the circle of friends toward us. Emmett lets go of me with his left hand while dragging his right hand over the width of my waist until he's no longer touching me and instead hugging Tyler. I'm suddenly jealous that his hands aren't on me anymore.

Damn, the night is still early and I'm already in trouble. I should not be thinking about this right now, but you can't blame a girl for getting hot and bothered in the club. Right? It's not insane. Emmett is just *here.* And he's being extra flirty and handsy and all I want to do is dance with him. It's harmless, I swear.

I don't need Smart Cassie to infiltrate my brain right now and remind me Emmett is bad news for me. Falling for an actor is not a part of my plan. Anyway, I don't have the time to make a relationship a priority. Between working, auditions, and acting class, I hardly have time for myself.

But that doesn't mean I can't have fun tonight. Lucy told me I deserved to have fun, so to hell with being smart. For one night at least.

Speak of the devil. Lucy enters the front door of the club and I wave my hands until she sees me and starts running toward the dance floor. She's sporting a little black dress with tiny spaghetti straps. Her auburn hair falls in loose, bouncy curls around her shoulders. It's almost shocking because I don't think I've seen her out of her work or painting clothes in months.

"Damn, Luce."

She smiles and turns in a circle. "Oh, this thing?" She glances down and gestures to her dress before looking back at me. "Dress to impress, right?" She smiles and pulls me into a hug.

When she releases me, she looks around and sees Emmett and Tyler. She holds out her right hand and waves at Emmett. "Hi! I'm Lucy, the best friend, if you didn't remember me from a few weeks ago at the diner."

Emmett nods and grins. "How could I forget? I'm Emmett, the uh…" he stumbles over his words, his gaze flickering toward me, and I silently urge him on with a raised eyebrow. "This is Tyler." Instead of claiming a title, he introduces Tyler to Lucy.

Tyler steps forward with the biggest smile I've seen from him. He gives her a small wave and says hi. When I told Lucy about Emmett and his friends, I may have mentioned that Tyler would be the one I thought she'd like the most. Lucy normally goes for more quiet, reserved guys, but I think she'd like a change. Tyler is the opposite of her ex, who I think I spoke to maybe three times in the few months they dated. He is more outgoing, talkative, and I'm sure just as supportive—which she needs desperately in her life.

"Join me for a drink?" Lucy says to Tyler. He nods. They both smile at us, Lucy winks at me, and then they're off to the bar.

Emmett turns to me. "Well."

"Well," I mock.

He looks around the room before meeting my gaze again. He takes one step closer to me and holds out a hand. "Want to dance?"

Do I want to dance? Yes. Most definitely. Do I want to feel his body close to mine? One thousand percent. Being around Emmett makes me nervous, but the good kind of nervous. The kind where my stomach is full of butterflies, but I try to hide it. The kind where my cheeks are constantly flush with red and hurt from smiling. I don't know what *this* is or what we are to each other, but it feels different from just friends.

I've had male friends before. I didn't get goosebumps or giddy thinking about them. I definitely didn't want them to touch me like I'm thinking about Emmett right now. Besides the few people I've dated, I've never felt this pull to another person before. It's magnetic, two sides pulling toward each other, begging to touch.

With a slight nod, I place my hand in his as Emmett pulls me toward him. I collide with his torso; the impact sends a jolt through my body as my hand connects with his chest. Emmett's hand is on my waist, his grip tightening with each sway as we dance to the rhythm, moving left and right.

The song transitions to "Miracle" by Calvin Harris as if the universe expected my wants. As Emmett spins me around, his hand effortlessly moves from mine to rest on my waist. The song is talking about how when someone touches you; you get vulnerable and I gotta say, I feel vulnerable as fuck right now.

We keep dancing, losing ourselves to the rhythm. The music grows louder, consuming the room with its energetic beats. Each movement brings us closer, the intense heat radiating between our bodies, overwhelming my every thought. I tease Emmett by pressing against him, grinding my backside into him. In response, his fingers dig into my waist, encouraging me to push a little more. I lean my back and head onto his chest, closing the small gaps between us.

The music continues to play similar songs, so we never have to break our dance. Emmett's head dips forward, breathing into my neck. My breath quickens, speeding up with the anticipation of his lips on mine. I think he's waiting for me to make the move or to give him some sort of sign that I want to cross the line we've drawn. Tonight is different for us, given the nature of the event. Hanging out alone in his apartment brings a different level of intimacy. That's when I get a version of Emmett that many people don't have the pleasure of knowing.

Here, I get the public version of Emmett and, because of that, I won't cross the line. Even if I want to.

The music transitions into a slower song. Emmett talks into my ear and asks if I want to grab a drink. I nod.

His hands leave my waist, but not before he gives me one last squeeze, which I can't help but overthink. I'm about to say "fuck it" and press my lips against his. This tension between us is going to be the death of me, I swear. Every time Emmett meets my gaze, I want to slam him into the nearest wall and declare him as mine in front of everyone in this venue.

When we get to the booth, I slide to one side. Instead of sitting across from me, he slides next to me and stops a few inches short of our legs touching. A soft, red velvet lines the booth, creating a cozy ambiance that pairs well with the vibrant lights. I've never been inside this club, but I would have thought the inside would have featured more blues and purples. You know, moonlight and all doesn't normally remind me of the color red. But, looking around the venue, there is a lot of red. Red lights, red chairs, red signs.

"What do you want to drink?" Emmett asks. He's looking at a menu on his phone from the QR code printed in the middle of the table.

"Any mocktail with lime would work for me. What do they have?"

"Would it surprise you to hear that the menu is custom for tonight based on my resume of movies?" Emmett winces. "Tyler thought it'd be hilarious."

Emmett slides his phone over to me and I look. There are a handful of normal wines and beers, but the cocktails are all named after a movie.

"To the Moon" is from one of his first big movies, where he played a hotshot engineer who saves a moon landing. Not kidding with that one, it was quite hilarious, and it was a plus that he was very hot and smart in that movie. It's also the reason I call him Hotshot. "Jungle Breeze" is from when he played a journalist. "Man of the Hour" was from when he played a CEO (which was his role in multiple movies). "Cash Money" must be from the bank heist movie he was in. I think "Too Hot to Handle" is from when he played a lifeguard and had his shirt off for 90% of the movie.

I giggle.

"Recognize any of them?"

I look over at Emmett. He has his left elbow on the table and is resting his head on his hand.

"All of them, actually," I answer truthfully. Sure, I could hide the fact that I know the movies he's been in. Except he'd catch me lying. It's not like his movies are indie movies or anything. These are blockbusters. Everyone knows them.

Emmett opens his mouth for a moment to say something, but he's interrupted when Tyler and Lucy come barreling on the other side of the table.

"Well, helloooo lovebirds," Tyler says, grinning ear to ear while sliding into the booth. Lucy follows suit and slides in next to him.

Emmett glances at me, rolls his eyes at the notion, and returns his gaze to Tyler.

"What have you two been up to?" Emmett asks. His hand that was once on the table slides underneath and lands on my thigh. He gives me one squeeze. To my surprise, he leaves his hand there. It suddenly feels hot in here again, having this little intimate secret between us. Since we're nestled into the booth and the venue is dark, his touch remains unseen.

Tyler glances over at Lucy and throws his arm around her shoulder. "Oh, you know, little bit of this, little bit of that."

"We got a drink." Lucy grabs Tyler's hand and moves his arm out from behind her shoulder. This is typical Lucy. Tyler is pushing his limit with her and he will find that out real quick if he doesn't tone it down a bit. She's single, sure, but only because everyone she's been with has never shown any serious, long-term interest in her. Lucy and Tyler share a glance. Maybe it's a glare. Either way, it's some shared moment that makes me wonder what they talked about while they got that drink.

A waitress brings over two drinks and smiles at Emmett when she places them both in front of him. She doesn't glance at anyone else, but slips a piece of paper to him with the drinks. I can only assume it's a phone number and now I'm wondering if that happens to him a lot. My mind feels like it's rapidly switching contexts tonight. I'm overwhelmed by the environment and all the people.

I can feel myself growing increasingly restless. Now that I have a drink, I find myself twirling the little straw in the glass. I take small sips and smile when I remember I need to act engaged. Tyler is rambling about something to Emmett in relation to the studio and work, but I zone out. When there's a break in the conversation, Emmett leans over to me and asks me if I'm alright. I meet his gaze and nod, trying to convince my mouth to form a better smile than what I'm sure is displaying on my face right now.

He squeezes my leg once. It's comforting to know that I am heard and understood.

"Let's dance?"

"Sure." I smile. A real smile. Anything to get out of this booth and occupy my mind.

He turns back to let Tyler and Lucy know we are going to go dance. He offers to have them join us, but they both decide to stay at the booth.

Emmett gives my leg one more squeeze before he removes his hand and slides out of the booth. I slide out after him, standing up and moving to Lucy's side for a moment. I lean down to be closer to her face before speaking. It's not too loud in the club, but I also don't want my conversation to be heard by everyone surrounding us.

"Will you be okay? Sorry for basically ditching you tonight."

Lucy places a hand over mine, which is resting in front of her on the table. "I'll be fine. I got this guy—" she glances back at Tyler before returning to face me, "to keep me company. He's a goof. Don't worry about me. You go have fun. Just let me know if you plan on leaving." She smiles and removes her hand from mine.

I nod. I don't know what I'd do without Lucy.

Actually, I do.

I'd probably be living with someone who cares more about themself than others. I'd most definitely not be working at the diner. I only got that job because of Lucy. If I didn't work at the diner, I wouldn't have met Emmett. I also wouldn't have the job at the studio, since I only applied for that when I was *with* Lucy and we stayed up too late watching a movie after work. Hell, I don't know if I'd still be living in Los Angeles trying to chase this dream.

"Let's go dance," Emmett whispers the reminder into my ear. My cheeks flush and I bite my bottom lip when I turn around to glance at him.

I let him take my hand and lead me onto the dance floor. He moves past the spot we were originally dancing and leads me into the far back corner, where it's empty and less illuminated.

"I want some alone time with you while I can," he says.

Before I can respond, his hands land on my waist and he puts enough pressure to spin me so my back is once again on his chest. I'm feeling spoiled by all of this close contact with Emmett.

I'm finding that he's very forward tonight.

I like it.

I like that I can always find his gaze on mine if we're in the same space. Our relationship has evolved since that first night to this moment on the dance floor.

It's no longer surprising that I crave his touch and presence. From tonight onward, I decide to welcome it.

But it'll be my secret. For now.

"Come back to me," Emmett whispers in my ear.

My body melts into his as we sway to the pulse of the music. I do my best to keep my head from wandering into all the *what ifs* and *I shouldn'ts* and enjoy the night. It's not every day that I let myself let loose and have fun.

The music continues, and Emmett and I keep dancing. When the song ends and transitions into a slower beat, he spins me around and pulls our chests together into a slow dance. His left hand moves to grab my hand, my other hand moving to stabilize myself on his chest. I rest my head in the nook of his neck and breathe him in. My nose fills with smells of cinnamon and sage. He smells like a forest in the fall.

The song ends and I pull away, letting go of his hand and moving it to my side. Standing up on my tiptoes, I lean my head close to his so my mouth is next to his ear.

"I should go find Lucy," I say. My heels return to the ground and I look at him to see his reaction.

He opens his mouth to say something but hesitates.

"You should go mingle. We can chat later." I smile.

He removes the hand from my waist and covers my hand that is resting on his chest. He gives it one squeeze. Our secret language. He raises his eyebrows. "This isn't over."

I don't know what *this* is, but I nod anyway. *This* could mean a lot of things. Too many possibilities that I don't want to think about at this moment. I don't need to feel overwhelmed by my own thoughts right now. The club is already enough to overstimulate me with the sizable crowds of people and loud music.

By the time I make it across the dance floor, I find Lucy still with Tyler at the booth. I move in their direction and sit back in my same spot as before.

"Where's Emmett?" Tyler asks.

Before I can respond, the booth sinks.

I look to my left to find Emmett sitting next to me. He must have followed me.

"I thought I told you to mingle."

"I thought I said this isn't over," he counters.

I know Tyler and Lucy are both looking at us, but I don't take my gaze away from Emmett. Instead, I turn my body toward him and continue to face him off. This is the hottest staring contest I've ever had.

Of course, I end up blinking first, and he winks at me before turning to the table. I sigh a little too loud, maybe on purpose, but find Emmett's hand back on my thigh with a squeeze following. This time, I place my hand over his, interlace our fingers, and give him a squeeze back.

"I think I'm going to leave," Emmett says to the table. "Cassie can drive me home. Right, Cass?" He turns to me and smirks.

"I suppose I *did* bring you here." I dip my head and follow the action with an eye roll. My signature response.

"Great. It's settled then. Let's go!" he says with a grin.

"Don't you have to say bye to everyone?"

"Sass, this is my party. I can do what I want and what I want to do is leave with you."

Like before, he slides out of the booth and grabs my hand. I say goodbye to Lucy and Tyler and he leads me to the back door of the venue.

Before opening the door, he peeks out to ensure there aren't any cameras waiting for us. I already forgot about that minor part of his life.

We head out of the venue, walking slowly to my car. I can't help but steal a few glances in his direction, and I'm glad I do, because I spot a faint smile during the entire walk. He drops my hand to open the door for me.

I get in and Emmett walks around the front of the car to get in the passenger seat. We pull out of the club, onto the road, and start making our way back to his apartment.

It's silent for a few minutes until Emmett speaks. "I'm glad you came tonight, although I'm sorry we didn't get to talk much."

"We would have talked more if we didn't spend most of the night dancing." I glance at him for a quick moment before returning my gaze back to the road.

He laughs.

"Fair point. Maybe you can stop by my apartment Monday after your shift?" Emmett says, looking out the window. The passing streetlights cast a soft glow on his face.

"Mhm, *maybe*," I tease.

"I can provide food." Emmett shifts his gaze from the window to me.

"Well, in that case, I can come over before my shift at the diner," I tell him.

When we get to his building, he has me pull into the garage instead of dropping him off at the front. I can only assume he asked for privacy reasons.

I put the car in park and look at him, placing my right arm on the center console. He has a look in his eye, like he is thinking about kissing me, but he's hesitating. Between dancing together and all the little small touches, the 10-foot wall I built is almost nonexistent. If he kissed me, I would kiss him back.

That's a scary realization. I was *so sure* that I was better off alone, but *maybe* I should take a chance. What would the harm be? If something went wrong, I could just quit the studio. It's not the worst outcome that could happen and I'm getting tired of keeping my guard up. I want to lean into the feelings building up between us. I want to know what it's like to wake up next to Emmett.

To my disappointment, Emmett simply lays his hand over mine and gives me a single squeeze.

"Text me when you get home?" he asks.

"I will."

"Okay, good." He hesitates again, his gaze dropping to our hands still intertwined.

For every second that passes, my breathing gets heavier and my heart beats faster. All my thoughts escape my head as his thumb moves back and forth in a rhythmic motion. He leans farther over the console, bringing our faces inches apart. At the last moment, he dips his head to the left and plants a kiss on my cheek.

He doesn't move, not yet, his lips hover over my ear as he whispers, "Goodnight Cassie."

When Emmett pulls away, a chill rushes over me and I have a strong urge to tug him back. A small smile appears as if he can read my mind, another single squeeze, and then he lets go of my hand.

"Goodnight Emmett."

I return my hands back to the wheel while Emmett gets out of the car. He turns to give a last wave before stepping into the elevator.

I drive off, headed for home, unsure of what to do with these feelings. That's tomorrow's problem.

12

EMMETT

I'M IN A GREAT mood this morning.

It is my birthday, after all. Max, Tyler, Lane, and Marcy are coming over later. That could contribute to my mood.

Although, that's not the primary reason for my happiness.

Images from last night flash in my mind, and I can practically feel Cassie in front of me if I close my eyes and think hard enough.

I *like* Cassie. More than a friend. I would have asked her on a proper date if I knew it wouldn't complicate things between us. I would have said "fuck it," she's worth it, I can try to date again. Except, she doesn't want to.

Well, after last night, I don't exactly know if that's true. Still, I can't cross the line yet, it's too soon. Plus, I wouldn't want to risk the foundation we've built. It's already thin as it is, and I wouldn't want her out of my life already if something happened.

I'm falling fast. I need to hold myself together for a little longer. Or at least figure out a way together to make something work, if she likes me as much as I like her. I can't be the reason she loses her job.

What if she doesn't like me? What if she doesn't want to pursue anything? Where will I put these feelings? There is no invisible rug to shove them under or trash bin to toss them in.

Before I have time to rabbit hole down that thought, my phone buzzes. Then it buzzes again. Then it starts ringing.

I finish pouring a cup of coffee and take my phone out of my pocket to find multiple unread messages and a missed call from my publicist. Before I have the chance to look into what they want, my phone starts ringing again, but this time it's someone I'd rather not talk to this early in the morning.

Ugh.

"Hi, Dad," I answer.

"I see you had fun last night."

Oh boy.

"I did," I answer with suspicion in my tone.

"I'm sure you did."

"Dad, just get to the point. What's up?" I ask, tired of the vagueness of his words.

"An article was published."

That's it? I'm not surprised. There *were* a lot of cameras there last night. The party was bound to be posted in some places, but I was hoping to avoid the limelight.

"You're photographed with some girl and you two look..." he pauses, "*cozy.*"

Ah, it's a photo with Cassie.

"She's just a friend, Dad."

He sighs. "You know how I feel about this type of press, Emmett."

Yes, I do. I know my dad hates any type of press that brings negativity to the Davis name. If he finds an article about him and he doesn't approve, he knows the right person to make sure it's shut down.

He's always been hard on me for any press I receive. Even when it's not anything bad. It's never good enough for him. My movie could hit record numbers and he'd still tell me I could do better next time. He has never once given me congratulations or told me he was proud.

Instead, I get berated anytime the press mentions my name. This isn't anything different. He's just mad it's not some girl he wanted to set me up with. Someone he knows and can control how they contribute to the family. At the end of the day, it's a transaction for him. It doesn't matter that I'm his son or that I'm old enough to make my own decisions.

Shit, do I have family issues, or what? I'm glad to be spending time with my chosen family today.

"Today's news is tomorrow's history. Isn't that what you always say?"

"Better be. I don't enjoy seeing the Davis name dragged down for miniscule reasons."

Dragged down is a bit of an exaggeration, but okay.

"I know. Listen, I'd love to chat for longer, but someone is at the door and I need to answer it," I lie.

"Alright, Emmett. Happy birthday, by the way. Call your mother when you get a chance."

"Thanks. Okay, will do. Bye, Dad."

I hang up the phone and set it on the island. I can't ignore him because he'd just show up at my apartment, but I'm tired of having these toxic conversations with him.

I tap at my phone to open the texts from my publicist. In addition to multiple "call me" messages, I find the link for this article. I click it open and sure enough, I'm holding Cassie's hand, smiling down at her. Only the back of her head is showing, which is good. No one will knock at her apartment trying to ask her follow-up questions because she's anonymous.

A message appears on the top of the screen, a text from Cassie.

Cassie

Happy birthday, Hotshot.

I smile and slide open the text to message her my thanks and also ask if she's having a good day. I want the conversation to continue, not end. I don't want to mention the article over text, I'd rather have that chat in person since it's not a big deal.

It's easy to fall into a conversation with Cassie. We're always asking questions to find out more about one another, or simply to show interest in whatever topic we're talking about. She frequently asks me about my writing. The first time she asked what I was working on, I didn't know how to respond. No one asks me about my writing. Not even Tyler, who sticks his nose in everything.

Also, how do I say I'm not writing something but I want to? That I have so many ideas floating in my head and written on random sheets of paper, but whenever I sit to actually turn my thoughts and ideas into coherent sentences, I can't form any. None. It's as if I've lost the ability to create.

I told her the truth. If anyone else would have asked me, I would have lied and said I was working on some script. If I can act in a movie, I can certainly pretend to be active with my hobby.

Ever since then, she's been checking in and encouraging me to journal. She thinks that maybe if I write my thoughts without some perceived stress around making my idea perfect, then I will at least be writing some words down.

So, that's what I've been doing. Except, I *may* have changed her request a bit.

She told me to write about my days: what happens at work, how I'm feeling, who I talk to, what my favorite moments are. What she doesn't know is my journaling just happens to be about her: when I see her at work, what we talk about, how I feel about her, what my favorite things about her are.

It's working too. I've written a few beginnings to some of my ideas and it's been freeing to be this creative again. All thanks to Cassie.

"What's got you down, birthday boy?" A voice comes from behind me.

I jump, spilling coffee all over the counter.

"Shit!" I grab a towel and start wiping it up as it drips on the floor.

I look to my left to find Tyler standing by the island, watching me clean up the mess that he caused.

"Your fault you didn't hear the door. I could have been a robber." Tyler smirks. He takes a seat at the island, still not offering to help.

"You're early."

"It's nice to see you too, lover-boy."

"The nickname is sticking, huh?" I glance at Tyler as I turn to the island and rinse off the towel in the sink to get the coffee out of it.

"Mhm. Sure is. Is she coming over today?"

"Who? Cassie?"

It's Tyler's turn to roll his eyes at me. "Yes," he says, exaggerating the 's' like a snake. "I thought you two made it official or something based on the article I saw this morning."

I give him my best side-eye and choose to ignore the comment. He knows I'm not allowed to be with Cassie, and he's trying to annoy me. I also don't want to talk about the article just yet. I'd rather it get buried in the rest of the news from today.

"I haven't thought to ask her," I respond instead. It's the truth, after all.

"Well, you should text her and ask. Lucy told me they have to work at the diner tonight, but I'm sure they would stop by before then," Tyler says with ease, as if he and Lucy are best friends after last night.

"Lucy, huh?"

"Nothing happened, before you ask me that." He points a finger at me in a warning. "We just talked and when I asked her what she was doing today, that's what she told me."

"Hmm." I nod. "Sure. Well, if you wanted something to happen, at least it could. With Cassie, I can't cross that line."

"Was it not crossing the line when you were grinding her ass?" Tyler smirks, grabbing a donut from a box I hadn't noticed. He must have brought it with him.

"I'm not answering that question." I grab a glazed donut and take a bite. "But I'll text her and ask." I'd use any reason as an excuse to see Cassie today.

I pull out my phone to text Cassie when the front door opens. I quickly type my message and hit send and when I look up, Max and Lane are walking toward the island holding a giant pizza. Tyler and I both wave hello.

I glance at my phone again and am surprised to see it's already time to eat lunch.

Max sets the pizza on the island and sits on a stool next to Tyler, who has not moved once since being here. Lane walks past the island and goes straight for the fridge, grabs a drink, and moves to lean on the counter behind me.

"So, Emmett, did papa Davis call you about the article?" Max asks, taking a bite of the pizza.

I groan. "You saw it too?"

"Dude, it's everywhere. People are obsessed with you." Tyler glances up from his phone to interject before quickly refocusing on his screen, the sound of an irrelevant video playing on.

I bring my hand up to my face and rub my temple, closing my eyes for a quick moment while I let out a big sigh. When I open my eyes, my phone buzzes, but before I have the chance to look at it, Lane decides to add to the current conversation.

"Wait, I didn't see it!" I wait a few seconds for Lane to look it up. "Oh shit, man!" he says to me. Then, looking at Max, he adds, "He definitely called about this photo. Look!" He holds his phone out, pointing to Cassie and I's interlocked hands. "They're holding hands! Definitely screams relationship." He pulls his phone back, zooming in and out, laughing.

"Are you done?" I ask, shaking my head back and forth in annoyance.

"Come on." Lane flashes me his phone screen, which is still showing the photo from the article. "You look happy."

I roll my eyes, but he's right. I *am* happy.

"Well, we're just friends. I'm not allowed to date anyone at the studio, remember?"

I look from Max to Lane, and then to Tyler to ensure they all heard me. I find them all nodding and muttering under their breath.

"Good. No one better bring this up when Cassie comes over."

"But—" Tyler starts to talk, returning his attention to the group.

I hold up a hand in front of his face. "Nope. I'm shutting this down now."

Wrinkles appear in Tyler's forehead as he squints his eyes and lets out a small groan. "You're no fun."

"At least I'm rich, eh?" I smile and hold both hands out in a *look at me* fashion.

A donut hits me in the face. I twist quickly to my left to find Marcy laughing at me.

"Hi to you too, Marce. Just come in, why don't you?" I walk over to the sink to grab a towel, running it under the water so I can wipe the glaze off of my face.

"Door was unlocked." Marcy takes the last seat at the island, sitting next to Lane on a barstool. Max has since moved to sit on the couch and is now flipping through movies available to watch.

"And the donut?"

"For the article, of course, you dumbass." Marcy grabs her own donut, jelly filled, and takes a bite. The jelly spills out of the opposite end, dripping onto the counter. I'm still holding the wet towel from wiping up my donut mess, so I toss it over for her to clean up her mess before I start stress cleaning.

"I promise, Marce, it's nothing. Don't look into it," I warn, keeping a straight face.

"Mhm." She shrugs, not impressed with my explanation.

"Anyway, Cassie and Lucy are coming over tonight before their shift at the diner, so you better cool it. I already warned the guys."

"I'm not scared of you," Marcy says. She hops down from the stool and moves over by Max, plopping next to him on the couch.

If I wasn't nervous about tonight, I am now. Marcy has a way of shoving her thoughts and opinions into my business, and normally I'm grateful for her help with obsessive fans, but I don't *need* her to protect me.

I walk over to sit on the armchair to the right of the couch.

"I'll be good, I promise." I look up to see Marcy looking at me, eyes softened. I nod and return a small smile.

It's moments like these that I wish my parents were kind and loving and wanted to be in my life. I have these great people around me, supporting me, not asking for anything in return, yet I can't help but feel *empty*. Alone. I wish my parents would ask me about my day or find an interest in my hobbies. Except, that's never been their story.

It's always about where I'm going or how much I can accomplish. I'd like to say my mom's better, but she's not. She supports my acting but always agrees and sides with my dad. I couldn't tell them about writing, they wouldn't understand.

Not that I've opened up to my friends either, besides the basics. They know I like to write and that I do it sometimes during my time off between contracts, but they don't know that I *love* writing.

Looking around the room, I want to tell them. I know they'd be supportive of whatever I wanted to do, but I can't help but question it. They have known me as Emmett, the actor, for too long. What would they think of Emmett, the writer? Just plain Emmett?

It's ridiculous, I know. To put these perceived opinions on them, but it's the circumstances of our friendships. Marcy is most likely stuck with me for life, as my adopted little sister, but we don't talk about our careers much besides surface-level things. Tyler is busy with his catering, and I love that for him, but we also don't talk about life things.

I talk to Max and Lane about writing the most. Since they started the casting business, I've been curious about the logistics and how they have made it successful. It's given me a lot of insight on what to look out for if I were to go off on my own and pursue my writing. I've told them I like to write screenplays, but that was a random point in time that feels like ancient history.

Cassie is the only person who's read my writing and has somehow turned into my own personal muse. That's gotta mean something, right? I mean, I can't explain the pull I get when I'm around her. It's *magical*. I see her and thoughts immediately start piling up in my head, overflowing and nagging at me to write them down.

It's both terrifying and exhilarating. A chain reaction that I can't stop or tame. That's how my brain feels when I'm around Cassie.

I'm pulled out of my thoughts by my phone ringing. I sigh and groan, slinking into my chair deeper.

Lane walks over from the kitchen, peering over my shoulder. "Mommy troubles?"

I grab the pillow next to me and toss it up into his face. I stand up to answer the call, and Lane takes the advantage to steal my spot.

"I'm taking that back." I point to the chair. Lane nods, then swiftly turns to watch whatever is on television. I didn't pay attention enough to figure out what they turned on.

I walk down the hall toward my bedroom, shutting the door before I hit the accept button on my phone.

"Hi, Mom."

"Hi, sweetie. Happy birthday." It's almost as if I can hear her smile and it makes me sad again. Not sad that they aren't here, more so sad that I don't think she realizes she's no longer a close figure in my life.

"Thanks, Mom. Staying busy today?" I ask.

"Mhm, mhm. The growth in my garden has been astonishing. You wouldn't believe it, sweetie. I mean, cucumbers, tomatoes, carrots, potatoes... I could keep going on, but I wouldn't want to bore you with the details." She adds an innocent chuckle.

"Not a bother. Happy to hear the garden is going well. Dad around?" Not that I want to talk to him, but I always ask. It's the same script every time we talk.

"No, he's out with some friends. Golfing, I believe. He told me you two talked though and informed me about your little friend," she says in a motherly tone. I can hear clashing tools and a bit of muttering. I can only assume she's trying to carry things and talk on the phone at the same time.

"Just a friend, yes. No need to worry. Dad already talked to me about it." I'm wondering why I bother to answer her calls anymore. They tend to just be a reminder of my dad's call. To push my buttons a little further until I'm about to pop.

"Okay, sweetie. I know. We trust you. We just want the best for you, you know?" I hum in response. "I hate to cut this short, but I think it might just rain. Dang weather. We'll talk later this week, okay? Love you."

"Love you too, Mom." I remove the phone from my ear and hang up with one last sigh.

Greetings from outside the room reach me, so Cassie must be here. I should get out there before the guys gang up on her for something or the article gets mentioned. Both of which I don't want to happen. I will say that Cassie seems to blend in with our group seamlessly, minus Marcy, who is still a little apprehensive.

I stand up from the bed and walk out of the room, shutting the door behind me. When I get to the living room, I'm hit with the smell of lavender and citrus. A scent I've familiarized myself with. Cassie is sitting in the other chair to the left of the couch talking to Marcy, who moved to the other side. Lucy is sitting at the island with Tyler. My gaze meets Cassie's, and she waves while giving me a small smile. I continue walking toward her and for once I have hope that maybe she's feeling the same way.

13

CASSIE

I WISH I COULD stop time and freeze this moment. Here I am, sitting in this chair in the last place I would have expected a few weeks ago. I smile at Marcy as she tells me about her family, which I take as a good sign that she's not mad at me. No one has mentioned the article Annie called to tell me about this morning, so I'm breathing a little easier.

This group of friends is special because they support and encourage each other in everything they do. Sometimes, I wonder if I would have made friends like this years ago if I had put myself out there. I've been so busy ensuring that acting is my number one focus and priority that I forgot to live a little. I've forgotten what it's like to not worry about if I'm behind or if I'll land an audition.

I've felt my mood shift over the past few weeks. I'm no longer as anxious when I go to acting class. In the past, I would obsess over scenes and practice nonstop. If I wasn't at the diner or having dinner with Lucy, I was rehearsing, trying to improve my craft. There's nothing wrong with being ambitious, but when it takes over your whole life, it becomes unhealthy, and I see that now.

I've let my fear of losing this dream chase away potential people that could have been by my side encouraging and rooting for me.

Looking at Emmett, who's currently in an intense conversation with Lane about the latest basketball game, I'm grateful. He somehow penetrated my wall and pulled me into this little group of his, even though I wasn't the most willing participant.

I can't help but stare at him, and when he catches me, his lips break into a smile and his eyes widen with delight.

"Hi." I mouth the word since he's across the room. We haven't had the chance to talk since I've been here. As soon as I knocked, the door opened to reveal everyone in the living room watching a movie. Lucy walked past me and went straight to Tyler, something we will need to talk about later. It's a little suspicious.

Marcy waved me over to sit by her, and part of me thought she would reprimand me for the article. Okay, well, most of me thought that. I definitely assumed she'd at least question me about it.

Lucy and I were eating breakfast when Annie called to tell me about the article.

"When were you going to tell me about you and Emmett?" She had asked.

She caught me off guard, but I wasn't sure what she meant. She knows I work with him, but she couldn't possibly know I was hanging out with him. Lucy didn't tell her and she's the only one that knows.

"The article, Cass! Really? You have a Hollywood article featuring you and you don't even know. I can't believe it." She scoffed.

Lucy pulled up the article, waved her phone to show me, and sure enough it was a photo of Emmett and me leaving his party.

"How do you know that's me?" I asked. My face isn't showing. It's just my back profile, which could be anyone.

"One, it's pretty obvious since I know you." I glanced over at Lucy for confirmation to find her already nodding in agreement. "Two, you're wearing our matching bracelet."

Shit. "And three?"

"Call it sister intuition." She chimed. I could picture her then, sitting cross-legged on her bed with a giant smile, proud of her discovery.

So, that was how I found out that what I thought was a small article was in fact larger than I expected. Then Emmett invited me over, and I thought he might want to talk about it or tell me we can't be friends, but he told me to bring Lucy and that everyone would be over. He acted like it didn't happen, or that he didn't know the article existed.

Which is *impossible,* right? He must not care, or maybe he doesn't want to talk about it. What if he's embarrassed by it?

Doubtful, but still a possibility. I have to look at it from all angles.

"You good, Cass?"

I whip my head in the direction the voice came from to find Emmett kneeling next to my chair. His brow is furrowed, creating deep creases on his forehead, as if begging to be smoothed out to erase the worry etched on his face.

My gaze lowers and my breathing quickens. I try to think of something to say, but my mind is blank. All I can think of is Emmett, in front of me, inches away from me, my arm brushing his chest.

I like a guy on his knees.

Emmett brows draw together, as if he knows exactly what thoughts are swirling around in my head.

Right. The question. I quickly nod, hoping my cheeks aren't as red as they feel. I offer a nervous grin, hoping it looks normal.

"Thanks for inviting me." My voice is almost a whisper.

Glancing around, I notice everyone is sitting around the island eating pizza. Marcy must have stepped away.

"They all decided it was time to eat," Emmett says, glancing in the same direction as I am.

"Mhm," I mutter. My stomach grumbles as if on cue. I move my right arm from the arm of the chair and cover my stomach.

Emmett chuckles and stands up, holding out a hand. "Come on, Sass. Let's go eat."

Of course, he adds a wink. It wouldn't be a normal Emmett conversation without a few winks that turn my insides into puddles and make my heart stutter.

I sigh, roll my eyes in return, and place my right hand in his. As soon as I'm up, he squeezes once and our hands come apart.

Out of habit, I'm about to reach for him again when my gaze meets Marcy's and I remember where I am.

In Emmett's apartment, with *his* friends, we aren't supposed to be anything more than platonic.

I walk to the kitchen to stand by Marcy since her gaze never left mine. I don't know a lot about her and Emmett's relationship, but I know that it's a little complicated with her working at the studio and also being one of his best friends. She's caught between being supportive and wanting to follow the rules. I get it, but I need to win her over.

"I'm so thankful you started when you did," Marcy says while grabbing another slice of pizza. She leans back on the counter next to me, facing toward the rest of the group.

Emmett's sitting next to Lane at the island. Our glances connect for a moment.

I shift my gaze over at Marcy, who's currently also looking at Emmett, who is looking at me. When her eyes finally meet mine, the urge to fidget is overwhelming and I think about making up an excuse to leave at this very moment.

"It's busier than I thought it would be," I say, trying to move the conversation in a more positive direction instead of feeling like she's shooting daggers at me.

She hums a response. "It is. I don't think they originally planned it to be that way, but once you joined and Ed saw the opportunity..." she trails off. "It worked out that you're getting more *comfortable* with the rest of the staff and crew." She's testing me.

I fight back the urge to tell her to chill the fuck out. Instead, I take a bite of my pizza and nod in agreement.

"Cassie!" Tyler calls from the other side of the island.

I meet his gaze and raise my eyebrows, waiting for him to keep speaking.

"What'd you think of the article?"

My jaw drops and my hand pauses bringing the pizza up to my mouth.

"Tyler." Emmett glares and gives Tyler a silent warning.

Tyler doesn't even bother looking over at Emmett. He decides to stir the pot.

"I thought it was funny, to be honest." Tyler leans back in his chair, crossing his arms over his chest. "Emmett hasn't had his face in the tabloids for a few months."

"Oh, um." I look around the room to find everyone staring at me, waiting to see how I will respond. "There's a first time for everything, I suppose. I'm just glad it didn't show my face." I take a bite of my pizza again, swallowing the nerves alongside the greasiness of the pepperoni.

"You're a dick, Tyler," Emmett chimes in.

Tyler's head turns toward Emmett, jaw slacked. "I just wanted to talk about the elephant in the room, so you're welcome. You've been so worried about what she thought about it, I thought I'd ask."

Emmett glances toward me, cheeks flushed, and returns his gaze to Tyler. "What a way to go about it," Emmett says, adding a humorless laugh.

"It's fine, promise," I say, trying to make the situation better. I genuinely don't mind the article, since I was anonymous. "Besides, it's false anyway."

"Hm?" Emmett looks at me. Obviously, he knows the article is promoting false news. I don't get why he wants me to spell it out.

I glance at Marcy, who's still standing to my right and patiently waiting for my reply like everyone else.

"The article stated we're together, which is false. We're just..." I trail off. I realize I don't want to assume we *are* friends, even though I don't know how else someone would categorize our relationship.

"Friends?" Emmett smirks.

I nod quickly, my cheeks growing hotter by the minute. Damn cheeks, showing my emotions like a star on a clear night.

I need a moment alone, so I excuse myself to use the bathroom. A tug at my wrist has me pausing in the middle of the hallway. I already know who it is before turning around.

"What are you doing?" I ask.

"I just wanted to make sure you were okay." Emmett averts his gaze, looking behind him to make sure no one followed. "I told him not to bring it up, but he never listens."

"I'm fine."

"Fine? I don't believe you," Emmett challenges, staring into my eyes.

"I'm *fine.*"

"And are we *honestly* just friends, Cassie?"

"No." I enjoy watching his eyes widen in surprise. "You're also a pain in my ass."

"You're warming up to me. I can feel it. Don't you?" Emmett leans his shoulder against the wall, his head following suit. His eyes never leave mine. "There's something between us, Cass. You can't ignore it forever." A small smile appears.

Before I can respond, Emmett winks and spins around to walk back into the kitchen. He leaves me standing in the middle of the hallway, baffled by what just happened. What *did* just happen? Do I *like* Emmett?

Of course I do. It started as a little baby crush, likely stemming from the flirting and small touches, and it might have turned into a medium crush last night at the party. He doesn't need to know that. I need him to keep believing that I want nothing to change between us, not just because it's forbidden by rules and *blah, blah, blah*, but because I don't have time.

I don't have the time to fixate on a romantic relationship while I'm still struggling to land a damn gig.

Running my hand through my hair, I realize I should use the bathroom like I said I would and return to the kitchen before someone wonders where I am and why it's taking me 10 minutes.

When I get back to the kitchen, I notice Lucy by the front door. She's still talking to Tyler, but at least she's putting on her shoes. I glance to my left to view the time on the microwave and it's time to go. If we don't leave now, we risk being late to the diner, and I don't think it would thrill Dave.

Lucy lets me know she'll meet me by the car. She's going to call her parents or something. I walk over to the front door and slip on my shoes. When I turn around to grab my bag off the hook by the door, I find Emmett. He's holding my bag and jacket for me. I take the jacket first, slipping it on, and grab my bag from him.

"I'll walk you out," Emmett tells me like it's a done deal.

I turn my head to look into the living room and kitchen, at everyone still in his apartment. "You don't need to."

"I want to." He walks a few steps forward, closing the distance between us. With his left hand, he reaches for the door handle, twists it, and starts opening the door. I sidestep once to the left to get out of the way so the door can open all the way. "Plus, they'll be fine." His head tilts to the right to gesture to his friends occupying his space.

"Okay."

I wave and say goodbye to everyone, letting them know I'll see them at the studio on Monday. Marcy doesn't seem elated that I'm walking out with Emmett, but I can't let that cloud my thoughts for the evening.

We walk in silence down the hallway, Emmett on my left, slowly making our way to the elevator doors. He leans across my body to press the down arrow button, meeting my gaze for a moment before returning to a standing position.

When we get in the elevator, he reaches for my hand. I let him intertwine our fingers together. With a quick, anxious movement, I bite my lip and purposely avoid meeting his gaze. I don't *want* to see how he's feeling.

I will not kiss Emmett. I will not kiss Emmett. I will not kiss Emmett.

The entire elevator ride is silent, my heartbeat echoing off the walls. It's loud, and beats a million times a minute. Instead of having a cheeky conversation with Emmett, I'm stuck with thinking of him. Thinking about how his hand feels in mine. It's *electric*. I notice every time his finger moves against my hand, every intake of breath, and every time Emmett shifts his weight. His gaze never wavers from me, as if he's trying to decipher my feelings and responses to our hand-holding.

After our hallway conversation, I'm so confused. This whole time I've been in Los Angeles and I've never felt like this with anyone else.

I've never longed to be pressed against the elevator wall. To have the elevator break and be stuck in here for hours with no escape. I want an excuse to be trapped with Emmett.

Unfortunately, the elevator dings to let us know we've made it to the garage level, which dispels my fantasy.

I look to see our hands still together and look to my left to meet Emmett's eyes. A small smile first appears. His bottom lip disappears under his teeth and I'm back to wanting to slam him against the elevator wall.

Emmett sighs and shakes his head in a way that conveys he's thinking very similar, frustrating thoughts. He gives my hand one squeeze and then lets go. He reaches out with the same hand to hold open the elevator doors to let me out.

"Text me?" he asks.

"Obviously." I tease, dipping my head, batting my eyelashes, and shaking my head a few times.

He chuckles.

"Goodnight, Cassie." Emmett gets the last words in as the elevator door closes between us and climbs back up to his floor.

It feels like the walk of shame as I strut to Lucy's car. Despite the early hour of 7:30 at night, there is a noticeable absence of people coming and going from the garage. It's a small space, so that makes sense. Most people that live here likely have drivers and leave out the front door.

Lucy doesn't even see me walking toward the car. She's looking at her phone and appears busy with furrowed brows. I can only assume it has something to do with her upcoming art show. There's always something that she's grumbling about. I can't keep it straight. Too many paintings, not enough paintings, maybe a different color scheme, tickets sold, tickets not sold, and 100 other various topics.

"Everything okay?" I ask as I buckle in, setting my bag by my feet. I adjust the air to blow more directly at me, turning the temperature in the car from a warm 71 to a cool 68. My body still feels like it's on fire after the elevator ride.

"Hm?" Lucy asks, turning her head to face me. "Oh, yeah, everything is just fine. Same shit, different day." She flips the music to play an alternative playlist and sets the phone in her lap before driving us out of the garage.

"How was the walk with Emmett? Talk about anything interesting?" Lucy glances at me.

I shake my head. "Please don't start. We are *friends*. Nothing happened. Nothing *can* happen."

Lucy just nods in response.

With everything in close proximity, we're already pulling into the diner parking lot a few minutes later, so we have little time to chat.

"Shit," Lucy mutters.

I look up from my phone to see the parking lot of Dave's Diner packed. Every spot is full. I groan. Tonight was supposed to be slow. I was *hoping* it would be slow. Slow means I can go home early and go to bed, which I desperately want to do. I didn't realize how exhausting these past few weeks would be trying to balance it all.

With the addition of last night and tonight, I'm drained and not sure I have the right mindset to wait on people.

"Lucy, I need to quit." I surprise myself by saying these words out loud.

She turns off the ignition after parking in an employee spot in the back. "Girl, I know. I do too. Can you at least wait until *after* this shift? You wouldn't be a great best friend if you left right now." Lucy grabs her bags from the back, full of books that she won't get to because of the crowd of people and food the guys sent with us to snack on later.

"Yeah, yeah. I won't leave you hanging."

"Just promise me you will still make time for me between your new boyfriend and the studio." Lucy wiggles her eyebrows.

I glare at her. "Not my boyfriend—"

Lucy holds up her hand in between us. "But he wants to be! He was eye-fucking you the *entire* night."

I roll my eyes and grab my bag. "Anyway, yes, I will obviously make time for you. It helps that we live together."

"True. You can't get away from me, even if you wanted to."

For the rest of the night, I can't get Emmett out of my head. Every time I overhear a patron talk about touring the studios, I have to bite my tongue and walk the other way. I'm afraid I'll say something about knowing Emmett, or ask strangers what they think about him.

I take time to talk to Dave, let him know that I'm quitting. Telling him in person is the least I can do for having spent so many years here. He's always been supportive, so I wasn't nervous to tell him. That was the easy part.

The hard part is now I'm relying on the studio and trusting myself to land a role before the end of the year. If I don't, it may be time to move on.

14

EMMETT

I KNEW I HAD it bad as soon as the elevator doors closed and the familiar butterflies in my stomach began to flutter.

Every time my thoughts wandered, they said '*Cassie, Cassie, Cassie.*'

When I arrived back at my apartment, we all agreed to watch a movie, which only made my wandering thoughts worse, as I had to sit in silence.

Luckily, Cassie texted to tell me she made it to work, and that it was busy, but she's going to quit. Then she sent 10 smiley emojis, and I had to bite my cheeks to prevent the biggest grin in front of my friends.

The rest of the weekend went by quickly. Sundays are my private rehearsal days. I go over the scenes for the week and make sure I know my lines and then spend the rest of the day relaxing. It's my day to reset.

I decide to go to the studio early on Monday. On my walk to my trailer, I browse social media, knowing I could get to my trailer with my eyes closed.

When I get to the steps, I look up to see Cassie standing at my door, waiting for me.

"Shit," I mutter and slam my right hand to my chest. "Warn a man, Sass, before you sneak up on them."

Cassie's looking at me, smiling. She's already holding her clipboard, stacked with papers for the week. I can tell she's happy, probably because she quit the diner Saturday. She's pairing high waisted jeans with a v-neck today, with her radio attached to her hip.

With a giggle she responds, "Sorry, I would have texted you but figured I'd surprise you with coffee."

"What did I do to deserve this?" I ask. I'm partially joking, but in truth I'm surprised to see her here. We texted a little yesterday, and I would have asked her to meet me this morning, but I didn't want to seem desperate to see her or clingy.

"I..." Cassie starts, but then averts her gaze. She bites her lower lip, and upon releasing it, she returns her eyes to mine. "I wanted to see you."

I nod, and a smile dances across my lips. "I figured it was only a matter of time before you fell for me." I lean against the railing of the stairs, crossing my arms, while I watch her cheeks fill with pink.

She shifts from one foot to the other, her eyes on the step under her feet. Although she's looking down, I can see a smile forming. "You wish, Hotshot." Her gaze snaps back to mine.

"Give it time, Sass," I say with a smirk, provoking another chuckle from her. "Want to come inside?"

Cassie nods.

I slip past her on the stairs and open the trailer door, holding it for her to go in before me. She turns to the right and heads to the couch, so I follow her. I choose to sit next to her. Not too close, but close enough to feel her warmth.

"Okay. First, know that it's hard for me to ask this," Cassie starts in a steady tone. She sits up straighter, turning to be fully facing me. "Second, you can say no."

"I won't say no."

"You don't even know what I'm going to ask." Her head dips down, eyebrows furrowing.

"Doesn't matter. I'd say yes to anything you ask." I lean back on the couch, wrapping my left arm on the back, intruding on her space. She glances toward my arm for a moment before returning to me, but she doesn't shift away. "I would say yes if you wanted me to jump off of a cliff."

"Woah now, let's not be ridiculous. I will definitely not be doing that, thank you." Her hands flail in front of her.

"Noted." I decide to push some limits and grab a piece of her hair, twirling it in my hand. Again, she glances but doesn't move.

"I wanted to ask if your offer to act out scenes for my acting class was still standing."

"Of course—"

"Remember, you can say no," Cassie interrupts, lurching forward to emphasize which brings her legs to touch mine.

I bring my hand that was twirling her hair and grab the hand that's resting on her leg. I offer one squeeze, something that has become a secret tell between us. Something to show that everything is okay and we're there for one another.

"I was going to say, before you interrupted me..." I raise my eyebrows. "Of course I will. I already said I wouldn't say no." Cassie rolls her eyes, her signature move. I think she does it because she can't believe how much she likes me. "Want to come over tonight?"

Cassie smiles. "That would be great, actually. I don't have class this week or next, so we can rehearse more. I'll bring the script over after work."

Right. Work. That's a thing.

"Okay." I smile. "Tell me more about this acting class."

Cassie stiffens.

I drag my thumb back and forth on her hand. "I'm just curious, Cass."

"Right. Sorry. I'm not used to others caring about my class or acting in general." She sighs. I continue to move my thumb on her hand, not letting go. "Um, so I told you I moved here five years ago? I already knew I was going to move in with Lucy, so I had just moved all of my stuff into the apartment before deciding I needed a break. I went to a coffee shop that was around the corner, saw a callout form for a local acting group, and that was it." She adds a shrug.

"And do you like the class? Has it been, I don't know, fun? I've never been a part of an acting group, so I'm not sure what they're like."

Cassie laughs and nods. "I like it. Yes." She pulls her right leg up more onto the couch. Our legs were just touching, but after moving, her knee is resting on mine. She leans back onto the couch, getting more comfortable. She laughs some more. "Okay, don't judge me for this."

I let go of her hand and slam mine to my chest, dropping my jaw. "Me? Never." I shake my head slowly, back and forth. Cassie playfully pushes on my chest with her now free hand, which causes me to lose my balance, my right shoulder going toward the couch. When I bounce back, I rest my hand on her knee instead of back in her hand.

"The callout form only had an address. No phone number, no building name, nothing. Literally just an address." She pauses. "Don't look at me like that. I know the risk I was taking, but I couldn't find any classes before I moved here that either had openings or didn't cost too much."

I realize my jaw is open, for obvious reasons. Someone could have robbed her or kidnapped her. I shut my mouth and let her continue.

"So the building looked abandoned, but when I entered the front door, there were signs leading up the stairs to a room that they were hosting this class in. Turns out their old building had water damage, and this space was the only temporary place available. Still sketchy as fuck, but it turned out to be a fun class and everyone was nice, so I stuck around."

"Wow. That's awesome how it all worked out. Kinda like fate, huh?"

"I suppose, yes. If you believe in that sort of thing," Cassie replies.

"We feel like fate, don't you think?" I ask before I have time to think about the words coming out of my mouth.

"Emmett." Cassie dips her head, playfully glaring at me.

I squeeze her knee. "I would love nothing more in the world than to continue sitting here talking to you, but I bet we need to get on the set."

She responds with a groan, throwing her head back onto the couch. What I would give to lean forward and press my lips on her neck, sucking enough to leave a mark for everyone else to know that she's mine.

I don't realize I'm squeezing her knee until her hand covers mine and gives my hand a squeeze. "Careful, Hotshot. You might leave a mark." She adds a wink and moves to stand up.

My hand regretfully slides off her leg, but my brain is still thinking about what she said. *You might leave a mark.* I would love to leave a mark. Multiple marks. One on her neck, a few on her chest, her hips, her inner thighs. I can tell my little touches are getting to her. Her pulse quickens when our hands lace, and she fidgets to distract herself from thinking about us too much.

She pauses by the door, turning around to look at me. I'm still sitting on the couch, afraid that if I get up and say goodbye, I won't let her leave.

"See you on set?" she asks.

"Oh, possibly, who knows," I say, smirking the entire time.

Cassie opens the trailer door cautiously, leaning her head outside to check for others. The coast is clear; she lets me know and says bye on her way out of the door.

I don't see Cassie a lot for the rest of the day. Ed has me running around and re-filming scenes because he wanted to "try" something to please his drifting brain of ideas that pop up while filming. I entertain his ideas because it normally helps the day go faster. I don't even make it to the cafeteria, I just eat food from the table on set.

Each time I catch sight of Cassie, our eyes meet, and we exchange a small smile, silently acknowledging each other from opposite sides of the room.

On my way out of the studio, Tyler catches me by the gates.

"I'm still irritated with you." I greet him with a stare and an even tone.

"Oh, shut up." He gently nudges my right arm, causing me to readjust my balance as we walk side by side. "I was helping you break the ice," he adds with a mischievous grin.

"You weren't helping anything worth for shit. You put her on the spot, *and* Marcy is already angry about the whole situation."

"Well, Marcy can get over herself. You're clearly in love with her."

"I am *not*." I like her a lot and I want to be around her all the time, but I don't love her.

"I was exaggerating. You two are fine though, right? I saw her in your trailer this morning."

I whip my head to the right to look at him. "How?"

"I saw her leaving." He glances at me. "After call time this morning."

"Great." Looks like we will need to be more careful about hanging out. I know Tyler wouldn't say anything, but staff at the studio like to gossip during their free time. I don't need an article written based on a story a staff member sold for a few bucks.

We stop walking when we reach the front gate. My driver is waiting outside and I know Tyler parks in the lot to the right.

"Just be careful," Tyler warns. "You know how some people get around here. Little gossip machines."

I laugh. "Yeah, I know. Thanks, man. Let's grab lunch tomorrow."

Tyler nods. "Sounds good."

As he walks away, I walk through the gate and get into the car's backseat.

By the time I get home, I already know Cassie will be here any minute. She texted me while she was leaving the studio to let me know she would stop home first to change into comfortable clothes before coming over. That was only a few minutes after I left, and ever since then I've been spiraling, thinking about what she meant by comfortable clothes. Why? *I don't know.*

Ever since deciding to not filter myself around Cassie, I'm falling faster and faster for her every day just from being around her and talking to her. Tyler wasn't far off, and I'm aching to cross a line with her. I want to *destroy* the barrier she has set up. I want to kiss her and hear the gentle moans she makes as my fingers graze her skin.

I need to get my shit together. These thoughts will make nothing easier when Cassie comes over. It's one thing to want to hang out and talk to her, it's another to want to touch her, and I can't. Or, at least I shouldn't.

I want her to make the first move. I need permission to touch her.

I walk into the kitchen and turn on the electric kettle to make tea for us. I have two cups steeping with some decaf chai when knocking comes from the front door.

"Come in," I yell, taking a moment to pour a little bit of honey in each cup.

When I turn around, I drop the spoon I was holding to stir. Cassie is wearing the *shortest* shorts. It's a matching pink sleep set. Simple, yet it's filling my head with dirty, *dirty* thoughts about dragging the shorts down and slipping the thin shirt over her head.

Clearly my thoughts are displaying on my face because when I meet her gaze, she winks. "Are you done eye-fucking me, Emmett?"

"Hardly," I respond, turning to grab another spoon to stir the honey in the mugs. I reach to pick up the dirty spoon and toss it in the sink. "That's what you consider comfortable clothes? Are you staying the night?" I slide the mug across the island as Cassie takes a seat on one stool on the opposite side.

She nods, taking a sip of the tea. "Yes, these are my comfy clothes. And no, I'm not staying the night." *Damn*, what I'd give for her to say yes.

"Well, drink up, Sass. We have scenes to rehearse. Do you have the script?" I ask.

"Oh! Yes!" She hops down from the stool, walking back toward the front door. She bends over and *dear god*, I know I should look away but I can't. My gaze remains on the way her shorts cling to her, leaving me wondering if she's chosen to go without underwear. Leaving herself bare for me, hoping tonight will lead to somewhere.

I get my composure back once she stands up and walks back to the island. "Here."

She hands me one of the pink folders with the word "RO-MANCE" written in the middle in Sharpie, keeping the other for herself. I lean forward on the island, resting my elbows on the counter. Opening the folder reveals three pages of paper, with words printed on both the front and back.

I take out the first page, skimming the scene. They're your typical romance scenes, full of cheesy lines and all.

"You don't have to do it, you know. You can still say no," Cassie blurts out.

I raise my eyes to meet hers and stand up from the island. Cassie looks at her hands. She's nervous, which is not like her.

"Come on." I move toward the living room. I look back to make sure she's following me. "You coming?"

She nods, biting her lip.

I stop in front of the couch and wait for her to stand in front of me. She stops, but not as close to me as I'd like. There are a solid two feet between us, a gap I plan to close once we act. Her eyes are looking at the scenes.

"You need to relax," I tell her.

"You're not supposed to tell a girl to relax." Her eyes shoot upwards, but her head remains tilted down toward the floor.

"Do you trust me?"

"I don't *not* trust you." Her lips turn up in a smile, then her eyes return to the script.

I roll my eyes. "Let's do this."

"And you're sure you don't have any problems rehearsing with me?" Cassie looks up at me again. "Even after reading the first script?"

"I wish you'd stop asking me that. Of course I'm sure."

"Did you read the whole script?"

"Yes. Are you asking because it ends in a kiss? Nervous you won't be able to resist me?" I tease.

She rolls her eyes this time.

There's my girl. Those three words echo through my head. I try to hold in a smile, but it doesn't work. My mouth forms into a grin.

She smiles but then bites her lip to stop herself from blushing, which does not work one bit. Her cheeks are a soft pink, increasing to the color of a rose.

"Okay, let's do this," Cassie finally says after what feels like an hour of waiting for her to go through the pros and cons of us running lines together in her head.

"It won't be any different from you being an extra, Sass, no pressure." I shrug.

Cassie takes a deep breath and begins the scene.

When she delivers the first line, I try my best not to drop my jaw. She's a natural. The perfect amount of emotion, not too much to be overly dramatic and not too little to seem dry. It's enough to distract me from responding with my line.

"Emmett, that's your cue," Cassie says, smirking at me. I blink my eyes a few times, considering I was just staring at her like she's some rare diamond. Can you blame me? This girl randomly stumbled into my life and has me on my knees. Not literally, although... *no*. I need to focus and not think about my head between her legs.

"Right." I look at the script and then back up to resume the scene. "Don't tell me to leave you. Not now, not ever." I improvise and reach out to grab her hand in mine. She flinches the slightest bit, surprised by my touch, so I give her hand a squeeze.

"It was never meant to get this far. You're better off without me," Cassie says. Dropping my hand, she turns around to face the opposite direction. She peeks back at me, giving me a slight smile, which I can't help but return.

I grab her left hand and pull, twisting her back around to face me. This time, she's mere inches from me instead of the original two feet. I wanted, no, *needed*, her closer to me.

It's time for me to deliver the closing line. I take a step closer and place my left hand on her cheek. "Don't you understand?

You're it for me. There is no one else." She leans into my touch, as if we've done this before and it's now muscle memory.

A single tear falls from her face. "It's always been you for me, too," Cassie replies, and with that, I lean in and press her lips against mine, sealing a single kiss.

If this was a Disney movie, fireworks would go off in the background and there would be romantic instrumental music playing right now. That's how this moment feels. It sure as hell doesn't feel like we're acting.

I take two steps back, dropping her hand, to give us space. It's clear she's as affected by the kiss as I am. It felt overdue. We've been dancing around each other, pulling at the tension between us, and flirting on the edge of pushing the boundaries for weeks.

"That was incredible, Cassie. Did you want to run it again?" I just wanted another chance to kiss her.

"Um, I have another scene we can do. If that's okay?" She glances down at the folder, opens it, and takes the next scene out. I can see her read the scene from left to right, skimming the words on the page.

I copy her, taking out the scene and doing the same.

Once I get done reading the page, I look up to see her already looking at me, studying me. She bites her bottom lip. She still has a slight flush on her cheeks from our first kiss. *Our first kiss.* It's not how I expected things to progress between us, but if I need to pretend with Cassie to show her we can be more than friends, I'll do it. I'll do whatever I need to do to show her I'm not the same as the other guys she's been with. I won't screw her over.

My mouth turns into a smile, and she responds with a small smirk back. The next scene is more intimate, with a little more touching and romantic lines.

"Okay, let's do this," I say, hoping that by the time we finish rehearsing lines, the wall Cassie built up will shatter and disappear.

15
CASSIE

Last week I hadn't considered running lines with Emmett, but after spending a few hot minutes in the elevator, I knew I needed more time alone with him.

My body craved his presence. I longed for his small gestures, like touching my arm or lower back, and holding my hand. I couldn't see him in the studio and not think about what it would feel like to have his lips against mine. Every time he winked at me from across the set, a blush would creep up my cheeks and my stomach would flutter with butterflies.

I know I shouldn't pursue Emmett. That's not what I'm doing. Even thinking about it complicates my plan. I wanted to rehearse scenes with him, knowing they have intimate moments, and just hope the lust and tension disappeared. I figured if I knew what it felt like to kiss him, it'd leave me feeling satisfied, content, and able to go about my day, no longer daydreaming about Emmett's head between my legs.

Fuck.

I was wrong.

So wrong.

It made me want him more.

The instant our lips touched, it was as if I lit the grand finale of a fireworks show in my belly and it's still going off. It's sending electric rhythms throughout my body and my brain is having a hard time deciphering what I should do versus what I want to do.

What I should do is not rehearse another scene that I know will probably lead to me saying something foolish. I should leave. I should say *thanks for the help* and *this means nothing* and *I promise I won't be awkward tomorrow.*

Except I'd be lying. Sure, I'm thankful for his help, but for selfish reasons. I picked these scenes on purpose, knowing it would force him to either say yes, and kiss me, or no. If he said no, I'd at least know he didn't like me. Or want me. Is there a difference? Or maybe our kiss would be terrible and I'd be able to forget about it even easier.

Also, this means *everything* and I will definitely be awkward because now that I know what it's like to kiss Emmett, I don't want to do anything else. I want to kiss him more.

So, we're rehearsing a second scene. A scene that I threw in on a whim, in case I wanted an excuse to pretend for a little longer. To pretend we are two people who are madly in love and alone at last. We are alone, but not *in love.* It's just a... I don't know. I like him. More than I want to admit to myself.

Especially as he openly stares at me, with the deepest of brown eyes that suck me in and hold me captive.

Without breaking his stare, I mutter, "Okay, I'm ready."

Emmett nods and smiles. He takes a seat on the couch and holds out his hand toward me. I raise my eyebrows and wait for him to explain what he's doing. I thought we were standing to run these scenes, as this scene doesn't call for anything different from the other one we just did.

"Sit on my lap." Emmett pats his leg with his left hand, waiting for me to make a move.

"Yeah, no, I get that. Why?" I look at the script to double check it doesn't call for this position. I hold it up in front of me to show. "It doesn't specify sitting in this scene."

"It's called improv, *Sass*." Emmett grins. "You asked for my help and I am a professional." He winks, and that alone turns my insides to mush. "Trust me?" He moves his hand toward me again.

I roll my eyes but place my hand in his, curious to see where this scene will lead. He pulls me toward him. I place a knee on either side of him, straddling his thighs. I don't know where to put my hands, so I opt to put them in between us. The script is still in my right hand in case I need to see the lines.

I shift, adjusting my body to sit closer to him. Emmett's left hand moves to my waist, gripping me. When I look to meet his gaze, he has flushed cheeks and soft eyes. He hardens under me, I'm assuming, because of the proximity of our bodies.

His hand grips me a little tighter, as if he's afraid I will change my mind and get up. Too late for that. Once I've set my mind on something, there's no turning back. I need to see this through to the end. I want to know what happens if I push him just a bit more, testing the limits of his patience.

Emmett glances at the script in his right hand, his eyes moving to find his line.

"I'm glad you invited me to come out tonight," he says, locking our eyes together.

I memorized these lines, so I don't bother looking at my script. I knew I would need to be in the moment with Emmett, so I prepared. When I asked him to rehearse lines with me, I wanted to give in to the tension between us. Just a little.

"Me too. It's been nice to finally have some alone time. Just the two of us." I move my left hand to his chest, rocking my hips forward to move our chests closer together. Emmett's breathing hitches and then settles, his following breaths deeper.

Emmett's gaze trails from my eyes, to my mouth, to between us to where our bodies connect. He sighs, closing his eyes for a moment, before looking back up at me and smirking. If I could read his mind right now, I know what he'd be thinking. *What the fuck are you doing to me? Do you feel this too?*

To which I'd respond, *I feel it all. Too much.*

He finally breaks our stare and looks back at the script.

When he looks up, a soft smile appears. "It was always going to be this way. You and me, you know? I always knew it'd be the two of us in the end."

I knew that line was coming, but I was not prepared to hear it come out of his mouth sounding like *that*. The honest tone of his voice is enough for me to throw all caution to the wind.

I know it's just a line in this scene, but it feels like way more. It's just Emmett and me in our little world, just the two of us. No one knows what we feel for each other, and we haven't even fully admitted that to one another.

I look at the script between our bodies, contemplating my next move. I could stick with the script, deliver the lines, and that'd be that. I feel prepared enough for the showcase. Although I know the reason this feels easy is because it's with Emmett. Romance scenes are always easier when you have a more intimate relationship with your partner.

You know what? The past few months, I've been sticking to my comfort zone and playing it safe. I've been working twice as hard and focusing on preparing for this showcase. I've spent hours and hours working on my craft, all with the goal of securing a role that proves to myself this move was worthwhile.

Fuck it.

I look up from the script, meeting Emmett's eyes with mine. I drop the script between us and move both of my hands slowly up his chest, to his shoulders, and clasp them behind his head.

I bite my lip, drawing his gaze quickly to my mouth before it snaps back to my eyes.

"I want to kiss you," I say in an even tone.

Emmett's eyes widen, his eyebrows furrow, and his head tilts by default. He turns his head to the right and looks at the script still in his hand. He quickly scans for the line I delivered.

Knowing him, he more than likely memorized my response to what he said, and the line I just said is not in the script.

By the time his eyes meet mine, his cheeks are flushed with light pink. "That's not in the script."

I shake my head, my hands still clasped around his neck. I rock forward, bringing our chests mere inches apart.

"It's called improv, *Hotshot*," I tease, throwing his words back in his face.

Emmett rolls his eyes, dipping, then shaking his head with a small chuckle.

With his head still dropped, he glances up at me through his eyelashes.

"Are you going to keep staring at me, or are you going to kiss—"

I'm cut off by Emmett's hand grabbing my neck, pulling my face to his. Our lips slam into one another.

This kiss differs from the first kiss. That kiss was short-lived, a small peck. It was like dipping your toes into the water, trying to feel if you want to go in deeper. This kiss is the opposite. It's a full on cannonball.

He reaches between us, grabs my script, and tosses it to the side. His hand reaches my jaw moments after, cupping my face and encouraging me to turn my head to open more for him.

Our pace slows, each movement becoming more deliberate and filled with passion. It's as though our mouths are exchanging secrets, savoring what we're not allowed to taste. We shouldn't be doing this. We're not allowed to be together. Except we don't care. We're acting on weeks of built up tension, colliding and exploding.

His hands trail down my back, pulling me closer until our chests touch. I move my right hand to his hair, grabbing and lightly tugging as our tongues dance around one another.

A low groan slips from his mouth, begging me to keep going.

He applies light pressure as his hands grab my hips, encouraging me to move. I move rhythmically, rocking back and forth. When our lips break apart, Emmett brings his to my neck. A breathy moan escapes my lips, which only causes him to grip me harder. I spread my legs wider, trying to close the small gap that remains between us. His dick strains in his pants, pleading to be let out.

I grab his face and bring it back to mine, kissing him with intention. The movement of my hips gets faster as his length hardens more beneath me. It only encourages me to kiss him deeper.

"*Cassie*," Emmett says between kisses, but I keep going. He growls, grabs my jaw, and pushes me away, separating our lips. "If you don't quit grinding on my cock, I won't be able to stop. So either we stop now while we're ahead, or I take you to my room and fuck you until my name leaves those beautiful lips." His hands drop back to my waist, tracing small circles with each thumb.

My cheeks darken, flooding with warmth. I bite my bottom lip and avert my gaze. What's happening between us is feeling real, very fast. I thought I was ready to progress things between us, but I didn't expect *that*. I didn't expect to feel the need for him like I do now.

I also didn't expect him to want me as much as he's showing me right now. I was dumb to think that this was merely a small crush, something that I could easily shake off and forget about.

Emmett's right hand cups my face, turning it to face him, forcing our gaze to meet.

"Where's your room?" My voice is barely a whisper.

The hand that was cupping my face moves to be behind my neck as Emmett pulls my face to meet his. Our lips touch, as we savor the decision to continue exploring this side of our relationship.

Emmett takes his hands and hooks them under my butt, lifting me off of the couch as he stands up.

As he walks toward his room, I break apart our kiss, giggling and resting my head in the nook of his shoulder. What should be a romantic moment is interrupted by my laughter, and Emmett holds me tighter, squeezing a little harder.

When we reach his bedroom, he walks to the side of his bed and lets go. I land on the mattress. Emmett holds himself above me, one hand on either side of my head.

"Is there something funny you want to share with me, Sass?" Emmett asks.

I shake my head, unable to form sentences at the moment. I place both of my hands on his chest and push, signaling him to let me up for a second. He obliges, leaning back and stepping to the side.

I hop off of the bed and turn toward him. He's not saying anything, but he's watching me. His gaze remains fixed on me, never missing a single movement. I grab the bottom hem of my shirt and lift it above my head. By the time I have my shirt off, Emmett has moved closer to me. He beats me to the clasp of my bra.

"Let me." Emmett takes a step forward and whispers into my ear. He dips his head and kisses my neck while his hands reach behind my back. I tilt my head to the right to give him more room. When he successfully unclasps my bra, he takes a strap in each hand and slides them down my arms, exposing my breasts. His gaze follows, along with a sharp intake, as my nipples graze his shirt.

After my bra slips from his grasp, he mirrors my action by shedding his shirt. His mouth moves to mine as his hands grasp the back of my shoulders, bringing us closer, as if it's possible to get even closer than we are now.

"Take off those little shorts and get on the bed," Emmett commands between kisses.

I loop my thumbs into my shorts, pulling them down along with my underwear, leaving myself bare.

I sit on the edge of the bed, leaving my legs spread for him. Like clockwork, his gaze travels from my eyes, to my breasts, to between my thighs.

I close my legs, causing his eyes to snap back to mine. Emmett's cheeks are flushed after being caught staring.

"What *now*, Hotshot?" I tease, knowing full well what he wants from me. I like to hear him say it.

"In the middle of the bed. Now."

I scoot toward the head of the bed until my back touches the pillows. Emmett follows me, crawling toward me. Gravity causes my legs to naturally open, giving Emmett the opportunity to move closer.

He moves to be in the middle of them, resting his still-strained cock between my legs. He leans to capture my mouth with his. Our kisses are now hungry, passionate.

Using his left arm to hold himself up, he takes his right hand and slides it down my body. He finds his way to the space between my legs and starts gently caressing my clit with his thumb, tracing small circles where I ache for it the most.

"*More*," I say with a breathy sigh.

Emmett applies more pressure while also increasing his speed. My breath hitches as I get closer to an orgasm, small moans escape my mouth.

Emmett moves his head down my chest, pleasuring me while taking time to lick each breast. He gives small kisses, navigating down my belly until he replaces his thumb with his tongue, my back arching in response.

He uses his left hand to massage my right breast, tugging at my nipple, which is currently a stiff peak.

He inserts one finger in my folds while continuing to lap at my clit, bringing me to reach my first climax of the night.

I grab his hair and pull his head up, cupping his jaw and pulling his face to mine. Tasting myself on his lips and giving myself to him. Finally breaking the barrier between us that's been doing nothing but causing tension.

Emmett sits up to slide off his pants and underwear, his cock springing from the confines of his pants.

I sit up, reaching for his dick. He stops me. I push out my bottom lip in a pout.

"I need to fuck you, otherwise I will come on you, when I'd much rather come inside you," Emmett says.

"Do you have a condom?" I ask.

Emmett nods. He leans over me and opens the drawer on the nightstand to the left of the bed. He pulls out a condom, which I take from him. Emmett stares at me as I open it and slowly slide it over his length.

He positions himself in front of me and teases my slit with his cock, sliding it up and down.

I put both of my hands around his waist, to his back, and try to pull him to me. I want him to stop teasing me and fuck me already.

He slams into me and drops his mouth onto mine to siphon off any moans coming from my lips. I open my mouth, once again inviting his tongue to dance with mine. Between the passion coming from our kiss and Emmett thrusting in and out of me, it feels like we will both hit our climax in record time.

He puts a hand between my thighs and starts rubbing my clit to help me reach another orgasm. I dig my nails into his back and arch mine.

"I'm almost there. Don't stop," I say with a sigh.

He thrusts harder, faster. He increases the pace of his thumb on my clit, causing me to say the one thing he asked for.

"Emmett."

And with that, we finish together, and the sound of our synchronized breaths fills the room with pure bliss.

16
EMMETT

I BLINK MY EYES open as the sun hits me *just* right from the blinds to the right of my bed. My right hand instinctively blocks the direct light while my left hand moves to the previously occupied space on the other side of my bed.

I jerk my head to the left, lifting to rest on my elbow. Cassie is across the room, under my desk, gathering her belongings that were thrown to various areas as last night progressed. *Last night*, what a night. And now Cassie is trying to sneak out.

"What are you doing?" I ask.

Cassie shuffles out from under the desk and faces me. She's still wearing one of my shirts while clutching her clothes and various other accessories in her arms.

"You're not trying to leave, are you?" I ask a different question, since she's yet to respond to my first.

"I'm..." she starts, averting her gaze and looking at the floor. She drops a sock. She leans over to pick it up, but as she does that, she also drops her bra and a tube of chapstick that must have fallen out of her shorts. "Shit," she mutters, trying to figure out a way to pick everything up and not drop anything.

"Come back to bed."

Cassie's still kneeling on the ground, but her gaze snaps up to mine.

"*Please*," I add. I move back the sheets from where she was sleeping, inviting her to come back to me.

Cassie stands up and looks around for where to put all her stuff. Her pile of things, since neither of us expected her to stay the night. She finally settles on the chair in front of my desk, carefully leaning over to set the pile down, ensuring that everything stays put in its place.

She tiptoes back toward the bed, only looking up from the floor at me when she gets close enough to slide under the sheets.

"I won't bite," I say, but then my mind flashes to last night and my cheeks flush as I picture my lips on every available surface of her body. "I mean, I won't bite right *now*. Maybe later, though." I smirk.

Cassie rolls her eyes, laying back next to me. She rolls over on her side to face me, wrapping her right arm under her head.

"I wasn't expecting you to wake up." Cassie finally speaks to me, although it's a whisper at best. She's transfixed on a single thread that's exposed itself from the edge of the sheet. She's currently twisting it in between her thumb and pointer finger.

Gently, I place my hand under her chin, lifting it up to meet my gaze. "I wasn't expecting you to leave without saying goodbye." Cassie looks back down before returning her eyes to me. My thumb softly glides across her jaw as I wait for her to reply.

She bites her lip, and her eyebrows furrow. "I didn't want to assume that you wanted me to stay. I wasn't exactly sure *what* to expect after last night."

This girl. Have I not clarified that I'm infatuated with her? That last night was weeks in the making for me?

"I don't want you to leave," I say, pressing my lips against hers in a single kiss. "Isn't it obvious that I like you, Cassie?" I press another kiss to her lips before letting her say something back. I lean back on my pillow, mocking her position.

"It's... complicated?" Her left shoulder lifts in a shrug, her eyebrows following the same direction.

It *is* complicated. "No one has to know, if that's what you're worried about. I hope you know I wouldn't tell anyone and risk anything with your job. I've been trying to be careful."

"Flirting with me in public is being careful?" Cassie counters.

"Would you rather I ignored you?" I ask. Cassie lets out a small laugh, which I'm grateful for, because it helps lighten the conversation.

"I don't think you could do that, even if you tried."

"You're right. Sure, it's complicated, but I *do* like you. And I *think* you like me too?" I ask. She nods, tucking her left hand under her head and snuggling more into the pillow. "Then I don't think it's a complication between us. It's things around us that make it complicated."

We both sigh, showing that we share similar thoughts about the "no dating" rule and our forbidden romance.

"There is a way to avoid the complication," Cassie says, and my eyes widen with curiosity.

"Go on..."

"We could do this—" she takes her left hand out from under her head and points from me back to her, "in secret."

"In secret," I repeat, thinking. It could work. I want it to work. We've already been public about our friendship, so it's not odd to see us together at the studio.

"I mean, we don't have to. I was just thinking out loud," Cassie quickly says since I'm clearly taking too long to respond.

"You should know I don't casually date. If we continue *this*," I gesture between us, parroting what she did, "you're mine. No one else's."

"I'm... yours." My eyes widen, and I furrow my brow at her lack of confidence. "You're insufferable. I'm yours, okay? Yours, no one else's, secretly," she adds, grinning at her response.

"I like when you're extra sassy." I extend my left arm and start sliding it under her arm and head, encouraging her to nest herself closer to me, which she does.

Just as I'm about to kiss her, the jarring sound of a phone ringing breaks the silence, pulling us back to reality. "I think that's yours," I whisper in her ear. She groans and boy, do I feel that way too.

Cassie rolls over, plants her feet on the ground, and walks over to the chair where her pile of things still sits. Miraculously, nothing has fallen over. She digs to find her phone, which was at the bottom of the pile. Everything is now back on the floor, surrounding the bottom of the chair. This time, she doesn't bother picking it up.

"Hi, Annie." She answers the phone with a smile, walking over to sit back on the edge of the bed.

As she talks, I sit up and move to sit behind her, leaning to kiss her neck. Distracting her. Taunting her. Torturing her. I know it's working because Cassie keeps fidgeting and glancing back at me while still trying to remain engaged in the conversation with her sister.

"Annie, I need to go. I'll call you later and we can chat about this." She pauses. "Yeah. No, I will not tell Emmett you said hello." I pinch her side. She whips her head back to me and glares. "Because Anns. Yes, I know him." A pause. "It's complicated." She glances back at me again. I wink at her. "Love you too. Mhm, okay, fine, if I see him I'll let him know your thoughts on his last movie. Great. Bye." She takes the phone away from her ear and presses the end call button.

"Emmett..." she drawls. She sets her phone on the end table before turning toward me.

She surprises me by pushing me back on the bed, pinning my arms with her hands. She then crawls close enough to throw her left leg over me, straddling me.

"Cassie."

She leans over and captures the end of her name with her mouth, giving herself to me again.

For the next hour, we lazily roll around in bed, pleasuring and giving in to each other. It's somehow different from last night. After last night, I knew we broke the barrier she had up. I know she can trust me because I have shown her time and time again that I have her best interests at heart. I would never betray her like past guys did. Acting not being my true passion helps, but it doesn't make her feelings any less valid.

She's used to being used, and stepped on, for others to cheat their way into roles. I don't blame her for putting up such a large front and not originally trusting my intentions with wanting to explore things with her. She made that clear from our first interaction in the diner when I asked her to sit with me.

Slowly, over the past month, we've become closer. A single hang out turned into smaller texts, which turned into occasional phone calls, and every step has led us here. It led us to the moment where we both admitted to each other that we like one another and that we were going to try to secretly be exclusive.

I don't know how it's going to go, or what our future looks like, but I don't want to ruin today by thinking about that.

I want to live in the present. In this moment, with her.

After our morning fondle, we quickly get ready because it's only Tuesday and we both have to be at the studio.

Cassie leaves first, and I leave 10 minutes later. I figured staggering our arrival is a good idea, otherwise we might have to come up with some excuse, and I don't have the energy for that. Not just because of my time with Cassie, but because I don't want to lie if I can avoid it.

Ed is waiting for me on the stairs of my trailer as I approach.

"Hi, Ed," I shout.

He looks up from his clipboard and smiles. He walks down the stairs to meet me.

"Emmett! I was hoping you had a few minutes to chat through something." He looks at his clipboard again, flipping through the first few pages. He never looks back up but continues walking with me up the stairs of the trailer.

"Yeah, sure, Ed."

I open the trailer door, walking through first. Ed follows me inside and stands by the entrance, not moving to take a seat. It looks like he won't be staying for long, so I wonder what he needs to talk about. I know we only have two months left of filming. I sit on a kitchen stool, waiting for him to finish flipping through the pages. If I interrupted him, he'd start mumbling something back to me in response, but more than likely it wouldn't be the topic he wanted to talk about because his focus was currently on whatever he's looking at.

So instead of doing that, I wait and finally he sighs and drops the clipboard by his leg.

"Have you decided what you're doing after this film, Emmett? I have been told you haven't signed any contracts," Ed says. There is no sign of judgment in his tone, just a pure question that leads me to believe he's curious to know the answer. Ed is more like a mentor to me than anyone I've had in this career, so he's been a part of some of my conversations with my agent since I trust him.

I haven't had a conversation with my agent in months.

"Um." I fidget with a napkin that was left on the counter, keeping my eyes down. "I'm not sure." I peek up at Ed to find him still just looking at me.

"Well, you know we stop filming in two months. As of now, I have nothing else lined up at the studio that I know of." Ed would have helped me land a role in whatever movie was filming here next. It's sort of an unspoken deal between us, since Marcy and the guys work here.

But he has nothing else lined up. It gives me an idea, but I don't know if it's a ridiculous idea. I *have* been writing more and I have a great start on a script that I started recently. I wonder, do I have what it takes to finish the script and get it produced? Could I *actually* stop acting? Would my friends still like me when I'm not an actor?

Of course they would.

I hope.

Still, I wonder. I've had this newfound sense of purpose for writing and it *feels* right. It's always felt too difficult and out of reach, but now... now it feels meant to be. It's kind of like Cassie. A few weeks ago, I was just a guy trying to get a girl's attention in a diner in the middle of the night. Today, we are *exclusive* and I've been writing more than I ever have.

"Emmett? You okay?" Ed pulls me out of my thoughts. I nod a few times.

"Yeah, Ed. I am. Let me think about it and I'll get back to you, okay? I have a few ideas," I explain, hoping it's enough for this conversation to end.

"Of course. Just try to let me know by…" He brings his clipboard back up to his face, flipping the first few pages, searching for a date, I can only assume. "Let me know in a few weeks. I want to make sure I'm available if you need me. You know how the end of filming gets." Ed chuckles.

Yep. The last few weeks of filming are typically our busiest, trying to film any last-minute scenes and saying bye to everyone on set. It's productive and emotional as hell.

I give Ed a nod and a wave goodbye as he leaves my trailer. While being caught up in my feelings for Cassie, I momentarily forgot about this looming decision about my career. What the fuck do I do? I have enough savings to take a risk and leave this sector of the industry, but what would that mean for my future? Would anyone take a risk on me? *What would Cassie think*?

Taking my phone out of my back pocket, I open up my messages with Cassie. I decide to text her and ask if she wants to come over for dinner tonight. I need *someone* to talk to about all of this, and I don't have anyone else.

I can't talk to Marcy about it because she'd likely just glare at me and tell me I'm "making a dumb mistake and I'll regret it." She would then later regret what she said and be supportive of whatever I do, but she can be a little bitter in the moment, especially on a substantial change like us no longer working together.

Tyler, Lane, and Max would understand, but I don't know how to explain it. It's *different*. I can easily go to them about other issues, like when I disagree with a script or have contracts I need advice on. This is a more intimate issue. It's personal. And for some reason, Cassie is the only person I want to talk to about it.

Well, I know the reason. I like her. A lot. More than a lot. A metric ton. I like her more than most people and I've known her for the shortest amount of time.

I sigh into my palm. I have it *bad*.

My phone buzzes with a text back from Cassie. She'll be over around six. That leaves me eight hours until I get to have her alone again. To distract my mind, I spend the next hour reading lines and doom scrolling on my phone.

The door to my trailer swings open. Marcy walks up the stairs. I side-eye her from where I'm sitting.

"What are you doing just sitting there? You're supposed to be on set." Marcy glances at her clipboard. No one around here would survive without one. She slides her pointer finger in various directions on the page. "Ah, yes, 10 minutes ago, hence why I'm here." She looks up from the clipboard, a giant grin plastered on her face.

"You could have radioed me." I stand up from the stool and push it back under the island. I walk toward her. She turns back toward the door, opens it, and starts walking down the stairs as I follow.

"I could have, but I was getting ready to head off-site and Ed asked me to check on you. He said you two talked and you still haven't decided what you're doing after this?" She glances back for a moment to see my reaction, which is why I ensure a neutral reaction. No one needs to see my struggle.

Also, why is everyone so worried about my next contract? My dad, Ed, Marcy, and I'm sure there are a few others that just haven't bothered me yet. I can make my own damn decisions and I have enough money to be without a job for the next few years if nothing happens immediately with my writing.

"I'm working on it." I keep it vague, hoping she doesn't decide to press me for more information.

Thankfully, she doesn't and just asks me about my week so far while we walk toward the studio. I scroll on my phone while giving her one-word answers, not in the mood for small talk today.

"Hi, Cassie!" Marcy greets and my eyes snap up to find Cassie coming out of the studio door, walking toward us. Marcy embraces Cassie in a hug. I find Cassie's gaze and raise my eyebrows in question. I wasn't aware Marcy was a fan of Cassie. I thought she still held some sort of grudge against her.

Cassie's cheeks flush in response as Marcy steps back from their hug. "Hi, Marcy. I'm excited to get lunch later."

Marcy turns to me. "I asked Cassie for lunch today to get to know her better. I figure if she's going to hang around the group more, it would be nice for us to become friends."

"Carla is joining us too!" Cassie chimes in.

Marcy turns to Cassie. "Oh! Great! Wonderful." She turns back to me. "Sorry Emmett, ladies' lunch. I'm sure you'll be fine with the guys."

"I have a scene during lunch today. *You* should know that, Marcy, queen of schedules," I tease and send Cassie a wink while Marcy is looking at her clipboard to check the schedule.

"Bye ladies!" I wave as I walk through the door to the studio set, the door closing as Marcy asks Cassie what she did last night after work.

I stand by the door momentarily, trying to figure out if I can hear what they are saying, but Ed calls my name from the other side of the room. Since I'm already late, I strut over to see him. I'm hoping today goes by quickly because I have dinner tonight with Cassie and I think we need to define what's going on between us and the rules for our being exclusive.

17
CASSIE

AFTER AN AWKWARD LUNCH with Marcy and Carla, I felt like I didn't stop walking for the rest of the day. Carla needed something from casting, so I had to go visit Max. Max didn't know where it was, so I had to track down Lane. I finally got some envelope to deliver to Carla, who left a note saying she had to run an errand. I took a *literal* five second breather before Ed's voice came over the radio to ask me to come to set to help catering restock dressing rooms, the long table on set, and find out if anyone has any dietary restrictions for dinner that evening. Why was I doing all of this? I didn't even have time to ask, and honestly, I didn't care.

It kept me busy. If I stopped for a moment, my mind would flash to last night. The memories set my body ablaze, making me feel like a walking inferno, and I couldn't shake the feeling that everyone could see it. So, I said yes to every task that was asked of me because that meant my mind had something to focus on before our dinner tonight.

Dinner. Tonight. Butterflies swarm my stomach, circling from one side to the other. My heart races even though I know it's just Emmett and it'll be like every other night we hang out.

I'm glad I get to talk to Lucy before heading over. I need to confide in someone. Lucy already knows I've been hanging out with Emmett, so I know it's safe to tell her. Plus, she's kind of an outsider to the studio crew. Sure, she's hung out with everyone, but she doesn't have to see them every day. I don't know if she still talks to Tyler. I'm waiting for her to tell me about what happened there when she's ready.

She has enough on her plate with her fall art showcase coming up. Likewise, my audition for the acting showcase is this weekend, which I find hard to believe. The actual showcase will take place in a few weeks. I feel like it was just yesterday that I was struggling with my scenes and trying to figure out how the *fuck* I was going to pull them together.

Then Emmett came along, rehearsed with me last night, which led to...*yeah*, and now I'm feeling great about this weekend. I'm motivated, more motivated than I've been the last year. I'm actually looking forward to this weekend instead of dreading it.

When I get to my apartment, my phone buzzes. I look to find Annie's name on the caller screen.

"Hi, Anns," I answer. I hold the phone in between my right ear and shoulder as I sling my bag over my opposite shoulder. We're lucky to live a few blocks off the main drive, so it's fairly quiet. I smile at a few others who enter the building at the same time as me and press the elevator button to go up to the 5th floor.

"She lives! I feel like I've been trying to call you all day."

"Ah, sorry." I step into the apartment and find Lucy sitting at the island. I give her a tight smile and mouth *"Annie,"* to which she nods and goes back to eating whatever's in her bowl. "I've been a little occupied with—" What do I even tell her? I can't tell her about Emmett. She would *flip out*. She's obsessed.

"Work?" Annie asks, clearly annoyed at my loss for words.

"Yep, work."

"Well, I was wondering something..." Annie trails off, which normally means she wants to ask me something.

"What, Annie?" I put her on speaker and place the phone on my desk in my room. I need to change before Emmett's anyway, so I might as well do it now while talking with Annie before I go chat with Lucy. I don't want to be late.

"You know how I'm on some of those movie chat boards?" Oh boy. I hum in response. I know she spends hours obsessing over celebrities, trying to learn the ins and outs of their lives. When she comes to college in the fall, she's planning to study public relations. Her dream is to work with celebrities, so whenever I give her shit about her near-obsession, she tells me it's for research. "Well, I was chatting with my friend June and she was talking about Emmett and how there has been no news of what his next movie is. And I may have told her you know him."

"Get to the point, Annie."

"Well, do you know what he's doing next? It'd help me earn the respect of some of the top posters if you knew something. Of course I wouldn't say how I knew, but—"

"No, I don't," I cut her off. It's the truth, anyway. "I don't know what Emmett is doing next. We haven't talked about that." Again, not a lie.

Lucy appears at my doorway, still wearing her overalls, which are covered in green and blue paint. She leans against the doorframe, crosses her arms, slings one foot over the other, shifts her weight to her left side, and listens to my conversation.

"Damn. Okay, well, if you *do* find out, would you be the best big sister ever and tell me?" I can practically picture Annie on her knees, begging for insider information. She's done this only a few times when I happen to be around people that are famous enough to have an article written about them. It's part of the reason she freaked out when she saw that article about Emmett and me and when she found out I'd be working at the same studio as him.

"I'll think about it. Gotta go, Anns. Love you." I click the end call button on the phone after Annie tells me bye. She's coming to visit in two weeks, so I'm sure she will ask me this same question then. She's visiting the UCLA campus while she's here, although our mom thinks she's just coming to see me. Annie still hasn't told her about moving here in the fall, but I'm letting her handle that. I don't need our mom thinking I'm influencing her decisions.

I glance over at the doorway. "You hear all of that?"

Lucy strolls into my room and takes a seat on the edge of the bed. I'm still trying to figure out what to wear tonight. A dress? No, too formal. Athletic wear? Not formal enough. Do I bring an overnight bag? Should I assume he wants me to stay the night?

"I did. And I can practically hear your internal struggles. What's going on? Things not going well with Emmett?"

Right, she wasn't here this morning when I made a quick stop to change before work. She was already at her art studio.

My cheeks flush red as I glance up at her quickly before returning to flipping through the clothes in my closet.

"Oh my god, Cassie Marie."

"That's not my middle name."

"What aren't you telling me? What could have possibly happened over the last 24 hours?"

With a sigh, I look up and accept that my face has embarrassment written all over it. I'm as red as a tomato. I walk over to sit next to her on the bed, rest my elbows on my knees, then drop my head in my hands.

"We slept together."

Lucy playfully shoves my shoulder, and I topple to the left onto the bed.

"Hey! What was that for?" I ask, pushing myself back up to a sitting position.

"I knew you liked him, and you tried to deny it. You've been denying it for *weeks*."

She says it like I didn't know that already. I've been denying myself absolute pleasure for weeks, and I know it. In my defense, it was for an excellent reason. I could lose my job. Why would I risk that? Well, Emmett sure as hell didn't back down and challenged that question. So, I'm risking it. I think.

"We may have agreed to be exclusive." I glance over at her before getting up from the bed and walking back over to the closet. I flip through my clothes again, one hanger at a time, like I haven't already done this exact action three times. "But I don't exactly know what exclusive means. Do you? Like, does this mean he's my *boyfriend*?" I furrow my eyebrows. I would think yes, but it's honestly been so long since I've dated anyone that I've never had to "define the relationship." It was always casual, never serious.

"Don't ask me. I don't know. You'll have to ask him."

I sigh, returning my gaze to the closet. I decide on a skirt with a high slit on one leg, with a cropped shirt to go with it. It's casual, but looks like I put in effort. The perfect combination for a last-minute date.

"Do you think I'm making a bad decision?" I ask Lucy, turning around to face her.

"What? Seeing him? Pursuing something?" she asks, and I give a gentle nod. "No, I don't think so. I think you're finally allowing yourself to trust someone else and let them in. You've spent the last five years focused on acting, and acting alone. You haven't wanted to include anyone else in your little bubble."

"I include you. And Annie," I argue, even though I know she's speaking the truth. All of my relationships at the acting class are surface level. I'm careful about oversharing and avoid asking questions. It keeps it easier. I don't feel pressured to remember birthdays, or kids' names, or where they are vacationing in the summer. It was the same with any guy I saw. A part of me frequently held back, preventing me from fully opening up to them. I always kept a wall up, even though it did nothing to protect me. I still got a role stolen from me.

"We don't count."

I shrug.

"But I will say to be careful. Like I heard, I know you don't know what he's doing next and if it's something at the studio, what does that mean for whatever you two have? Will it always need to be this secret? Will it force you to quit the studio in order to be with him? Maybe ask him that tonight."

"That's a good thought. Okay, thank you. I don't know why I'm overthinking it. I'm trying *really* hard to live in the moment, I swear. Thanks for talking this out with me."

Lucy leaves the room, heading out to change before going into work at the diner. I do the same, getting dressed to go to Emmett's. I decide to bring an overnight bag, knowing I'd rather be prepared and have it.

I take a deep breath and one last look in the mirror, trying to calm my racing heartbeat. "It's going to be fine." After one more deep sigh, I gather my thoughts and feel ready to go.

On my way out of the apartment, I snatch my keys and slip on a pair of white shoes. I call out to Lucy to let her know I'm leaving. She replies "don't get caught" which is funny because it's true. We can't get caught. I would have avoided Emmett like the plague if I knew my feelings would start getting in-volved in this. I like him, truly like him, and it's annoying.

I was doing just fine before him, working at the diner and trying to make something out of my acting. He just *had* to come in that night and look at me with those eyes. Those beautiful, big brown eyes that just draw you in from the start. As soon as he winked at me and my stomach twisted in knots, I should have known that he was going to be a distraction.

Emmett has found his way into a little sliver of my heart. I don't know what to expect from this, but I'm at least willing to put myself out there. If shit hits the fan, I'm hoping Em-mett will at least defend me and I won't lose my job. I can't lose another job in the industry and have more people think negatively of me because I'm sleeping with the principal actor of the movie.

On my drive to his apartment, I think of ways to avoid Emmett at work. I could stay away from the set, eat at weird times, and try to steer clear of the trailers. I can't fully avoid him, but I know myself and now that I've gotten to experience Emmett in bed, it's going to be hard for me to not flirt with him or just stare at him. Someone will find it odd when I can't take my eyes off him. I also don't want to distract him. I know it's a busy week at the studio and they can't afford to re-film every scene if his mind is elsewhere. And I know it would happen because it did yesterday, and they had to re-film three scenes.

The guard at the garage waves me through. I still don't understand how he knows who I am. Is it the color of the car?

Like when you go to pick up groceries and you state the model and color of your car? I shake my head. It's not something I need to go down a rabbit hole on. I know my mind is currently latching onto anything to distract myself from thinking about Emmett.

I carefully look around, making sure no one was following me, even though it's late and I *know* no one followed me. Still, it's fun to pretend. When I make it to his floor, I stand outside his apartment with my back to his door. Should I knock? How should I knock? A few light taps? Do I announce my presence? Why am I suddenly questioning how to knock on a damn door?

I decide to text him. Except, when I'm in the middle of composing a succinct text message, the door opens behind me.

Emmett's hand wraps around my right wrist. I'm pulled into his apartment. Emmett slams the door shut and pins me to it with his mouth on mine.

My hands are still by my side when he removes his mouth from mine. I think I'm in shock because I don't speak first.

"Hi, Sass." He smiles, letting go of my wrist and walking into the kitchen. He glances at the bag in my hand. He says nothing, but he smiles to himself before he turns away. "I made chicken parmesan. I hope that's okay." He glances over his shoulder at me, then returns his attention back to the oven to pull something out of it.

"That's great." I set my things by the door and slip my shoes off. I walk over to the island, and immediately the perfectly set table draws my eyes. Before there was nothing on the table, but now it's lined with a table runner, two already lit candles, and a vase of flowers. My gaze trails down the length of the table and lands on the kitchen, on the island specifically, which is currently loaded with food. Yes, he made the chicken parmesan, but there's salad, and bread, and another kind of salad, and 10 different dressings, and two dessert options.

"I know, it's a lot."

I look up at him to find him already looking at me. He has a sheepish grin on his face and a slight tint of pink on his cheeks, which could be from the vulnerability or the heat of the kitchen. He takes the kitchen towel that's in his hand and tosses it over his shoulder.

"I didn't know what you like. I just wanted this to be perfect."

I walk around the island to where he's standing. Touching his left shoulder, I stand on my tiptoes, leaning toward him to plant a kiss on his cheek.

"It's great, Emmett. Thank you. Can I help with anything?" I look around to find something to do, but it looks as if he's somehow did everything.

"Nope, you can take a seat. I'll bring everything over." He leans toward me, this time leaving a kiss on my temple before turning back around to tend to something by the stove.

Just as I'm about to turn and walk to the table, I pause, realizing that I haven't taken in the details of Emmett. Not just glancing in his direction, but letting myself take him all in.

His hair, dark as tree roots, dangles neatly around his face. No matter what he does, a few strands of hair always find their way in front, shading his eyes. He's wearing a simple shirt, but I've *never* seen someone wear a t-shirt like Emmett wears a t-shirt. It hugs his shoulders and emphasizes all the right places while still leaving room for comfort. He's wearing my favorite pair of dark denim jeans, complementing the stark white color of his shirt.

"Cassie."

I take my time returning my gaze to his eyes, drifting from his legs, up his chest, to his face. "Hm?" I ask, my mind not all the way there as I study his eyes.

"If you don't stop looking at me like that, we won't be eating dinner."

I do a once-over again, my eyes looking down and back up. "What if my appetite has changed and I'm hungry for something," I lower my gaze to his cock, "*else.*"

In a low, husky tone, he growls, which isn't helping to convince me it's food I should stick down my throat.

"*Fuck*, Cassie. I promised myself I'd take it slow tonight."

"Don't you know you shouldn't make promises you can't keep?" With a subtle lift of my eyebrows, I issue a challenge. I stick my left leg out, causing the slit in my skirt to rise a few inches, revealing more of my exposed skin.

He lets out another low grunt. "Fuck it."

In record time, Emmett turns to the oven and changes it from bake to keep warm, turns back to face me, and closes the distance between us in just two large steps. He bends the top half of his body toward my waist, and before I have the chance to ask him what he's doing, he throws me over his shoulder and starts walking to his room.

18
EMMETT

"We should probably eat dinner."

I turn to look at Cassie. She has her arm tucked under her head, while the sheets barely cover her naked body. We've spent the last hour exploring and memorizing one another. The sheer contentment I feel in this moment makes me wish I could freeze time and stay in this state for hours.

"Emmett."

"Hm?" I drawl, slowly raking my eyes over her body and eventually meeting her gaze. "Right, dinner. Yes. We should do that. We need the energy for what I have planned tonight."

Her eyes widen. "What happened to taking it slow?" Her lips turn up, forming a slight smile.

I furrow my brow. "Sass, we both knew that plan was destined to fail. You're just—" I allow my eyes to trail her body again: the curve of her breasts, the dip of her hips, the slow intake of her breath. "*Irresistible.*" My eyes return to hers.

We eventually get out of bed, getting dressed in minimal clothes to eat dinner, knowing that we will just tear them off in a little while.

"So, there was something I wanted to ask you," Cassie says after we sit down to eat. She's avoiding my gaze, staring at her plate, which is her tell for being nervous.

"Anything."

Her eyes snap to mine. "When you said we were exclusive, what does that mean, exactly?"

Did she not want to be exclusive? Did I do something wrong? Does she not like me the way I like her?

"Let me clarify." She puts down her fork. "We talked about keeping this a secret since we both work at the studio, but I guess I didn't know how long we'd have to keep this a secret."

Oh. *Oh*. She thinks either we keep it a secret, or she might have to quit her job in order for us to be public.

I shake my head. "Not long, Cass. I wouldn't have started something with you if I knew I was putting you in a tough spot."

She bites her bottom lip, processing what I said. I continue eating as I wait for her to respond.

"But you started something." Her eyes reach mine for a moment before returning to her plate.

"Like I said earlier, you're extremely irresistible."

That earns me a chuckle and a flush of red in her cheeks. "Then what's the plan?"

The plan. The same question everyone has asked me. What is Emmett Davis doing next?

"I'm still working through it, but I don't want to hide us for long. You're too important to me, Cassie." I stand up from my chair and walk over to the other side of the table to where she's sitting. I hold out my hand, which she takes, and I pull her up toward me.

She nestles her head right under my chin in a space that was made for her. "But, since we are exclusive," I pull back a little so I can look at her face. "I wouldn't mind putting labels on it. For us."

"You want me to be your girlfriend?" Her eyes widen and her jaw opens.

"Don't look so shocked! Yes, my *girlfriend.*" I kiss her forehead.

She chuckles again. "Okay, *boyfriend.*"

I don't know why I suggested we put a label on our relationship, but I know I wanted her to continue being mine. Sure, we agreed to be exclusive, but I wanted another reason for us to be attached, for her to be mine in every way imaginable.

When I met her in the diner the first night and she looked at me with those sultry, ocean-blue eyes, I knew she would be mine. One way or another, it was going to happen. It *had* to happen. She set my heart on fire, and, like I already admitted, gave me butterflies immediately.

From that first night, I should have known that I had sealed my fate. I cannot imagine my life without her now.

Over the next few weeks, we fall into a routine. Cassie always leaves early in the morning to go back to her apartment before getting to the studio. It's easier to keep us secret and hidden from everyone that way. Well, everyone besides Lucy. I would tell the guys, but I worried they would say something in front of Marcy, and until my contract is up, I don't want to risk it.

It's safe to say I'm already falling for Cassie even though I've only known her for a few months.

When I'm with Cassie, I'm home. She fills a hole in my heart I didn't realize was there from my parents' lack of interest.

We're great at keeping it a secret. We've even hung out as a group a few times to keep up appearances, always at my apartment. Tyler, Max, Lane, Marcy, Lucy, Cassie, and myself. We always sit on opposite sides of the room because otherwise I'd do something dumb like pinch her butt or give her a kiss. That doesn't stop her from eye-fucking me the entire night, causing me to keep my mind on things other than her naked body, otherwise I'd end up with a raging hard on and would have to answer some questions.

Since we live so close, she goes home with Lucy and then drives back in her own car.

At the studio, we have a similar routine. We eat lunch together some days, starting as a group and ending up with just the two of us.

Those are my favorite times at work. Cassie has this habit where she bites her lip but smiles at the same time to stop herself from laughing. Her cheeks turn bright red. She rolls her eyes. Then, she places her head in her hand and sighs, raising her eyes to meet mine. It's the cutest fucking thing. I would have fucked her over the table if we weren't in the public cafeteria at the studio.

I only have a few more weeks, maybe a month, left in this contract before we don't have to worry about sneaking around anymore.

It cannot come soon enough.

Our first date is going to be the best. We'll probably get dinner somewhere secluded, with great food. Maybe pizza, which has become our favorite.

Tonight is Cassie's show with her acting class. She auditioned last week and, of course, she landed the role of the main romance actor. I knew she would. The scenes differ from the ones we rehearsed, but they still have the same depth and emotion.

Since it's Friday, Cassie didn't ask anyone to go. She told me, but since we aren't supposed to be seen in public alone, she said I didn't have to go.

But, being the best boyfriend ever, I got Lucy to take off from work and told Tyler, Lane, and Max they had to go. I think Marcy is meeting us there, too.

We're going to surprise her. I'm bringing her a dozen tulips, which I know are her favorite flower from her sister, Annie.

I met Annie when she was in town a week ago. She nearly fainted when she found out we were dating, but she held it together. It was cute. She asked me about 100 questions regarding my movies. *"Did you really fight that guy in the bar scene?"* or *"What is the craziest thing that happened while you were filming in the middle of the jungle? Did you get attacked by any animals?"*

I didn't say they were normal questions. I, of course, answered all of them while Cassie sat next to me, holding my hand, shaking her head at Annie every time she asked me about something ridiculous she likely read about on the internet.

I don't do a lot of interviews about my movies, so there are always a lot of rumors or speculations about what occurs on set and in my personal life.

I hadn't known if Cassie wanted me to meet Annie since we were still so new. She told me what happened with that dick writer she'd dated, which helped everything about the first week I knew her make a ton of sense. So, the fact that she was okay with me meeting family, especially her sister, was pretty huge for me.

Seeing the way Cassie and Annie interacted made me want a brother. They hardly communicated with words. Annie would start saying something like, *"You know that one place with the plants..."* to which Cassie would say *"What happened this time?!"* and then Annie would answer with literally two words like *"Balloon fight."* Which made no sense to me, but they would break out in laughter and continue laughing for the next five minutes until tears were streaming down their cheeks.

That's typically when I would refill snacks or drinks and let them have their moment. I knew it had been a while since they'd seen each other. It was great to see a different side of Cassie. Sometimes we spend all day ignoring each other on set, and we hardly talk when we see each other. Our hands never leave one another and we spend most of the night in bed.

Every morning, I wish I could be with Cassie. Every evening, I'm grateful that I am with Cassie. I hate this being a secret.

That's why I'm glad everyone could come support Cassie tonight. I would have come by myself, but since no one knows we've been dating for the last few weeks, it might have looked weird since, as far as anyone but Lucy and Annie knows, I only see Cassie on set and when we hang out as a big group.

We get to the theater where I have six seats near the front reserved for us. I sit in the middle. When she looks into the crowd, I want her to see me. I want her to know how damn proud I am of her for chasing her dreams and not giving up. I want her to know that nothing would have stopped me from coming tonight.

The show is amazing. There are three acts before Cassie's and one after, making it five total for the evening.

When it's time for Cassie's act, she enters stage right and captivates the audience from the start. Her emotions are authentic and the chemistry she has on stage with her partner is believable. Cassie has a natural edge to her acting that is so critical, I find myself daydreaming of acting by her side, for real, not just practice.

After the final curtain falls, everyone stands in applause. The cast, including Cassie, come out on stage to give their final bow. They lift the lights in the theater so the actors can see the people who came to support.

Everyone is still applauding, myself included, when Cassie sees me. Her eyes go wide, her jaw ajar, and the biggest grin forms on her face. I give her a wink.

If I thought I was falling for Cassie before tonight, this is the moment that confirms I've already fallen deeply in love with her.

Sometimes you just know, and I know with Cassie.

Lucy's been to previous shows, so she helps guide us to the backstage area to greet Cassie.

Cassie comes out of the green room and makes her way to us. Everyone takes their turn giving her hugs.

"Cassie, you were great," Tyler exclaims.

"Thanks, Tyler."

"Yeah, girl, I did not know you could act like that!" Marcy leans in and gives her a hug.

"Same here," Lane chimes in.

"I almost cried," Max says.

Cassie laughs. "Thanks, all. It means a lot. I didn't even know you were all coming!" She turns to Lucy. "Thanks, Lucy."

Lucy gives Cassie a hug and then points to me. "This was all him."

I raise a hand and wave, then realize I'm still holding the bouquet of flowers like an idiot.

"You were great, Cass." I lean in to give her a hug.

I didn't want to let go, so I let our hug linger a little, giving her an extra squeeze since I can't kiss her in public.

"Get a room, you two! Geez!" Tyler has to interrupt, of course.

I turn to him and give him a playful shove.

I turn back to Cassie. "These are for you." I hand her the flowers, which leads to Cassie blushing and giving me the smile that I love so much.

"Thanks, Hotshot." It was her turn to wink at me. Winking has almost become a secret language between us in these past few weeks. We've been using them to communicate when around others when something means more than what we can say with words. Her calling me Hotshot low enough that only I can hear was purely for my benefit.

"So, anyone up for a late dinner? Maybe we can go to the diner?" Lucy asks the group.

Of course everyone loves going to the diner, so we decide to head there.

"Do you mind if I catch a ride with you?" I ask Cassie loudly. "A driver dropped me off and everyone else rode together."

"Yeah, of course. Let me just grab my bags," Cassie says before anyone can offer a different solution. She turns to the rest of the group and lets them know we will meet them there since it might be a few minutes.

Luckily, no one asks questions. So as they leave, I follow Cassie back to the greenroom.

Cassie opens a door, pulls me inside, and switches on a light. We are not in the greenroom, but in a small storage closet with a rack for jackets and a shelf on the back wall. It leaves little room to move, forcing our bodies to be flushed against one another.

"You don't have to grab your bags, do you?" I ask.

She shakes her head. "I already threw my bags in the car."

"Then what are we—" I say before Cassie interrupts me by putting her lips on mine.

I kiss her back with every intention to revel in this private moment before we're forced to return to our group. Her hands wrap around my waist. Mine cup her jaw, deepening our kiss. Hers then gently glide across my back, tracing delicate circles, moving up and down.

I'm five seconds away from taking her right here in this closet when we hear a group of people walk down the hallway.

As much as I don't want to stop, I know we should head to the diner before our group of friends think something happened to us. We can't exactly say "sorry we were making out," and I can't think of any other excuse.

"Cassie," I say when I'm finally able to get a word in, but she keeps kissing me. She's being overly persistent. I gently push her face away from mine. "Sass."

She finally stops and pouts. She's so damn cute it hurts my heart.

"Don't look at me like that."

"It's not fair."

"I know." I kiss the top of her head. "Soon."

She nods and kisses me one last time before we step out of the room and head to her car to drive over to the diner.

The drive to the diner is short. We get there in 10 minutes, and I sneak in one more kiss before we get out of the car.

Before we are about to enter the diner, we're cornered by a reporter. This is why I don't go out a lot.

"Emmett, look here! Who are you with tonight?" The reporter shouts as if he's 10 feet away from me, instead of just a few.

I quickly shuffle Cassie to my left side, blocking her from the scrutiny of the reporter.

"Hey, you know the rules!" A shout comes from in front of me.

Looking up, there is an older gentleman hovering outside of the right door. He's shaking his fist and mumbling about how cameras aren't allowed in his diner.

"Come on, you two." He waves to usher us inside.

"Thanks, Dave." Cassie smiles.

"No problem, kiddo. I know you don't work here anymore, but I'll always be there for you. Your friends are at the big table in the back."

I nod to Dave as we pass, silently thanking him for removing the reporter. Taking a deep breath, I look in front of me to see Cassie looking back at me and smiling. I slowly blink once, capturing this moment forever, hoping that I can figure out what I'm going to do with my career so I can keep Cassie forever.

19
CASSIE

WE MAKE OUR WAY into the diner after Dave runs off the reporter and find our group sitting at a table in the back left corner. On one side are Lane, Max, Lucy, and Tyler. The other side has two open seats and Marcy. There are only a few clusters of people in the diner tonight, but our group of friends talk loud enough to know where they are the minute we walk through the door.

I see Dave again and give him a smile. I've only been in a few times since I've quit, and every time, his face lights up and he always wants to catch up. I wonder if that's what it's like to have a parent that cares, that asks you questions about your day and if your job is going well. Dave filled that semi-parent role over the past few years since my mom is practically absent from my life.

We sit at the table and find they have already ordered what appears to be one of every appetizer. It is enough food to feed double the amount of people we have.

We spend the evening eating too many fries and talking about the movie coming to a close.

"I don't know about you all, but I cannot wait for a break," Tyler says. He leans to the middle of the table to grab a fry and shoves it into his mouth.

"You think *you're* ready?" Marcy practically yells across the table at Tyler, throwing a fry at him. "I've been running around between not one, but two sets! If I didn't have Cassie, I would seriously go insane." She looks over at me and we both start laughing.

"You're welcome," I say with a smile. I grab a fry for myself, dip it in some ketchup, and stick it in my mouth. Emmett squeezes my leg under the table. I glance at him. I should glare, but I'm smiling and trying to stop myself from saying something out loud that would make what's happening obvious to the others. Instead, I resort to trying to give him a mental "Will you stop that?!" before he forces my hand and I say something to give us away.

"It's been fun for me, though. Obviously, it's been great to meet you all and become friends." I smile at everyone around the table.

"It's been great for me, too. There are so many things I've loved about this film," Emmett says. I look over at him and find him looking at me. I grab more food to eat, trying to hide the fact that this man is causing me to blush like a horny teenager.

"Same here, dude," Max thankfully chimes in.

We eat and chat. Lane tells us about the next project he and Max are working on. Tyler comments on the food and somehow relates it to his catering.

Marcy talks about the film that she's been working on off-site. Apparently, that director has asked her to help in the next movie they're shooting.

People ask Lucy about her art and she mentions her show is coming up this fall if any of them want to go. She doesn't know that we have all already bought tickets and plan to support her, like everyone supported me tonight.

I should have known they would come, but I didn't want to be optimistic and then find that no one showed up. Everyone knew my show was tonight, but I never asked if anyone was coming. I would have asked Emmett, but I didn't know if it would be a good idea, since it was a public event.

At past showcases, we have had a few people who could be considered celebrities attend. They were mostly lower-level actors or directors there to help scout for extra roles or smaller indie films. But Emmett is on a whole other level. Not only is his dad a known actor, he's one of Hollywood's best. Seeing the way people reacted was interesting, considering Emmett's fast-growing reputation as an actor in America. Emmett didn't have any bodyguards or anything, and luckily everyone was respectful of his space, but I got a few questions backstage and texts afterwards from people asking how I knew Emmett.

I simply answered that we work together and left it at that.

Somehow, two hours have passed, and all the food is gone on the table. We were so busy chatting and snacking that I didn't even realize how late it was.

"Emmett, do you need a ride back home?" Lane asks.

"Cassie offered to give me a ride home when we were on our way over here, but thanks, man," Emmett says casually, tossing Lane a smile.

"Yep, no big deal," I say.

I didn't even realize Lucy wasn't at the table until she walks back over.

"Okay, dinner is all covered. Dave said it was on the house tonight to celebrate your showcase, Cass," Lucy says with a grin.

If Dave has one quality, it's that he is overly supportive. Working in a diner that has a target demographic of actors and people who work with film, you have to be. Most people who work here dream of working in the industry in some capacity. They're just waiting for the right person to walk in and give them their first chance.

Is that what happened with Emmett? Even though I wasn't looking for anything or anyone, he just stumbled in here randomly one night when I was already having a long day and somehow has become this constant in my life.

A day doesn't go by where I don't see him. I didn't know how I was going to handle secretly dating Emmett, but it's not bad since we live so close and we are still friends at the studio, although I have to ignore him a bit. I am afraid I will push him into a closet like I did at the showcase or that he will pull me into his trailer and people will start wondering why his trailer is rocking back and forth. It would not be a good look.

It's been nice getting to know him privately. I like the moments we spend together no one knows about, so it's just for us and no one else. We can pretend to be a normal couple instead of a celebrity couple where cameras are waiting on every corner. I don't know what to expect when we go public. Part of me feels like it's too good to be true with him, like all of this has a ticking timer and when we don't have to hide our relationship anymore, he will realize that I'm just me and not the girl he envisioned.

But I look at Emmett like I am right now in this diner and he gives me this look that makes me forget all my worries and doubts. When he looks at me, it feels like the rest of the diner fades away and it's just the two of us.

We say goodbye to everyone and get in my car. Since it's Friday, we won't be seeing our friends again until Monday. I might see Lucy if I make it back to our apartment, but for everyone else, we have a free weekend and don't have to be at the studio.

I plan to spend a long time with Emmett. Particularly in his bedroom. We'll get food delivered, drink too much coffee, and watch movies. It's going to be the perfect weekend.

I let Emmett drive us to his place. It's a short commute, but I think he enjoys driving when he can since he normally has a driver take him everywhere. His touch on my thigh sends a tingling sensation through my body as he gives it a gentle squeeze. I take my gaze from the window and glance over at him. In a fleeting moment, his eyes meet mine as he steals a quick glance, a smile blooming on his lips.

"You were great tonight, babe," Emmett says with another squeeze on my thigh. His hand trails higher, and the heat spreads through my body.

I'm unable to resist rolling my eyes in response. "You have to say that."

"I don't have to say anything, Sass. You were great, really, really great. I almost teared up."

I slap him on the arm. "Shut up."

We both start laughing.

"Thank you for being there. It meant a lot. You know, it was the first time I had people come to see me." I shift in my seat and grab his hand with mine, looping our fingers together.

"Lucy's never gone?"

"She has, but she works a lot of the time and I tell her it's not a big deal."

"But it is a big deal, Cass. You deserve to be seen," Emmett says, pulling into his apartment complex and into the garage. I look out the window and turn back to him, getting ready to say something.

"It's late, no one is around. We don't have to worry about going separately." Emmett answers the question that I was going to ask.

"Oh, okay. Great," I reply.

He helps me grab my bags from the car and we head to the elevator to go upstairs to his apartment. I've been in this elevator a lot over the past month. The beige carpet has slowly grown on me to the point that it's calming. The elevator music plays just loud enough to get stuck in your head for the next five hours. Normally, I'm alone and I have to pinch myself to remind myself that this is real and not some long-standing dream.

This time, I'm with Emmett. I look over at him and find he's already looking at me. I'm not surprised. He's always looking at me when I glance his way.

"What are you thinking about?" I ask as we get out of the elevator. We walk to his apartment. He reaches into his back pocket for his keys, opens the door, and lets me in first, closing the door behind me.

"You," he replies, taking my bag from me and setting it by the door.

We walk into the kitchen. I take a seat on a stool at the island. Emmett walks over to the cabinet and grabs two mugs, starting our nightly routine of drinking tea and talking about our day. At the studio, we don't typically talk about things other than work because we're always around others. Here, we use the first hour to chat about everything else. We talk a lot about our childhood and what it was like growing up, taking time to learn more about each other. It's become my favorite part of the night, well, one of my favorites because what normally follows this is also great.

Tea and sex. Two things you normally wouldn't put together, but it works for us.

Emmett leans onto the island. He is looking at me with a focused gaze, as if we've known each other for far more than just a month. I smile, the warmth of the tea in my hands comforting me as I take a sip.

"I have something I want to show you," Emmett says, stepping away from the counter. He walks around to my side and holds out his hand. I grab it, then follow as he leads us down the hallway and into his office.

Taking a seat on the couch, a mix of excitement and curiosity bubbles inside me, and I wonder what he wants to share.

"You're not going to tell me you've written a script about me, are you?" I tease.

Emmett looks at me from over his shoulder and chuckles. "No promises." He winks, and I blush instantly. My body has a consistent response whenever Emmett persists with his winks.

He walks over to the bookcase and grabs a box from the top shelf. Holding it in his hands, he walks over to me and sits next to me on the couch.

I don't know what's inside the box. It's a cube box, kind of the same size that fits in those IKEA cube shelves. I think it's normally for random stuff, or maybe pictures, so I'm not sure what he's keeping in here.

"I've kind of been busy when we aren't together..." Emmett starts and stops, taking a deep sigh. I put a hand on his and give him a squeeze. "If you can't tell, I'm nervous. Cassie, I thought I would be an actor for my entire life and always just wonder what my life would look like if I wasn't. I've been writing. A lot. About anything that comes to my mind. I didn't write for a long time because I had nothing to write about, but now I have you."

"Are you saying I'm your muse, Hotshot?" I tease again, enjoying seeing the flush of red on his cheeks from my response.

"Maybe." Emmett smirks at me and pulls off the lid. There are notebooks and folders inside. Few, but enough to fill the box over halfway.

The top notebook has a title printed across it, "One Last Time—Emmett Davis." He takes it out and hands it to me, but he doesn't let go right away.

I look up at him from the notebook to find him looking at me, like always.

"You *have* been busy."

"Be nice, okay? I know you read my past work, but this is recent." Emmett finally releases the notebook.

I open to the first page. It's the synopsis of a film. I turn to the next page and find the opening lines of the script. I keep turning the pages to find they are all filled with scenes and lines. This whole notebook is full. There are no empty pages.

"Are these all scripts?" I ask. He nods but says nothing.

I hand back the notebook which Emmett files back in the box. He puts the lid back on and takes the box back to the top shelf where it was.

"I've wanted to be a writer for as long as I can remember." Emmett turns to me, walking back over to join me on the couch. "But my dad has always made it seem like I wouldn't be good enough. You know? Like if I didn't follow in his footsteps, then the Davis name would be worth nothing once he's gone. It's obvious he cares more about the family name in

Hollywood than his actual son, but for some reason I feel like I can't stop acting."

"Even if it's what you want?" I loop my fingers with his.

"I'm not sure anymore. Seeing you chase your dreams is helping me, Cassie. You have so much drive. Hell, you moved here because of your dream and you work your ass off to make it happen. I can't even stand up to my dad, even though what I want is to be a writer."

"I think you could do it, for what it's worth. You're stronger than you think." I nudge his shoulder and give him a smile, which gets a laugh out of him.

"Thanks, Sass." He leans over and presses a kiss on my forehead. "I just wanted to show you what I've been up to lately when you're not around, and I guess thank you for showing me I can still achieve my dream."

"I'm glad you did. It suits you, you know. I mean, you're great at acting, don't get me wrong, but I could also see you as a writer. You can do whatever you set your mind to, Emmett. I think people think getting older means we need to remain content with whatever we're currently doing, but it doesn't have to be that way. If I woke up tomorrow with a new dream to... I don't know, open up my own coffee shop, I could do it. We create our own glass ceilings and sometimes they need to be shattered."

Instead of using his words, Emmett lets go of my hand and pulls me on to his lap so I'm straddling him. A surprised squeal escapes my lips. My hands grab his shoulders, then quickly find their way to the back of his head.

Emmett pulls me closer. I dip my head and press my lips against his. Our kiss is full of passion and heat. I've never felt like this before with anyone. I've never had this desire to want to get to know someone, to wake up next to them in the morning. With Emmett, I'm safe. I'm able to be myself. Like I could wake up one day and decide to do something different with my life and he would support me.

For the next few moments, we remain like this. Our hands moving around each other's backs, memorizing the shape of each other. I turn my head to the right to deepen our kiss.

Emmett's hands find my face, and he gently separates us.

His hand tangles in my hair as he takes a strand and tucks it away, leaving a soft, lingering touch.

"I don't know why fate put us together now, but I'm falling for you." Emmett's lips find my neck. My lips part, releasing a soft moan.

I lean close enough that my lips are almost touching his left ear. "I'm falling for you too, Emmett Davis," I say with a shy smile, my cheeks turning a rosy shade. Because of Emmett, I've started believing in happily ever afters again.

As soon as I finish getting his name out, he wraps his hands around my butt, lifts me from the couch, and guides us into the bedroom, his lips never leaving mine.

20
EMMETT

"EMMETT. EMMETT, WAKE UP."

The first detail I notice when I open my eyes is Cassie isn't in bed anymore, she's standing next to me, repeating my name to wake me up. The second is the smell of coffee wafting into the bedroom from the somewhat opened door. The third is voices, a pair, echoing in from the living room.

I sit up immediately, knowing who would show up unannounced this early in the morning.

"Emmett," Cassie repeats for the tenth time. "Your parents are here." Her voice is barely a whisper, her head whipping from my face to the door and back.

"Why are they here? Why did you let them in?" I find a pair of shorts within arm's distance and a shirt to match, throwing them on and grasping at Cassie's waist. I pull her toward me, pressing a kiss to her forehead.

A sigh escapes her as she says, "I don't know why they're here. I came to wake you up as soon as I let them in, which I wasn't going to do at first. But then I accidentally dropped my book, and your dad heard and *demanded* to be let in."

"Ah, so you got his good mood today." I try to joke.

"Very funny." Cassie groans, pulling away from my embrace. "This isn't how I pictured meeting your parents."

I grab her hand, interlacing our fingers one by one.

"There's no great way to meet my parents." My lips turn up, but I know it doesn't reach my eyes. This isn't how I wanted her to meet them either. "What did they say to you?"

"Barely anything. It was awkward. Your dad asked if I was the girl from the article and when I said yes, he just hummed a response. I only recognized them from pictures online."

"He's such a dick. I'm sorry he said that to you." To help calm her, I move my thumb up and down her finger.

"Thank you, but it's okay. I just told them I'd come get you and here we are."

I nod, thankful she wasn't with them alone for long. "Let's go see what they want, Sass."

Cassie nods and follows me out the door.

When we reach the kitchen, my dad is standing with his arms crossed, nose to his phone. My mom sees me coming, a smile plastered on her face. I walk toward her and give her a hug, ignore my dad, then move to the island to stand next to Cassie.

"Hi, sweetie. We are sorry to drop in. Your dad thought to see if you wanted to go out for breakfast. And we met Casey here." My mom smiles and looks at Cassie, then back at me.

"Cassie," I correct.

"Yes, we were just talking to Cassie about how we didn't know you were seeing anyone," my dad chimes in, finally looking up from his phone to acknowledge our presence. What a dick.

"I am," I say, keeping my tone neutral, careful not to reveal anything he could use against her. I pull Cassie toward me by wrapping my arm around her waist.

"Well, it must not be serious enough if you didn't tell us, son," my dad says. He looks over at my mom.

"Honey, let's let them enjoy their morning."

He looks back at me. "Keep me updated about your next contract, Emmett. You can't be having—" His eyes linger on Cassie for a moment before refocusing on me. "Distractions."

"Cassie isn't a distraction," I say, my tone laced with anger. Cassie's hand tightens on my waist. "I'll call you later, Mom. It's nice to see you. We need to plan something soon."

"Okay, sweetie. No worries. It was great to meet you, Cassie."

Cassie smiles at my mom. My dad keeps looking from me to Cassie and back like he's trying to figure us out.

On their way to the door, my dad stops by the end table next to the couch. He leans over to pick something up, turning back to me.

"What's this? Are you daydreaming again, Emmett?" He scoffs, holding up a script I was working on.

"It's nothing that concerns you," I reply, trying to get him to ignore it.

"What do you mean it's nothing?" Cassie asks, looking at me, begging me to stand up for myself.

I start to open my mouth to reply, but my dad interrupts me.

"You can't seriously think you can become a writer, not without me backing you. Tell me, son, what are you doing next after this movie of yours is done filming?"

My eyes widen. This is not a conversation I want to be having right now. I'm not ready.

"I–I..." I stutter, not knowing how to respond. "I don't have anything lined up." My heart is racing a mile a minute.

"You don't have anything? What about the contracts your agent sent?"

Of course my agent sent them to him as well, keeping my dad in the loop with all my decisions.

"I said no."

"No? What do you mean you said no?" My dad starts pacing, still holding the script in his hand. His gaze is on the floor, but I can see his brows furrowed.

"I haven't decided what I'm going to do yet."

"And it's all because of her." My dad points to Cassie with his free hand and she shrinks, her body sliding down and back from mine.

"Mom?" I ask, pleading for her to say something.

For a moment, I think she might, but she looks at my dad first and when she turns back to me, I hardly recognize her. "Your father's right, sweetie."

"Oh, for fuck's sake. I'm my own person, okay? Has it ever occurred to you that I might not want to be like you?" My voice is elevated and I'm furious. There is a void at my side, letting me know Cassie has retracted her hand. I whip my head to look at her, but she won't meet my gaze. I reach out to cup her cheek with my hand. When her eyes finally meet mine, my heart shatters into pieces. She bites her lip, blinking rapidly to keep the tears in her eyes before shaking her head out of my hand.

I watch as she walks out of the kitchen and back toward the bedroom.

"You need to leave," I snarl at my parents, not giving a fuck what they say to me.

"We won't approve this Emmett. She's not worth it," my dad says like I care about his opinion in the matter.

"You know what? She's worth everything. And fuck, I don't want to act anymore. Okay? I'm a writer, Dad. A fucking writer. And if you can't accept that, then I think we are done here."

My mom's jaw goes slack and her eyes widen with shock.

"You're going to regret this," are the only words my dad says before he leaves the apartment.

After hearing the door click, I turn around to find Cassie standing in the hallway.

"Is he going to say something?" she asks.

"Knowing him, I don't doubt it."

"Emmett, I can't lose my job."

I make my way to Cassie, tugging on her shoulders to embrace her. "I won't let that happen."

"I think I should go." Cassie starts to pull away, leaving a void again.

"I don't want you to go. I want to work through this, together. Please."

Cassie remains silent, her gaze to the floor. She's thinking too hard, and I'm starting to worry she's actually going to leave.

"You're too important to lose, Sass. I don't want to live in a world where I don't get to see your smile everyday. Please. Stay." I'm five seconds away from kneeling, begging her to keep giving this a chance. Keep giving us a chance.

"Okay."

"Okay?"

An eye roll makes its appearance. "Okay," she replies, and I'm wondering if she remembers the first time I asked her to hang out, our conversation ending just like this one.

"So, what now?" Cassie asks.

"Breakfast?" I grin and watch as her lips form a smile before nodding in agreement.

"Pancakes sound really good right now." Cassie turns to walk to the kitchen. She stands on her tiptoes to reach the flour from a cabinet, then proceeds to gather the rest of the ingredients.

For the next half hour, we alternate making pancakes while talking about our plans for the week. I keep catching myself watching, staring, not being able to take my gaze away from Cassie. She carries herself with so much grace that I find myself being struck by her sassy demeanor that's hidden from most people. What I love most about her, though, is how determined and motivated she is to achieve her dream. Nothing can stop her. I won't let anything stop her, not even my parents.

"So, have you heard from Annie recently?" I say, flipping a pancake, hearing the sizzle of the butter.

"Oh, yes. She still hasn't told our mom about her moving here." Cassie struts to the other side of the island, plopping on a stool.

"When do you think she'll tell her?" I turn to rest my backside on the counter.

"Soon, hopefully."

She opens her mouth to say more, but my phone buzzes, radiating on the island. Cassie leans to the left, reaching out to slide my phone closer to her.

"Someone named Logan is calling you." The buzzing ends as I walk over to the island, spatula in hand. "Actually, he's called you a few times."

I reach out my hand toward Cassie for my phone. "That's my agent."

As soon as the words leave my mouth, Cassie's eyes widen and her jaw slacks. My phone starts vibrating again. We both know what this call is about without answering it.

"Are you going to answer it?" Cassie mumbles, fidgeting in her seat.

"Should I?" I ask.

Cassie winces. "Yes, but I'm scared." Her lower lip disappears as her gaze trails from my eyes to the island.

"Hey, look at me." I walk to Cassie, twisting her seat until she faces me. I wrap my arms around her shoulder and nestle her closer to me. "I won't let anything happen."

Her gaze flickers from me to the floor as she mumbles, "I know."

"I promise."

Cassie's eyes find mine, her lips curl inward, and she nods.

"We are in this together, Sass. You and me," I remind her.

"Together," Cassie agrees.

"Okay." I give her shoulders a squeeze before removing my hand and stepping back. I reach for my phone on the other side of the island just as Logan is calling again and click the accept button.

"Logan, what's up?"

"Emmett. Finally. Sorry to call on the weekend, but we have a situation," Logan says.

"Does this situation have anything to do with my dad?" I ask, rolling my eyes in Cassie's direction.

"He tipped the media that you were done acting because of a girl, he didn't name names. And, the only way I know this is because he called me to tell me that he's doing this for your benefit," Logan explains.

"Of course he is. How bad is the press? What are our options?"

"Well, I can try and keep some of the outlets quiet. Mostly anything that would be printed tomorrow or next week. But anything that's online is going to be difficult."

"Okay. Well, is there anything we can do?"

"We can put out a quote letting them know that it's false information."

"Any other options?" I ask, knowing I'm not ready to tell everyone the truth.

"Um, we can let it ride and hope people forget about it next week? It's purely speculation, since they can't name your dad as the source. That'd look bad on him if they did."

I look over at Cassie, trying to gauge what she wants me to do. Neither option is great, but Logan's right. People will likely forget about it without there being a solid source. But my dad did mention Cassie, which we will need to figure out. There are a few people who would piece together who the *girl* the articles refer to is.

Cassie mouths, "Let it go" and shrugs, also unsure if it's the right decision.

"Let's let it ride, Logan. Just keep me updated if anyone spins the speculation negatively, then maybe we can decide something else." My chest still feels tight with dread.

"Okay, alright, that sounds like a plan. I'll keep you updated," Logan responds.

The line goes silent, but my mind is on full blast. My dad would mention Cassie. He knows I don't care about the world knowing about my career being over, it's something that would be surprising for a moment but then forgotten. But he had to mention something that would get under my skin, something to make me hurt.

Cassie and I can solve this together. I won't be the reason she loses her job.

21
EMMETT

"I'M GOING TO CALL Marcy," I say, already opening the contacts app and searching to find her name.

"What? Why? Emmett, she's *against* us. She doesn't want us to be together, remember? I don't see how that's going to help," Cassie says.

"I think she'll see reason."

"See reason? Is that possible? It's her literal job to prevent this—" Cassie gestures from me to her, "from happening. Can we trust her to be on our side?"

"I trust her, yes. And chances are, she's already aware. Knowing Marcy, she'd hold it against me for blackmail to get something she wants." I chuckle, thinking of the time she threatened to call my dad for ditching a charity dinner in exchange for me telling Ed she needed a week off of work, no questions asked. It worked.

"Plus," I continue, "It'll be better to talk to her here, now, before she sees it on her own."

"I suppose you're right."

"I know I'm right, Sass," I say with a wink, then I dial Marcy's number.

Within seconds, she answers.

"Emmett, I'm not very happy with you right now." I can feel her glare through the phone.

"Hello to you too, Marce. I'm great, thanks for asking. How are you?" I say, sarcasm laced in my tone.

"I warned you."

"Can you just come over here? We want to talk," I ask, just wanting her to give us a few minutes to explain.

A knock comes from the front door.

"Hey Marce, hold on. Someone's at the door." I drop my phone to my hip as I walk to answer it.

I barely get the door unlocked before it's pushed open and someone comes barreling in.

"You two," Marcy greets us, shaking her head, walking straight toward the kitchen. "You made pancakes?" She looks at me, holding the plain pancake in her hand to show me like I don't know, then proceeds to take a bite.

"We did, um..." I walk to the kitchen, stopping to stand next to Cassie. "I-we would like to talk to you."

"Mhm." Marcy leans her backside against the counter, crossing one arm over the other. Even though she's a few years younger, she likes to act like she's an older sister bossing me around. "Continue." She takes another bite of the pancake.

"You know we have syrup, right?" I ask, and immediately regret it because Marcy is shooting daggers at me. "Anyway, we want to tell you that we are dating."

I pause before saying more or asking for help, waiting to hear or see how she'll react.

"I know that, dipshit." She takes one last bite, finishing the pancake, before sauntering closer to the island.

Cassie stiffens a little, which I can only assume means she's uncomfortable about the situation and unsure what's going to happen next. I'm sure she's worried about her job, which we knew was a risk when we got together.

"I expected you two to be a bit more…Oh what's the word? Oh yeah, secretive," Marcy berates us.

"We were secretive," Cassie says, finding her voice. "We didn't expect his dad to come here today."

"You should always expect him to show up when you least expect it," Marcy fills Cassie in, raising her eyebrows in a "duh" expression.

"Can you help us, Marce?" I ask.

"I don't know. How do I know this is for real?" Marcy asks.

"You've got to be fucking kidding me." I pinch the bridge of my nose.

"Yes, I'm kidding. I already helped."

I look at Cassie, who's already looking at me, both of our mouths open, eyebrows furrowed in confusion.

"I take the silence as a thank you, so you're welcome." Marcy leans forward on the counter, grinning to herself.

"How?" I ask.

"Easy, told Carla, filed some paperwork, then filled Ed in. Easy peasy."

"When?"

"Oh, gosh, when was that? A month ago?"

"A month? Marcy, for fuck's sake. What does that even mean?" I ask, trying to keep my tone neutral.

"It means you two can see each other without worrying about anything happening. Stop looking at me like you're trying to decide whether you want to hug me or slap me."

"I'm just trying to understand," I say.

"Or you can just say, 'Thank you Marcy?' 'You're the best Marcy?' Either works."

Cassie walks over to Marcy and pulls her into a hug. "Thank you Marcy."

"We should probably tell Tyler, Lane, and Max," Marcy says as she pulls back from Cassie.

"We can do that tomorrow," I say, not wanting to add another tense conversation to today.

Marcy just nods, understanding that it's already been a long day even if it's not even lunchtime yet.

"Text me if either of you need anything, I mean it. I can talk to Logan if you need," Marcy offers before we exchange goodbyes and she leaves.

Once the door is closed, I pull Cassie into a hug and sigh into her touch.

She lifts her head off my chest, and her eyes meet mine.

"Have I told you that you're my favorite person in the entire world?" I say.

Cassie's eyes go wide for a moment before they soften and a smile follows. She kisses me once before finding my eyes again, shaking her head. "Not unless you've been whispering the declaration to me in my sleep."

I kiss her gently, savoring the sweetness of the moment as time seems to stand still.

It's been different having Cassie around. I'm used to being alone most of the time, keeping to myself and doing my job when I need to. I questioned nothing. Whatever came my way, I accepted it and occasionally forced myself to leave the house a few times a week. I never saw myself attached to someone like I am to Cassie.

I can't remember the moment where I accepted being comfortable with where I'm at in life. Maybe it was when I officially moved out and got away from my dad? Maybe it was when my first movie did so well that I didn't have to worry about judgment from others? Or maybe it was when my agent always had contracts on my desk with offers?

Either way, it's been a long time before something or *someone* has come into my life, held it in their hands, and shook it like a snowglobe. All of my thoughts about my life floating around like tiny snowflakes.

Before Cassie, it was easier to remain content and not push myself to grow. Except, that's when life loses its vibrant colors and passion fades away, leaving you stagnant. A sense of unease and discomfort often accompanies growth. So, naturally, I avoided it.

It appeased my dad. I didn't have to deal with question after question about my contracts and what was next for me. The less I had to communicate with him, the better. I thought it was healthier to ignore the problem than to try to find a solution. If I kept acting, and the films I was in did well, then I didn't have to confront my relationship with my dad. It could just be.

Cassie helped me see I don't have to be an actor to be valued. That there are people out there that love me for me. Not because I'm the son of a famed actor. Not because I can give them something.

I look at my girlfriend, who is now nestled under my arm.

After finally warming up our cold pancakes and eating breakfast, we move to the couch where we stay for hours. Her head rests on my chest. Our hands intertwine. A romantic comedy movie she picked is currently on the television.

I dip my chin and give her a kiss on the top of her head. She smiles and looks up at me.

"What's that look for?" she asks.

"I think I know how I want to announce that I'm done acting next week."

Her eyes go wide. She pushes off my chest, sitting up. She readjusts how she's sitting, tucking her legs under her butt, and placing her hands on her lap. I wait to say anything more until she is ready, because she's too cute trying to look all proper and serious.

"You ready?" I say, lifting an eyebrow.

She nods but says nothing. She's waiting for me to continue, giving me time to process. Somehow she's managed to know me better than anyone in the time that we have been dating.

I take a deep breath. "I think I want to do an interview, and I want you to be there with me."

If I thought her eyes went wide before, that was nothing, because they're currently about to fall out of their sockets. Her jaw drops. I've rendered her speechless.

I reach out with a hand, grab hers, and give it a squeeze.

My lips curl upwards into a contented smile. "Is that okay? I know it might be a little much to be in the spotlight. I know we haven't had to worry about paparazzi or anything. If I'm being honest, I haven't thought about this *at all*, so this is more of a conversation between the two of us. So, this could *easily* be not the right decision." Oh boy, I'm rambling now and talking with my free hand because she's not saying anything. She stares at me, her expression unreadable. "I promise I won't push you if you're not ready. I just figured it'd be good timing, ya know? And I'm tired of hiding you and—"

With a simple squeeze of my hand, she silences me. I drop the hand that was waving in the air like a damn inflatable arm tube man back on my lap.

Cassie takes one of her hands and cups my jaw, bringing my eyes to meet hers. "I would love nothing more than to be with you when you announce the biggest news of your career." She presses her lips to mine.

"You know, if this blows up in our faces and you leave me, I won't be able to focus very much. It would shatter my heart into a million pieces," I tease.

"Mhm, I'd be the one to crush your heart, that's for sure."

I give her one more kiss on the forehead before releasing her from our hug. "I've wanted you since the first time I saw you, Cassie, pretty sure I knew from the beginning that you'd be the death of me."

22

EMMETT

THE NEXT MORNING, WE busy ourselves with coffee and movies, enjoying each other's company. Even though Marcy and Lucy already know about us, the guys don't. And no one knows that I'm actually quitting acting. Everyone assumes the article was false, or at least they let me believe they think that.

"We have an hour until they get here," I say, standing up from the couch to grab a drink from the kitchen.

"I'm already stressing out about it." Cassie leans her head back on the couch, closing her eyes and releasing a big sigh.

I walk over from the kitchen and lean to kiss her neck from behind. "Want to go shower before everyone gets here?" I whisper in her ear. She nods.

We walk to the end of the hall and enter the bathroom. I turn on the shower, turning the knob to make the water hot but not too hot. Comfortable enough for the both of us.

The faint brush of air against my back alerts me to Cassie's presence as she steps behind me. Her hands find the bottom hem of my shirt. I lift up my hands and help her take it off. As she places her hands gently on my back, she traces small circles with her fingertips. When I turn around, I'm met with the sight of her standing there, entirely naked.

I lift an eyebrow. I don't know when she found time to do that, and she must see my shock and awe because she chuckles.

Cassie traces more circles around my chest, leaning in to leave small kisses on her trail. Her hands find the band of my pants and she tugs them down, kisses still following her every move.

Her little touches and kisses are enough to make me come, but luckily after being with her for the past month, I've kept myself together long enough to enjoy more time with her like this. Our intimacy is nothing like I've experienced.

Our emotional intimacy is so strong that it amplifies the physical attraction we have for one another. Every touch is intentional and has meaning.

Before Cassie can continue any further, I pull her back up to standing. "It pains me to say we don't have time for this, but I'd rather not be inside you when the company arrives." I give her a kiss on the nose.

She chuckles. "Fair. I guess you'll have to think of me all night until they leave, hm?" Cassie walks past me and into the shower, teasing me more than she knows just from the sight of her bare ass.

We still fool around enough in the shower and quickly get each other off before I have to remind myself we have people coming over within the hour. There's not enough time to accomplish everything I want to do to Cassie.

I want to take my time with her, memorizing every area of her body. Know all the ways to make her moan my name. *Later*.

"I'm glad I didn't scare you away that night in the diner," Cassie says to me as we dry off. She's at one sink while I'm at the other. She pulls out a hair dryer and plugs it in.

"You had me at first eye roll." I look over at her and wink.

23

CASSIE

Part of me wonders if everyone suspects Emmett and me, and the other part of me is freaking out that we're about to tell our friends we're dating. I went from not wanting anything to do with any guys, ever, to falling for Emmett. I did not see that coming. Sure, we flirted, but I thought it was harmless. I didn't want to open my heart again to the possibility of being hurt. But he just wouldn't let me go. He kept pursuing me, hanging out with me, breaking me down one wink, one touch at a time.

It was exhausting to pretend I didn't care for him, that I wasn't starting to like him. I knew he was different from the first time we met, the way he winked at me and said things to me that no other man would say. He wanted to fight back and push me to my limits. Even once I was working next to him, he wouldn't leave me alone. He was like a puppy dog, always needy and clingy and by my side.

Normally, I would hate that, but with Emmett, it was different. I wasn't any better. I just kept things hidden. He consumed my thoughts. His texts brought a smile to my face. I couldn't even contain my feelings enough because Lucy figured out I liked him from the beginning. I knew he was trouble, yet I ignored all the red flags.

I hung out with him alone. I danced with him at his birthday party. Despite everything, I don't have any regrets. Maybe I would have if things didn't go the way they are now, but I don't want to dwell on the what-ifs. I want to focus on the positive things.

The showcase on Friday surpassed all my expectations and was the best I've ever had. All of my friends were there. Friends, plural. I've had no one besides Lucy that I could rely on coming to see me. I've tried to make friends here, but no one has any time to hang out. Or at least, they don't choose you as a priority. Plus, between working and everything, I guess I didn't make it a priority either. I had Lucy and Annie, and with Annie moving here this fall, I had my little circle. I was acting well enough, and I got the job at the studio, so I felt like I was moving forward with my life.

But I wasn't. I was just comfortable with where I was at and I wasn't growing in the places that mattered. When it came to acting, I realized I wasn't pushing myself out of my comfort zone. I only accepted gigs in genres I was familiar with and felt confident I could nail effortlessly. I wanted to avoid more rejections.

I also was fine with the limited people I had around me. While I was growing up, my mom spent most of her time alone, and she appeared to handle it well. She didn't thrive all the time by any means, but she didn't seem lonely. I guess a small part of me deep down thought that since my mom was fine, I didn't need anyone either. It wasn't worth the heartbreak to find out whoever I chose wasn't in it for forever, or wouldn't want me once we had a family. I didn't want to go through what she went through, so I thought it was easier to be alone after what happened with the last person I was seeing.

Emmett is different, though, and he's proven that to me. He has layers that I would have never thought to look for. I see something new in him every day. From the way he always makes sure I eat breakfast, to how he just looks at me when we wake up in the morning. He makes me feel appreciated, wanted, safe.

Now, we just need to get through this dinner. I'm not scared anymore, though, because I trust Emmett won't treat me like the previous guy did. I know he won't leave me and I know he would stand up and defend me if anyone thinks I got a role because of him. He knows I have his back and would never use him to advance my career.

Communication is important. Without it, relationships fall apart because you're not on the same page as your partner. Communicating about each other's fears, wants, and wishes has been one of my favorite things about these past two months with Emmett.

Getting to know each other in the comfort of his apartment is something I won't take for granted. I don't think it would have been the same if our relationship was public from the beginning. We would have had a lot more to worry about. More cameras would have been around to capture our relationship, for one. For two, I think there would have been more pressure to be perfect. To have a face for our relationship, some script where we say nice things about each other.

I wonder if Emmett would have quit acting or if I would have been comfortable working with him at the studio. But again, I don't want to dwell on the what-ifs because that's not the timeline we are in.

Things happened the way they did for a reason. He came to the diner. I got a job at January Studios, and we fell for each other when we least expected it. Or at least, when I least expected it.

There's a knock on the front door that breaks my train of thought. It's probably for the best because I'll keep thinking about how perfect all of this is, and I'll start crying, and Emmett will wonder what's wrong because we have literally just been sitting here watching a movie in silence.

"I'll get it," Emmett says. He stands up and walks to the front door.

Tyler walks in. He's talking to Emmett about some movie he just watched. I swear these men are movie obsessed. He finally looks over and sees me sitting on the couch, watching him. I give a small smile and wave.

"I knew it," Tyler says. "You two *are* fucking."

Emmett laughs and I blush. Yep, pretty accurate representation of how we respond to things.

Tyler shoves Emmett's shoulder. "I had a feeling that things were about to get interesting when you brought up Marcy's new assistant in the trailer." I roll my eyes and stand up from the couch, walking over to give him a hug. "I would have stolen you for myself if Emmett didn't already stake his claim."

"Mhm, yeah, sure, that's why," Emmett says, walking to the kitchen. He opens the fridge to grab a drink for Tyler. We've talked about Tyler a lot, and we secretly think he's into Lucy. I thought there might have been something going on at Emmett's party, but she never mentioned him after that. She wouldn't hide it from me, or at least I wouldn't think so, since she knows about Emmett and me.

Max and Lane are next to arrive, driving together like always. If they notice anything, they say nothing. It could be because Tyler is already here, so maybe they just thought I also arrived here on time. Marcy shows up next, walking in with Lucy. They're chatting about Lucy's art show that will be here before we know it.

I help Emmett grab drinks and snacks for everyone. I set them on the coffee table and take a seat in one of the big chairs instead of on the couch.

"Alright, so what's the meaning of this dinner?" Marcy asks. "Not that I don't love y'all, but I had plans tonight, and Emmett made me cancel them because he said I just *had* to be here and to trust him."

Emmett looks at me, so everyone else does too. The familiar rush of nerves floods through me. I shouldn't be so nervous, considering telling them that Emmett and I are dating is small compared to telling them that Emmett is quitting acting.

We have decided to announce our relationship first because, although it will be shocking, the news that he will not act after this movie will upstage it. At least, he won't pursue any big time movies. I can see him still acting in smaller films because I know deep down he loves it.

Emmett walks over to where I'm sitting and places a hand on my shoulder. I nod in confirmation that it's time. We wanted to get it over with right away before we eat because pizza is a good way to win over all of them and apologize for hiding this from them at the same time.

"Cassie and I are dating," Emmett says. At first no one speaks. They're just staring at us, taking it in. I wonder what's going on in their heads. I know Lucy and Marcy already know, so I don't expect them to look shocked. Both of them are currently snacking and looking around at everyone else, trying to also gauge everyone's reactions.

Tyler already confirmed his suspicions. Max and Lane are going back and forth between looking at us with their jaws dropped to looking at each other with wide eyes.

"Wait, did you know?" Tyler says, looking at Marcy.

"They told me last night, but we all already knew anyway." Marcy throws a piece of popcorn in her mouth.

Tyler looks back at Emmett and says, "I can't believe you told Marcy before me."

Emmett shrugs. "We needed her to confirm Cassie's job would be safe."

"Alright, I get that," Tyler says.

I glance over at Lucy, wondering if maybe she told Tyler the truth.

"I didn't say a word. Don't look at me," Lucy mutters.

"No, Lucy didn't say anything. You two just don't hide it that well," Marcy says.

Okay, now I'm confused. I thought we were doing a great job hiding our relationship from anyone. We made sure to not spend a lot of time alone in his trailer and I barely talked to him on set.

"But why didn't any of you say anything?" I ask Marcy.

I *barely* knew Emmett and did not know if he was the guy I wanted to be serious with. I needed the time we had to confirm that what we had was something worth taking risks for. That I would be okay in a public relationship with someone who has some pull in the industry.

"I've known Emmett for most of my life and have never seen him as happy as he is now. I knew something was up when he stopped complaining about the little things and started smiling more. Laughing more. And of course, you two were eye-fucking literally all the time on set. It was getting to be annoying. All of this sexual tension because you two were trying to keep this a secret," Marcy says. She fills us in on how everyone had a hunch that we were together and just pretended with us they didn't know. Even Carla knows and said nothing. Apparently, Carla rooted for us too much. She sent me with mail to his trailer so many times, it all makes sense now. She was just meddling and knew all along that we were together.

I laugh. Emmett gives my shoulder a squeeze, which reminds me of the other news we wanted to announce.

"Well, since you all know so much about my life, I hope this doesn't come as a surprise," Emmett starts. I grab his hand and give him a squeeze. It feels good to show my affection to him now, in front of everyone. It doesn't feel as weird as I thought it would, but maybe that's because everyone seemed to already think we were together in some capacity.

Emmett takes one last deep breath. "I'm going to announce at the end of this week that I'm done acting. Or at least, not pursuing any more big roles. I want to pivot to focus on my writing."

Again, no one says anything.

Finally, Lane gets up from the couch and walks over to Emmett, who is still standing next to me.

Lane reaches out to Emmett and pulls him into a hug. "It's about damn time," he says.

Emmett chuckles. "Yeah, I know."

And that's that. What we thought was going to be a big deal turned out not to be a big deal at all. When you have people around you that care about you, you find that not much will shock them. They normally know you more than you know yourself. Like they knew that Emmett and I were together, or something of the sort. And even though everyone didn't know too much about Emmett's writing, they were more than willing to support him.

We sit and chat for a little longer about the interview that we're going to be doing later this week. Emmett still needs to work with his agent to get something scheduled, but we think it's going to be a video interview instead of a print interview.

Eventually, Tyler speaks up and lets the entire room know that he's hungry, so we all move to the dining table.

I realize at this moment, looking around the table at everyone, that this is what I've been missing. I've been missing a community of people to support and push me. After what happened, I wasn't sure if I wanted to stay here for another year. I was constantly pushing aside doubt, reminding myself that acting was my passion. It seemed like my spark was slowly fizzling out. Something that was once a passion of mine was feeling more like a chore. Then Emmett came around, and it no longer matters that my plan has failed. It no longer is my only priority to land a major role.

Now, my plan is simply to be happy and enjoy life with Emmett, however that looks for us in the future. I won't forget my dream, but I also won't let it hold me back from having a life like this, surrounded by friends.

My lips curve into a smile as I catch Emmett's eye, and he responds by smiling back at me.

I realize that regardless of how this week goes, we will be okay. All our friends are behind us. I will be there for Emmett as he announces the next chapter of his career. Even if his parents try to convince him otherwise, he will know that I am here for him. The only task left is to get through the interview.

24

CASSIE

THERE'S NOT MUCH HAPPENING during the last week of filming. Even though we aren't announcing our relationship until the weekend, I notice how everyone acts around Emmett and me.

I first notice Carla. What would have been normal to me last week is not this week. She hands me mail for Emmett's trailer and when I ask if any other trailer has mail, she says no. I wouldn't have thought much about it except for the fact that she's still smiling while looking at her keyboard. I can tell she's hiding a laugh and is acting giddy for no reason.

"Carla," I say. I put my hands on my hips and wait.

She looks up at me, her eyes widen. I might have been a little too stern when addressing her, but too late now.

"I know you know. You can drop the act."

"Hm?" she asks, looking back at her clipboard.

"I know you know about Emmett and I. You can stop pretending. It's a little obvious now that I know you know and I can't stand it." I take a seat in front of her desk, which I never do. I'm normally in and out, trying to keep my mind busy during the day at work.

Carla looks back up at me and practically slams her clipboard on her desk. She lets out the biggest sigh as if she's been holding it in all morning. "Oh thank god, I thought I was going to burst. I am not good at keeping secrets."

I laugh. "Well, unfortunately, you need to keep it a secret until Saturday. Emmett and I are doing an interview to announce it to the world."

"Okay, okay." She nods about 10 times, probably talking to herself in her head. "I can do that." She doesn't sound convincing, but if she has said nothing to me or anyone else in the past two months, I'm sure she can keep quiet for the rest of the week.

We chat for a few minutes, and I realize I don't know much about Carla because I haven't given our relationship any time to develop.

She reassures me that once we go public, nothing will happen to my job, which I already know because Marcy told me, but it's nice to hear it from her as well. I look at the clock and it's already almost nine, so I decide I should probably go check in with a few people and start the day.

I say goodbye to Carla, head downstairs, and find my way to the set. I check in with Ed to see if he needs any help with any scenes today since it's the last week. I've seen the filming schedule, and it's all over the place. The last week is for re-filming anything that was put on hold or any scenes that Ed may have reviewed and he just wasn't happy with.

After that I stop by the wardrobe department to see if they need anything. I already knew they would say no because I left that room pristine last week and set them up for success. I've come to love this job. It's been fun to get to know what goes into making a movie. I think back to my first week here, having to be an extra, and think about how much that changed the trajectory of my life.

I know Emmett coming into the diner was the start of something, but if I didn't get the job at January Studios, nothing would have happened. I wouldn't have tried to seek him out, and he wouldn't have returned to the diner that often. He likes to say he would have, if he didn't see me the next day on set, but I know how much that man loves pizza. He would always choose Al's Pizza over Dave's Diner.

My phone buzzes as I'm leaving wardrobe. I reach into my back pocket and hit the accept button, putting the phone to my ear.

"Hey Anns! On your lunch break?" I texted her last night to give her an update on what's going on with Emmett and myself and to call me, so I know that's why she's calling me right now.

"I am, yep. I cannot wait to move by you this fall. I'm soooo tired of working at this damn place," Annie says with a big sigh. She's started working at a local diner, like me, except hers is full of college students that make her want to bash her head in the wall. Her words, not mine.

I continue walking, heading to the trailers to deliver some scene changes Ed gave me when I passed him on set.

"Have you talked to Mom yet?" I ask.

"Um."

"Annie, it's already August! You're leaving next month."

"Have you told her about you and Emmett?" Annie counters.

"That's different and you know it."

"I plan to tell her at dinner tonight. Don't worry. I know I need to tell her, and I can do it by myself. I always thought I would need you as a buffer, but I've decided if she doesn't want to support me as I chase my dreams, then... I don't know what then, but if you're okay, I'll be okay, right?" Annie rambles.

"Yes, you'll be okay and I'll be here for you, always. We all know that there are a lot of opportunities out here for you to work in PR once you graduate and I think she'll feel better with you moving by me."

"Yeah, you're right." She sighs. "Thanks, Cass. Alright, I need to get back at it, but please call Mom and let her know before the interview goes live. You know she'd like to hear from you first that you're actually seeing someone."

"I know, I will. Text me later and let me know how things go with Mom."

"I'm sure she'll call you to fill you in, so you can probably use that as an opportunity to tell her the news. I'm happy for you, Cass."

Annie *would* almost make me cry this morning. "Thanks Anns."

I hang up, and somehow I've found my way to the trailers. My subconscious definitely took over while Annie was talking to me and I've delivered all the updated scenes besides Emmett's.

I'm not surprised to look up and see him standing at his trailer door. He's smiling at me, and my heart does a little tumble. He's already in his outfit for the day, a simple white button up paired with a pair of jeans. A classic look, yet I can't help but imagine taking his shirt off one button at a time...

"Are you done eye-fucking me?" he asks.

I give him an exaggerated sigh. "I have a special delivery." I walk up the stairs and give him the script updates.

"Thanks Cassie. How kind of you." Emmett winks.

"Gross, you two," Marcy says from behind. I spin around to find her standing at the bottom of the stairs, arms crossed.

"Shh, leave us alone," Emmett chimes in.

I give his shoulder a slap and then walk down the stairs to Marcy. "Have a sec?" she asks. I nod. I look back at Emmett and say goodbye, wishing him luck for his last week on set. A moment that to anyone else would look normal, since it is the last week of filming, but knowing that he's done acting means a different thing since it doubles as his last week on set for the foreseeable future. At least, the last week of his acting. He'll still be around the set, but it will be different because he's a writer of whatever film is going on. I realize I haven't even asked him what movie he's going to pursue or what next steps are for him. I don't know much about the behind the scenes of turning a script into an actual movie.

When we get back on set, Marcy stops by the snack table. This reminds me of my first week, following Marcy around trying to figure out what my job was going to entail.

She grabs a muffin, places it on a plate, and turns to face me as she takes off the muffin liner.

"Have you heard anything about the new movie being filmed after Emmett's movie ends?" she asks. She takes a bite of her muffin, briefly closing her eyes before opening them back up. It must be good to enact that kind of reaction.

"No, why?" I grab myself a muffin and take a bite. It sure is a damn good blueberry muffin.

She walks toward the hallway, so I'm assuming she's heading toward the offices. Apart from the entrance I use in the mornings, there's not much else there, so I can only guess we're going to see Carla.

Marcy explains while taking glances back every few feet to make sure I'm following her. This hallway isn't that big. I've learned to stay to one side because there is always someone running the opposite way. Sometimes it's because of a wardrobe malfunction, other times it's because Ed ordered a coffee from some assistant.

I find out from Marcy that January Studios has agreed to let an independent movie be filmed here during the three-month break between the current and the next movie. Not only that, but apparently Ed has agreed to stay on as the director, which she says never happens. We're on our way to talk to Carla because someone saw my recent showcase and wants me to star in the leading female role.

"What?" I mutter. I stop walking. Marcy takes a few more steps and when she looks back, she sees I haven't moved.

Instead of repeating herself or giving me shit for just stopping in the middle of the hallway, she walks back to me, loops an arm around mine, and pulls me forward.

"You heard me," is all she says as we walk up the stairs.

"I did." I give her my best side glare. "But I don't understand how they knew to find me here, of all places."

"Oh, don't worry about that. Just trust me, okay? It's going to be fine. You actually aren't auditioning against anyone." If that wasn't enough of a shock, she dropped my arm and headed into Carla's office. I wasn't even able to respond. She didn't turn around to see my facial expression.

I don't even get into the office before Carla is walking... wait, she's moving fast, she's speed walking toward me. "Cassie, oh thank god, I'm sorry I totally forgot to talk to you about this movie thing this morning." She hands me a folder and turns back around to walk to her desk. She said "this movie thing" like it wasn't a big deal, when in fact it is a big deal.

Marcy is already sitting in one chair in front of Carla's desk, so I move to sit in the other one. She's busy flipping through some of the top pages on her clipboard, taking her phone out to type something every few seconds.

I open the folder. I pull out the first page, which has the title of the movie on it. "A Little Bit Extra." It doesn't say who wrote it, but there's a short blurb about the film. It's written as a short film based on a true story. It's a romance, but it doesn't tell me much about the story besides the fact that it focuses on a main couple and how they slowly fall in love.

It's similar to the scene that I ended up performing at the showcase. I smile at the paper. I don't know how this happened, but I've decided I will not ask questions about it. I know that happened the last time I landed a role. It ended up terribly. Not only did I lose the part, but I shut myself off from new relationships. Without Emmett, I wouldn't have even acted in this last showcase.

I put the front page on the left side of the folder to find that there are no other pieces of paper. It's just this one page in the folder, which seems odd. I don't know why Carla didn't just hand me the piece of paper like she does every other time she needs to give me something. Instead, she made a bigger deal about this. Her love language is stationery and office supplies, so I guess it made sense to have it packaged up and in a folder. It gave me something to open, which, in return, caused my initial reaction to be for myself and not for her and Marcy.

"So?"

I look up to find Marcy staring at me. Carla is staring too, but it's Marcy who speaks.

"I mean..." I close the folder before I look back up. "The title is great and, I mean, it honestly aligns with my personality, but where is the rest? Don't I get a sample script or schedule? How does it affect my job here? I don't want to quit on you all last minute—"

Carla cuts me off. "It's all handled. Jeez, and I thought I talked a lot."

We all laugh. It's true, if I knew anyone for talking a lot, it's Carla. I'm the one with the extra personality. We know Marcy for the broody attitude, even though we know she's a softie under her shell.

We sit in Carla's office for a few more minutes talking, and I'm asking questions every other second about this film. Luckily, Carla reassures me that more information will come on Monday and I'll have a week off before filming. I let them know I need to talk to someone first. They know by "someone" I mean Emmett, but I'm still trying to be careful about saying his name here in case others are around.

I stand up to head out of the room. Marcy already handed me what I need to do for this week, mostly just tidying up and organizing, which is nothing new. I will need to find time to talk to Emmett, possibly at dinner tonight.

I walk down the stairs and take out my phone, opening the messages to my mom. The last time I texted her was for her birthday earlier this year. Her response was a simple *"thanks sweetheart."* Our relationship has gotten better over the years. I used to refuse to text her, and Annie would beg me to say hi to her over our video calls. I visited for Christmas two years back and she actually asked me about my job and seemed interested enough to talk to me. She kind of apologized about how the previous three years were, which I took as a good start. I owe it to Annie to try and reconnect. I type out a small message asking her to chat tomorrow. There, done.

Now that that's off my mind, I immediately start thinking about the acting job. I want to accept, but without receiving a lot of details, I'm not sure why they asked me to play the leading role. I know it's a short film, but I still don't understand who discovered me. It helps that it's going to take place here and Ed will be directing. That's honestly the only reason keeping me grounded with this project and has me leaning toward saying yes. If it was anywhere else, I would have a hard time accepting an undisclosed project.

I say hi to the doorman at the bottom of the stairs, turning to head down the hallway. I find Emmett on set with Max and Lane.

"Hi!" I wave to them as I walk over. They are also getting blueberry muffins. I'm not surprised since they were good. Word must have gotten around. "You guys heard about the muffins I take it?"

"Mm. So good," Lane says with his mouth full.

I respond with a laugh and a nod.

Emmett winks at me. Even though Lane and Max know about us now, we're still keeping talking in public to a minimum.

"So, last week on set, huh?" Max says to the group.

"I'm excited. This film schedule has been exhausting," Emmett replies. He turns back to the food table, grabbing another muffin. He gestures to me with it, and I nod. I definitely want half of that.

I was going to ask them if they knew anything about the new movie being filmed here, but Ed walks up and joins the conversation. Then I think maybe I shouldn't if it's not supposed to be public yet. So I stand there and talk with them about the week ahead before I decide to check things off my list.

Moving about the day is simple. By the time lunch rolls around, I find a seat across from Tyler in the cafeteria.

"Hi!" I set my tray on the table and take a seat. "Your day going okay?"

He nods, his mouth full of whatever the sandwich of the day is. "Busy, but that's pretty normal for it being the last week. What about you?"

"Eh, doesn't feel too bad. Just a lot of running around, making sure everyone else is all set, you know?"

"Yeah, I get that."

We talk about our weekends and what else we did after we all hung out. I'm not surprised to hear that what we did was similar; a movie marathon and lots of snacks. Eventually Lane joins us, sitting next to Tyler, and he fills us in on some casting issue that I honestly can not sum up because I have learned to zone out. There is always some sort of casting issue, so I've learned it's best to just listen and nod.

Max comes next and takes a seat next to me. He's on the phone with someone, but when we ask him who it is, he just waves us away. Lane says it's some new girl he met the other day, and that gets a glare from Max. It's most definitely a girl.

Marcy joins us, but she doesn't sit. She's always on the move, so she stands at the end of the table saying her hellos. She leaves just as fast as she came muttering something about needing to grab a sandwich on the way out. I tell her I'll text her later. She gives me a thumbs up. I want to let her know I want to do the movie, but not until I talk with Emmett first.

Eventually, Emmett wanders over and sits on my other side. He leans over and bumps my shoulder with his. I do the same back.

It's nice like this. Most days are like this, actually. Sometimes I see everyone at lunch and we get a few minutes to chat and catch up about the latest studio gossip. Other times people come and go, but at least I see everyone during the day.

January Studios has become a home for me. Or at least the people here have made it that way. It doesn't feel like I'm working most of the time, and it definitely makes me grateful that I accepted a position I wasn't even interested in to begin with.

I try to live in the present, but when I look around at this table and see Emmett, Max, Lane, and Tyler laughing and talking about some memory, I'm blessed to have met them all.

I figure I should get back to things, since we have been sitting in the cafeteria for over an hour. I know their schedules are pretty loose, but I have a list of things I need to get done before I'm able to leave today.

I get up and say my goodbyes, receiving waves and "see ya laters" in response.

My phone buzzes when I reach the doors to the trailers. I place my tray by a trash can and pull my phone out of my pocket as I push open the doors to the outside.

Emmett

6 days until I can kiss you in public and let the world know you're mine.

I sigh and smile. The world will soon discover that Emmett is no longer acting and that we are in a relationship. I'm not as nervous about that as I am about his parents' reaction. I don't let that take over my thoughts right now. No, right now I smile at my phone knowing that I've managed to not only land a role as a lead actor, but find someone who believes in me and likes me for me. Just when I was starting to come to terms with the fact that I may have to make some changes in my life, I'm about to check off the remaining item on my plan.

25
EMMETT

AFTER SEEING CASSIE ACT in her showcase, I *knew*, 100%, that my script had to be turned into a film. Why? Well, it's our love story. The problem is, I wasn't sure how to go about doing that. I knew actors got movies made all the time, but I didn't want just anyone making this movie. I wanted it to be filmed at January Studios, my home studio.

Everything needed to happen quickly. I needed to figure out my next move prior to the interview, so I asked the one person I knew could help me for assistance.

Ed.

Ed has been there for me, frequently, over the years. Even before I signed on for these last two movies, we knew each other just from being in the same circles. He has always rooted for me.

I asked him to come to my trailer early Monday morning, knowing that I would have a few minutes before I saw Cassie for the day. When I told him my idea, he sat there and listened, not saying anything the entire time, besides humming here and there.

When I asked him if he knew anyone I could talk to, he made the most surprising proposal. He mentioned he was looking for a short movie to produce and direct, since the next movie being filmed at the studio wasn't for another three months.

I was *speechless.*

He called Carla, gave her the heads up to set up some meetings for him, and told me we would talk more details later this week once they wrote the paperwork up. I had to ensure it was okay if I wanted Cassie to be the main actress, to which he responded with one request: that I act alongside her. Our chemistry is what will sell the movie.

He couldn't have said anything else to convince me otherwise.

So, that's how I took a tiny script and landed a deal with January Studios. The short film is expected to last around 30 to 40 minutes, including credits and all.

My mental load is lighter. The last week on set is normally quite emotional, but knowing that I get to stay here with my girl, I'm not sad. Instead, I'm looking forward to the coming weeks as we finalize everything and get started on the film.

I'm keeping my fingers crossed Cassie will say yes. I don't want her to think that I handed her this role. It's important to me she knows she's earned it, considering the effort she has invested, this is the reward she deserves. If only to see her smile, I would give her this role and more.

It wasn't even my original idea to ask Cassie. I knew she had an issue with past relationships, and I didn't want to cross a line by asking her to act in a role that was based on our relationship. The movie will follow our so-called "meet cute" and the development of our relationship over the weeks, filled with our secret dating and sneaking around. Max was the one who suggested Cassie when I showed him the script a few weeks back. Of course, this was before I decided to quit acting, when I was just throwing around the idea of getting the script produced.

I was glad that a few others could see Cassie when she performed both as an extra and at her showcase. Her ability to connect to a character on an emotional level and step into their shoes is unbelievable, and I'm hoping she will say yes to being a part of this.

I think she will. Once she arrives at my apartment, which will be any minute now, she'll definitely bring it up to me. I've asked that it's not revealed that it's my movie, I want to save that for the interview. She needs to understand first that we offered the role to her because of her ability to act, not because of me.

A knock comes from the front door before Cassie comes striding through it. She walks over to me and gives me a kiss.

"Hi. I've been itching to do that all day." She walks back over to the front door, taking off her shoes and setting her purse down. She's started keeping clothes and necessary items here, so she doesn't even bring an overnight bag anymore.

I've been wanting to ask her to move in, but I know she loves living with Lucy, and we can't take that next step until we're public and all is well with that. It would just cause extra eyes to be on our relationship before we're ready.

"Something on your mind?" I ask. Cassie is practically pacing the apartment. She stops mid-stride and looks at me with a curious eye.

"Hm, yes, *Igotofferedajobasaleadingactress.*"

I walk over to her and take her hand in mine. "If I understand your gibberish, you said you got offered a role? Is that right? When?"

"This morning."

Cassie fills me in on what happened this morning. She tells me about how Carla apparently already knew about us and how Carla handed her a folder with nothing but a title page. How Marcy and Carla wouldn't tell her anything but asked for her trust. No, she knows nothing; she swears. We end up sitting at the island to keep talking about the movie and what little she knows about it. I make us tea, since that's part of our thing. We sip the hot drinks while chatting some more and she lets me know Annie is telling their mom about her upcoming move to LA.

"Wait, Annie is telling your mom tonight?"

Cassie nods. She takes a sip of her tea, closing her eyes to relish in the warmth and comfort it's bringing her at this moment.

"Well, okay, then you telling her you're doing the movie will put a nice little bow on things and she will forget all about Annie leaving her."

"I didn't say I was taking the movie," she says mid-sip, cup still inches from her mouth.

I dip my head and uptick my brows in question.

Cassie sighs. "Okay, fine, yes, I'm accepting the job. I knew I would accept it this morning, but wanted to talk to you first about it. I wanted you to know that I would be there for you after the interview on Saturday and offer to go somewhere or do something with all the free time we'll have. I didn't want to be the person to force us to remain in the same spot because I—"

I cut her off. "Sass, you should know that I'm proud of you." I let go of my mug and place my hand on her left thigh. I give her one squeeze before returning my hand to the cup. "I'm more than thrilled to support you and be there for you while you film this. This is your dream. Maybe I'll even hang out on set with you, ya know, keep you company. It'll be you now with a trailer." I wink at her.

She laughs.

"I didn't think about having my own trailer. Okay, fair. Well, just know whatever you want to do with your writing, I'll support you."

She's already helped me more than she knows. Not only has she been my muse while writing this script, she has given me the courage to face my parents and chase my dream. It's only natural for me to want to help her achieve hers.

We talk for a while about the most random topics. We chat about the upcoming holidays, and I learn about what her family does to celebrate. I find out that she broke her arm in the third grade from jumping too high on a trampoline, which I tell her is cliche. I tell her about the time I got caught trying to sneak into a rated R movie when I was 12, one downside to having a famous dad. With every question she asks, I delve deeper into my past, painting a picture of my childhood experiences. We don't normally talk about my parents, because it's never a fun topic for me, but after she met them this past weekend, I find myself wanting to tell her more, so she understands why our relationship is the way it is.

We find our way into the bedroom after we finish our tea. Our conversation trails us as we get ready for bed together like we have done for the past two months.

Lying in bed, Cassie turns toward me to speak, her voice soft and gentle. "How do you think your dad will respond to Saturday?"

That's the number one question in my mind, too.

"I don't know." I roll over onto my back and look up at the ceiling. To ease my mind, I pause and take a deep breath. "I want to think that he'd be proud of me, you know?" I roll back over to face Cassie. "I've actually found my own thing and I love it. I love writing. I love acting too, but it's not the same. Acting has always felt like something I had to do because of my dad. That because it was his thing, I had to follow in his footsteps. When I met other writers at a young age, they inspired me to write my first script. It was terrible, but I didn't expect to love it so much."

"Why do you love writing?" Cassie asks. Not in a judgemental way, but because she's curious.

"Writing started as my escape. I found freedom in writing. I got lost writing about these fictional characters and I could step into their shoes and pretend to be them. Even if it was for a little while, I didn't have to be Emmett, son of a famous Hollywood actor. I think it helped me heal from whatever fucked up childhood I lacked."

"I get that. Well, I don't know how Saturday will go, but we can't control that. All we can control is right now, the present."

I don't have time to respond before Cassie pushes me onto my back and straddles me.

She leans and places her lips on mine. I grab her hips and kiss her back with passion and intention. Cassie's hands trail my arms until they wrap behind my head.

Her head leans to the side, begging for our kiss to deepen. I answer by shoving my tongue in her mouth, tracing and memorizing.

Cassie moves her hips forward and backward, rocking on my now-hard cock. A small moan escapes her lips, and my hands tighten on her hips in response. I want more.

She must want more too because she breaks apart our kiss and scoots off my lap. Her hands reach for the band of my pants and she pulls. I lift my butt up with enough room for her to slide my pants and underwear down. She stops once my cock springs free from my underwear, grabbing it with her right hand. Gradually, her hand moves up and down, the rhythm matching the beat of my racing heart.

I lean my head back, resting it for a moment on the headboard. A sharp exhale escapes my lips as her tongue traces the head, sending shivers down my spine. Little circles, enough to drive me insane. I'm about ready to tell her I need more when she takes more of my length into her mouth.

I lean forward, stretching my arm to grab her head, begging her to move faster. Cassie's touch becomes more intense as she massages my balls with her left hand while engulfing me. I let out a soft moan, unable to contain my pleasure.

"Cassie," I say. I need her to stop before I come in her mouth.

She looks up at me with only her eyes, my cock still in her mouth.

"My turn."

With one last downward and upward motion, she lets go of my cock. With a gentle tug on her hands, I pull her toward me, positioning myself beneath her. I reposition us so that I'm the one on top. Using my hands, I trail her body and lower her pants to her ankles. She reaches to grab the bottom hem of her shirt, pulls it up over her head, and throws it on the ground.

My hands instinctively reach up, tracing the curves of her hips, moving upwards toward her chest, and gliding back down. Cassie reaches toward me to grab the bottom hem of my shirt and tugs upwards, so I help her by taking it off.

"Tell me what you want," I whisper into her ear.

"You," she whispers back.

I glide down her body, positioning myself near her legs. Placing one hand on both knees, I put a little bit of pressure on them to get her to open up. I hook my hands around her knees and pull her forward so she's in the middle of the bed, giving me more access to her pussy.

I lean and place soft kisses in the sensitive area between her thighs, shifting sides until I settle between her legs. Cassie's right hand rests gently on her breast, while her other hand tangles in my hair. I use my tongue to pleasure her, her hips arching in response to the sensations. With each moan, her voice trembles, and my name escapes her lips in a soft whimper. I slide one finger inside, followed by another, causing her breath to grow heavier in response.

"Come for me, baby," I say and return my mouth to her. Following the rhythm of her breaths, I pick up my pace and observe her slowly unraveling. Her hand gets caught in my hair and tugs on it gently. My pace slows and her breath gradually returns to a steady rhythm. I lean up and press my lips against hers, the softness and warmth anchoring me. The night is just getting started.

I lean over to grab a condom from the nightstand. Cassie takes it from me, opens it, and slides it down my length.

"I need to be inside you," I groan.

Cassie scoots back toward the headboard, laying on her back, waiting patiently.

I press my hand to the outside of her left leg, applying pressure to get her to turn over. "Flip over, Sass."

"So demanding." She wiggles her eyebrows, teasing me, but she rolls over. She lifts onto her knees, her chest still laying on the bed.

I position the tip where she needs it most and slowly push into her, the sound of our breaths interwoven like threads. No matter how hard I try to maintain a slow pace, she presses against me, provoking me to pick up speed. My left hand explores her body, while the other finds its place on her slit, responding to the ebb and flow of her breaths.

"Emmett," Cassie sighs, her voice filled with both fatigue and relief.

When we finish, we take the time to clean up before snuggling back into bed, intertwining in each other's embrace.

"You know, I never thought I could have something like this," I say to her, my head propped up on my arm, my elbow resting on the mattress. Cassie is laying on her back, her head tilted in my direction.

"Why do you say that?"

"Growing up, my parents..." I pause, adjusting to lie fully on my side, moving my arm to be underneath my head. "I didn't have a lot of love at home. It was a lot of public love, but nothing in the privacy of our home. We didn't eat dinner as a family, we didn't take vacations unless it was for the media, and they never cared to ask what I wanted to do with my life. I suppose I never thought I could have love like this." I bite my lip. "I guess what I'm trying to say is, I am completely and utterly in love with you." With my thumb, I gently stroke her jaw, back and forth.

Cassie leans in toward me, pressing her lips to mine. "I love you too, *Hotshot*."

I playfully push her away, our laughter blending with the sound of our conversation as we unravel the depths of each other.

26
CASSIE

My phone ringing awakens me from my peaceful slumber. I open my eyes to find Emmett no longer beside me. I squeeze my eyes shut, then open them wide to try and wake myself up. Neither of us have to be at the studio until 11, so we definitely took advantage of that *and* each other last night.

I roll over to my left side, facing the nightstand, to find "Mom" on my phone display. Ugh. I don't even know what time it is.

I click accept. I was going to talk to her today anyway, might as well be now, before I forget to call her.

"Hi, Mom." I yawn.

"Cassie. Am I waking you up?"

"I mean, yeah—"

"Good!" My mom cuts me off. "When were you going to tell me about Annie?"

She's angry. I'm not surprised. If I found out my last child was not only leaving the house to go to college, but doing so over 2,000 miles away, I would also feel a bit hurt and enraged.

"Um." I sit up and rub my eyes with the heel of my palms. I'm in desperate need of a caffeine boost in the form of a steaming cup of coffee. "What about Annie?" I try to play dumb.

My mom sighs. "Annie is moving by you. You're both going to be too far from me. What are we going to do for the holidays?"

"Annie is chasing her dream, Mom, just like I chased mine. She needed to tell you herself. It wouldn't have been any better coming from me." I shift so I'm facing the side of the bed, placing both feet on the ground. I make my way to the kitchen, greeted by the warm glow of the morning light streaming through the window. "And for the holidays, I don't know. We can still come to you or you could come visit over here. Depends if you want sunshine or snow."

She sighs again. I enter the kitchen to find Emmett by the stove, making eggs. He glances in my direction, and I mouth that I'm currently speaking with my mom. Nodding, he reaches for a coffee mug and pours it full to the brim for me. Oh, this man. How did I get so lucky? I mouth the words "thank you" before settling into my seat at the island.

Something changed between us last night. The thought of living without Emmett is no longer an option for me. I take this time to stare at him a little longer while my mom rambles on about Annie. He's wearing one of my favorite outfits, his bare chest is exposed and gray sweatpants hang low on his hips. In my mind, I visualize myself ending the call with my mom, moving toward Emmett, taking hold of his hand, and kneeling in front of him.

It's like he hears my thoughts because as my gaze travels up his back, he turns around and meets my gaze. He smirks at me, a hint of amusement in his face. That jerk.

"Cassie? You still there?" Oh right, shit. I swivel the stool around so I'm facing away from Emmett. I can't pay attention with him standing there, taunting me with his body after the night we shared.

"Yeah, Mom, sorry. What was the last thing you said?"

"I said that at least you're out there to watch her and take care of her if she needs something. I was angry at first. Not because she was moving out, but mad at myself because she thought she couldn't talk to me about this. I just wasn't ready to be alone yet."

It had always been the three of us. Since I moved away, it has been just the two of them. Mom tried hard to get Annie to stay. She found special programs and paid for her to pursue unpaid internships in the city. She went on trips with her to help her not feel stuck, hoping she would choose to attend a local university. In the end, Annie still wanted to get out and experience somewhere else.

I don't blame her. I did the same. Mom will be okay. Lonely for a bit, maybe, but she will adjust. She knows that. She just needs some reassuring that we will come home.

"Well, we could start doing more regular FaceTime chats and maybe when Anns gets here, I can plan a visit back home with her. Maybe in the fall? I might bring my…" I hesitate for a minute. Glancing over my shoulder, Emmett's eyes are locked on me, his coffee mug cradled in his hands. He's supporting me while also giving me the opportunity to chat with my mom.

"Bring who, Cassie?"

"My boyfriend. I'd like you to meet my boyfriend, Emmett." Emmett smiles at me. I turn back around to face the living room again.

"Oh, Cassie, that's great. I know we haven't had the best relationship these past few years, but I'm happy for you."

I'm happy for myself too.

We chat for a few more minutes as I tell her about the interview on Saturday and that she can't go posting things on Facebook yet until that's live. She understands, thankfully, but that doesn't stop me from reminding her one more time before we hang up. We promise to talk a little more, and try to strengthen our relationship. We'll see.

"I'm assuming Annie told your mom?" Emmett asks from behind my shoulder.

I nod and swivel back around to face him. Emmett gestures for my mug with the coffee pot, seeing that I already need a refill. I slide my mug toward him.

"Yeah, went about as well as I expected," I tell him. It's the truth too. Mom took the news okay and, like Annie predicted, was in a better mood after I told her about Emmett and the interview.

Emmett walks around the island and presses a kiss on my forehead. "Good. I'm going to get ready for the day. Feel free to come join me." He winks, knowing that I will most definitely be joining him in the shower.

We still need to drive to the studio separately, so I arrive before him. I go to find Carla, like normal, and begin my tasks for the day. The interview this weekend has me so on edge that my mind feels occupied, leaving no room for other thoughts. The interview itself doesn't make me nervous; I just have to hold Emmett's hand. No one should even prompt me to speak. I am nervous about Emmett's parents and what will come from them. Emmett doesn't want to talk about it. He always just says *'Whatever it is, we will handle it together.'*

My feet carry me to the cafeteria without me realizing it. I take my phone out of my pocket and it is indeed lunch. I open the door and find Lucy sitting at a table with Lane and Max at the back of the cafeteria. She's facing the wall, so she doesn't see me, but Lane and Max do, so they wave at me to come to them.

As a result, Lucy turns around. Her eyes light up with joy as she catches sight of me, prompting her to stand up and make her way toward me. She greets me with a warm hug, her cheerful "hello" filling the air as we make our way back to the table where Max and Lane sit.

Once we sit down, I turn to Lucy. "What are you doing here?"

"After you texted me about the movie, I wanted to congratulate you in person and I had about an hour to kill until I had to be at the diner."

Right, I accepted the role in the movie this morning. Carla's response was unsurprising; she informed me she had already accepted the role on my behalf, fully expecting my agreement. She's not wrong. We have a group chat with the seven of us: me, Emmett, Lucy, Tyler, Max, Lane, and Marcy. I let the group know I accepted the role in the movie via text. I had to follow up with a brief explanation because Lane, Tyler, and Max did not know I was even offered the role. They were in the same boat as me, knowing about the movie because of their job, but still in the dark.

"Oh, thanks. I still don't know much about it, but Carla assured me I'll know soon." I'm beginning to suspect that Carla is the only one who knows anything about this movie, and she's not saying a word.

After lunch, I walk Lucy out of the cafeteria.

I give her a hug. "Thanks for stopping by Luce, it means a lot. And we will hang out soon, okay? I promise."

"I know. Okay, well, I have to go before Dave calls my phone and asks where I'm at."

I give her one last hug and wave goodbye as she gets in her car and drives across the street to the diner.

I head back inside the studio to complete my tasks for the day.

The rest of the week is the same. Same routine, different day. Each night I go over to Emmett's and we do a little bit of preparing for the interview. I'm thankful because I'm getting more nervous as Saturday comes closer.

When Saturday comes up in our nightly conversations, we talk about the kinds of things that might come up in the interview. He tells me they might ask my opinion on a few things. What are these things? When I ask, he says they might ask about our relationship or how I feel about him quitting acting.

If I can get through it without passing out or cursing, then I call it a success.

I've been texting my mom and Annie more often this week, too. My mom is already trying to plan for when we can all see each other, even though we literally just talked about it the other day. Annie is planning to move here within the next few weeks before her semester starts in September, so we talk about that. I already plan to help her move in and get settled. I tell her Emmett already has Max, Lane, and Tyler looped in, so we have extra hands.

We lay in bed Friday night and I can't help but think about how much my life is about to change.

The world is about to know about Emmett and me. The world is about to know about me, little old me, who apparently is starring in some new short film. That won't be in the interview, since it's about Emmett, but they will ask about his writing and what he plans to do next. Emmett still hasn't told me anything about what his current project is. I know he has something in the works and his schedule is going to get busy again, but he won't tell me more. He deflects and kisses me, which I want to say I'm strong enough to resist, but once his lips hit mine, I'm a goner. I figure he will tell me when he wants, and for now I'll enjoy him and his body and all the fun things we do in the late hours of the night.

I never knew I'd find someone who completes me the way Emmett does. He likes to rub it in my face that he knew from the moment he laid eyes on me I was meant to be his. I like to tell him he's full of shit, which always causes us to laugh because we know it's me that's full of shit. He knows now how painful it was for me to resist him. Even though I tried hard to keep my heart closed and push him away, it didn't work.

In the end, he wore me down enough to find his way into my life. Little by little, without me noticing, he found a little space to occupy in my brain and now I can't imagine my days without him. When you find someone you love, it's as if the world suddenly becomes brighter and more vibrant. When you think about what you'll be doing a year from now, you're no longer alone. In those dreams, it's never just you; it's always the two of you, intertwined.

I'm not scared of a lot of things, but I am scared for our relationship to change. When we become public, we will have less privacy and the world will think they know us. Emmett has been doing a great job of preparing me for a life where cameras follow us constantly. There are ways to be private, like now in his apartment, but whenever we travel or leave the house, we will always be in the public eye.

We'll adapt though, I'm confident about that. There is one detail that I am sure of—Emmett's love for me is everlasting, and my love for him knows no bounds.

Emmett is holding me, my back to his chest. His lips brush my ear as he leans closer. "I know your mind is going a hundred miles an hour right now, but try to get some sleep. We have our first date tomorrow night. I love you." He plants a kiss on my cheek and settles back on his pillow.

"I love you too," I reply and smile. Our first date, I almost forgot. With this past week being super hectic and the interview in the morning, it slipped my mind that Emmett wants to take me somewhere public for our first official date.

That night, I dream about our first date and wake up the next morning brimming with excitement to shout to the world my love for Emmett Davis and how proud I am of him for pursuing his dreams.

27
EMMETT

THE MORNING GOES BY in a blur. Cassie is already stressing out, even though she's trying her best to hide it. After asking me for the 5th time if she curled every piece of her hair, I knew she was getting stressed out about this interview.

I did my best to reassure her, but I also know that she has every right to be stressed out about today. It's going to change a lot for us. She doesn't even know that I'm going to announce the movie yet. I want that to be a surprise. I hope she doesn't slap me while we're filming.

We agreed to do the interview at the studio since it's where we both spend most of our time. Being the primary filming location for my movies, it's the ideal place to symbolize the closure of one chapter and the exciting beginning of another.

We still arrive separately, just in case we have any lurkers outside the studio with cameras. I find Cassie exploring the set inside, her footsteps echoing in the empty space. Even in its stripped-down state, Ed's chair remains a focal point in the center of the room.

A warm smile graces her lips as she spots me coming toward her.

"You ready for this?" Cassie asks. Before the person interviewing us arrives, I lean to plant a soft kiss on her lips.

"I should have done this a while ago, so yes, I'm ready." She nods because she's the only one who truly understands. I rarely open up about my parents, but Cassie's probing questions have shed light on why I chose to pursue acting. She also knows that without her helping me work through my past and question my career, I wouldn't be doing this interview. I wouldn't be quitting acting, and I sure as hell would not be making a movie next week.

That last part she still doesn't know, but soon she will. It'll be the last question that gets asked in the interview. To avoid any surprises, I took the responsibility of approving the questions for today. I knew the interviewer would bring up the movie and prompt Cassie to share her thoughts. We have done a bit of preparation, but her response will be unscripted and in the moment.

I'm being a little selfish with wanting her to be a part of the movie. The prospect of being on set together, collaborating, and bringing art to life fills me with excitement and fulfillment.

Finding Cassie was never in my plan. I didn't know what I was going to do after this movie, but I just figured I'd sign some other contract to appease my dad and keep him off my back. Sometimes I fantasized telling him I've had enough and being truthful about what I want to do. But then he'd encourage me to take a deal or my mom would call and talk to me about acting. I didn't have someone on my side, not like Cassie is. My friends have always been supportive, but I haven't been as open with them about how unhappy I am as I should be.

Today that changes. Within the next hour, everyone will know that I'm done acting.

The person interviewing us walks in, accompanied by two others. One person handles the camera, while the other person takes care of the audio. The interviewer offers a warm smile, extends her hand, and introduces herself as Mia. In order to conduct this live interview, we only need a small crew.

Cassie and I sit next to each other and Mia is across from us. I reach over the arm of the chair separating Cassie from me and intertwine my fingers with hers. She looks over, her eyes meeting mine, and gives me a nod and a small smile, letting me know she's ready.

The interview begins.

"So, Emmett, first off. Thank you for letting us do this exclusive interview with you. I know you don't do a lot of them, so thank you for giving us the honor." I nod. "Now, let's start by talking about the lovely lady sitting next to you. I want to get into your current movie, but I know viewers are probably dying to hear who she is." Mia pauses to let me respond.

Cassie and I prepared for most of these questions, so we knew this one was first. I give Cassie's hand one squeeze.

"Of course, yes, this is—" I look over at Cassie and back over at Mia, "Cassie. My girlfriend."

"Lovely! So the rumors a few months back were true, huh?" Mia raises her eyebrows. I chuckle.

"Well, at the time, Cassie and I weren't together. We were truly just friends, but over time we became more. We wanted to wait until after the movie to announce our relationship."

"Cassie, how was it keeping things private? How do you feel about your relationship being made public?"

I look at Cassie and smile, a sense of unwavering support evident in my eyes, letting her know she's got this.

"Keeping things private was intentional. We didn't know where things were going to go, and workers aren't allowed to have relationships with actors for that reason. Things go wrong, actors getting distracted, you know, so we kept things private and allowed our feelings to develop naturally. We had a few articles that tried to make our relationship public before we were ready, but we got through it together." Cassie looks over at me and smiles, squeezing my hand once. "Now, I'm more than ready to announce our relationship. Over the past few months, I've gotten to know Emmett, genuinely know Emmett, and I love him."

Mia grins.

"I love you too," I say and lean over and plant a kiss on her cheek.

"Gosh, you two are adorable. Okay, let's switch gears a bit. Emmett, you had something you want to announce. Is that right? Is it what movie you're acting in next?" Mia asks. I didn't disclose the purpose of this interview to her, but since I rarely do interviews, the content didn't matter to them.

"Actually, Mia. The opposite." I let my words sink in before I continue. I can see the confusion on Mia's face. She keeps opening and shutting her mouth, but no words form. "I am stepping away from acting and shifting my focus toward a career in writing."

Mia's jaw drops, but she quickly closes her mouth once she remembers we are live. She's as stunned as I expect the rest of the people watching to be. I can already picture my dad pacing his room, getting ready to give me an earful. I sent my parents the interview link, and told them I had an announcement. My dad obviously took that as something different, thinking I was announcing my next movie like Mia did, but I didn't bother correcting him.

"Not acting? Well, that's one way to make this weekend more exciting," Mia says joyfully. We all laugh a little. "Well, Emmett, if you're not acting and instead writing, what is next for you? Do you plan to write movies instead?"

"I do. With Cassie's love and support, I've decided to stop pretending and start chasing my dream, which is not acting. I want to write. So, I did just that. I wrote a movie. The movie's plot, which is inspired by a true story, holds a special place in my heart."

I can feel Cassie's penetrating stare, but I resist the temptation to look back at her. Not yet. I keep my eyes on Mia, waiting for her to ask her next question.

"Can you share anything about this movie?" Mia says, sounding way more excited than before if that's possible. This interview has evolved from being an exclusive interview with me to announcing some of the top news in Hollywood. Her company is going to be thrilled with the amount of traffic they'll get after this.

"Yes, thank you for asking. So this movie is a romance movie. It's about a couple that goes through life searching for love, acceptance, and understanding. They end up finding it in each other and fall in love over a short period. It's called *A Little Bit Extra,* and we start filming next week."

"What?" Cassie says and then covers her mouth with her free hand. "Sorry, Mia."

I give her hand a squeeze and look at her this time. She has a look on her face that I enjoy, slightly irritated, slightly amazed, but mostly surprised.

"Wow, that's so soon, Emmett. Well, I can't wait to hear more about it. Tell me, do you have a cast yet?" Mia asks.

"We set the cast. Cassie is playing the lead role, and I will actually act alongside her. It's our story."

Cassie's hand goes back over her mouth.

"Cassie, I can see from your expression that this is news to you. If you don't mind me asking, can I get your thoughts on what Emmett just talked about? It looks like you didn't know about the movie?"

Cassie's hand slowly leaves her mouth. She looks at me once, gives my hand a squeeze, and returns her gaze back to Mia.

"I knew about the movie. Well, I knew they cast me as the lead in *A Little Bit Extra.* I knew the plot, to an extent. It's honestly why I accepted the role. They only gave me the title page and a short synopsis of the movie. They didn't even give me a script. But, after reading about it, I could envision myself being a part of this movie. I related to the main character in a way I couldn't understand, and now I know why. Because it's my, *our*, story."

"That's great, Cassie. Well, thank you both for sharing your story with me and the rest of the people tuning in right now. Emmett, I wish you the best on this new journey and can't wait to see your film. You can count on me to be there when it premieres." The interview is over. Cassie remains silent until Mia and her crew pack up and leave.

"You're in trouble, Emmett Davis," Cassie says. My gaze meets hers and I'm met with her intense stare and defensive stance, arms crossed firmly over her chest.

"Oh, come on, Cass, you can't be mad at me."

Cassie is trying extremely hard to hide the smile that's appearing beneath her fake frown.

"Why didn't you tell me it was your movie?" she asks.

"You wouldn't have accepted the role if you knew from the beginning. I wanted you to know that you got the role because of your talent, not because of me. It was important to me that you knew how ridiculously talented you are. You deserve the world, Cassie. I just wanted to help move the needle and give you an opportunity to chase your dream. You've given me so much these past few months and have asked for nothing in return."

I walk up to her and stand a foot away. I tip my jaw down and give her my best puppy dog face, earning me a chuckle. She steps forward and throws her arms around me.

"You're the worst," Cassie says into my chest.

"You love me."

"Yes, I love you."

Cassie looks up and I meet her halfway to press my lips against hers.

My phone buzzes in my back pocket. I sigh and reach around to grab it. It's my dad. I'm not surprised. I honestly thought he was going to call as soon as the interview was over, so giving me 10 minutes is a record.

"You don't have to answer it," Cassie says, and I know she's right, so I press the decline button.

If my parents want to support me and my writing, that's a decision they will make over time.

"Want to talk about it?" Cassie asks.

I shake my head. With our first date on the horizon, I don't want to delve into it. When I have the love of my life standing in front of me, I don't need to think about my parents. She's the one who's given me the courage to face my past and look at my future. Cassie reaches out with her hand, intertwining her fingers with mine.

The world now knows that I'm done acting. They know about Cassie and I.

We don't have to hide anymore, and I feel so relieved.

We walk hand in hand out of the set doors to find our friends waiting by Cassie's car.

"So, your movie, huh?" Tyler walks up to me and gives me a hug.

"It appears that way." I smile.

We walk a few steps over to the rest of the group. Everyone comes up to me to congratulate me on my career change, the movie, Cassie. It's a lot. I didn't expect to become an emotional person today, but having formed my own chosen family, I have a lot to be grateful for.

Three months ago, I didn't know where my life was headed. Then one evening, a little sassy woman by the name of Cassie flipped my world upside down. All it took was one look from her and I knew I was a goner.

I shift my gaze toward her, taking in her presence. She's deep in conversation with Marcy. They're talking about something, their laughter bubbling up and filling the silence.

Walking over to her, I lean in close, my lips almost brushing against her ear as I whisper softly, "Let's go, Sass. We have a date to get to."

A warm smile spreads across her face.

We say goodbye to everyone and get into Cassie's car. I settle into the driver's seat and reach over to gently rest my hand on her thigh.

We pull out of the parking lot and I can see the sign of the diner flickering in the distance, inviting us in for a meal.

"We're here," I say and look over at her.

Cassie's gaze finds mine, and I am drawn into the depths of her piercing blue eyes.

The diner is the place where we began. We didn't quite know where our relationship would end up, but I knew from meeting her I couldn't let her go. The pull between us was too great to ignore. I know she feels the same way based on the way she's looking at me, her gaze filled with unspoken emotions.

What started as a friendship blossomed into something neither of us saw coming. The tension between us kept escalating, like a rubber band stretched to its breaking point, until it finally snapped. Now, it is impossible for either of us to dream up a life that doesn't include the other.

The girl who was once an extra has become a permanent character in my life story, and I've fallen in love with her.

I gently grasp her hand and bring it to my lips, planting a soft kiss on her palm.

"Let's do this, shall we?"

With a playful grin, she leans over the middle console, her lips gently brushing against mine.

"Let's."

28

EPILOGUE: CASSIE

TWO YEARS LATER

"Cassie, you have 10 more minutes before we leave," Emmett calls from down the hall. I stand in the bathroom and stare at my reflection in the mirror, making sure every detail on my face is perfect.

It's been two years since we announced Emmett's movie, our movie, to the world. After filming *A Little Bit Extra*, we took a month's break to do some traveling before my next project. I accepted a role in the next movie being filmed at January Studios, wanting to stay there as long as I could. Working there as an actress has been a dream, and they have a wide range of films, which is great because I get to have a resume of movies from different genres.

Emmett has written a few more scripts that are in the works to be produced. January Studios now exclusively consults Emmett when a new movie wants to use their set to film. He's gone back to acting in some minor roles, but only if he *genuinely* wants to.

We have our movie premiere tonight, and it'll be the first red carpet I've been able to be on.

"Cassie, seriously, we need to go. The car is—damn, Sass, you look beautiful." I turn around to see Emmett staring at me.

I'm wearing a dark blue, floor-length dress. A slit runs up the right leg, which is honestly my favorite part. I have meticulously styled my hair, using several bobby pins to secure it, and deliberately leaving certain strands to frame my face. For my makeup, I've gone for a natural look, but I couldn't resist adding a pop of color with a bold red lip. It's become my go-to as of late.

I lean against the bathroom counter and look at Emmett. Starting at his shoes, I trail my gaze upward. To complement my dress, he has chosen to wear a pair of dark blue pants paired with a white button-up shirt, leaving the top two buttons unfastened. He looks incredibly handsome.

"Enjoying the view?" He smirks.

"Very much." I smile and walk toward him. "Let's go, we're going to be late." I drag out the word 'late' to tease him, and he rolls his eyes.

"Annie is going to give you more shit than I will, so prepare for that. She's all PR lady now that she's interning for that firm, and it thrilled them to get a pass for tonight's event." Emmett fills me in as we walk to the car.

Annie moved out here two falls ago to start at UCLA and she's since gotten an internship at a PR agency. So, when I was asked who represents me, I naturally chose my sister, even though she didn't hold a formal position at that time. Annie has been great at helping me keep my social media in check and has helped with brand opportunities. I don't think she needs to stay in college, but she wants the degree and experience, which I understand.

Mom has been out to visit twice, and she's coming tonight, so it'll be a fun family reunion after the movie.

Our limo arrives at The Regency Theater. Outside my door, there is a long red carpet, flanked by photographers capturing every moment.

I'd like to pretend that I'm comfortable with the constant spotlight, but truthfully, it still unnerves me. I have come a long way since two years ago. The number of people around me now, since I started dating someone as famous as Emmett, is unlike anything I've experienced before. We have actively avoided events like tonight for this reason, and Emmett has always expressed his dislike for them.

With a single squeeze, Emmett lets go of my hand. He steps out and walks around to open my door. He opens the door and extends his hand. "Ready, Cass?" He smiles.

I return the smile and place my hand in his. "Ready."

A chorus of shouts bombard us, each person trying to catch our gaze when we step out of the car. We walk down the red carpet and the sound of clicking heels and murmurs of excitement fill the air. To make it to my seat without any mishaps,

I have to concentrate on smiling and taking measured steps, being cautious not to trip over my high heels or the flowing fabric of my dress.

We approach the door to the theater. Emmett abruptly stops walking and pulls on my hand, urging me to pause.

When I turn around, I am taken aback to see Emmett not only stopped on the red carpet but down on one knee, a crowd of onlookers gasping in anticipation.

"Cassie." He gives me a huge grin.

I shake my head, a small chuckle escapes my lips as I return the smile. What is this man doing? I cannot believe, wait yes I can, I can believe that he would want to do this in front of so many people. He's loved that our relationship has been public and takes all opportunities to let everyone know how much he loves me after being forced to hide it for two short months.

"From the moment I saw you, I knew you were meant to be mine. It's not every day I meet someone who's as sassy as you are." We both laugh. "I didn't expect to meet my best friend and partner that night in the diner. Without being drug out of my room, I would never have predicted how much you were going to rock my world. Every time I saw you, I had to resist the pull between us. That was until you started looking at me. Touching me. Giving me more opportunities to be near you. We once acted in a scene together, and even though it was practice, I knew at that moment that I fell in love with you. You're it for me, Cass. It's you and me. So, would you do me the honor of being my wife and marrying me?"

As payback for doing this in front of one hundred cameras, I give him a minute to sweat. I can see the panic setting in as he glances nervously at the ring and back to me. He tilts his head, and that's when I know it's been long enough. I give him the answer he wants.

"Yes." I nod, and in an instant, Emmett is on his feet, his lips pressing against mine, leaving me breathless.

Screaming and cheering fills the air around us. Once I finally break away from Emmett, I notice our friends and family waving and clapping. Everyone is here. Further down the red carpet, Lucy, Tyler, Lane, Max, Marcy, Carla, and Annie are all beaming with excitement and waving. Our parents are also here, both of us having done some work to repair the relationships and boundaries. We still have room to grow, but at least everyone is supportive of our endeavors.

"You just had to do this in public, hm?" I whisper in Emmett's ear.

"I did. Tonight's important. It's the first time our movie is being shown to the world, and I wanted everyone to know that you're going to be mine for forever. Our movie is only the beginning of our story. We still have a long way to go until it ends." Emmett leans closer to me, and I eagerly meet him halfway, our lips pressing together.

Just as I predicted, the movie was wonderful. I didn't know how I would feel watching myself on a big screen. I've waited to watch anything from this movie because I wanted to see it for the first time with Emmett.

From start to finish, the movie revolves around my perspective and my relentless pursuit of living a life of stardom on the big screen.

When I look at Emmett, I can't help but notice his piercing gaze, never wavering from my own. I then notice his lips subtly moving, silently reciting the words that effortlessly shattered my defenses and led me to willingly embrace the idea of loving him.

"It was always going to be this way. You and me, you know? I always knew it'd be the two of us in the end."

Acknowledgements

THANK YOU. You've made my year by choosing to read my debut novel. When I started reading again at the beginning of '23, I decided to start a Bookstagram account. Little did I know, I'd discover indie authors, best friends, and a new dream.

I want to first thank Kristen for being the best writing partner and friend. Without our weekly writing sessions and constant encouragement, this book would not be what it is today. I'm thankful to be on this journey with you!

To Beth, I'm so glad our paths crossed. Thank you for taking a chance on my debut and for helping me make this story better. I appreciate you so much.

Lindsay, because of you, Emmett and Cassie are visualized in my brain. Thank you for working your magic and creating a cover that's perfect.

To my "Bookish Babes," thank you for answering my questions, hyping up my books, and being there for me.

To my beta readers, thank you for putting in time to read and provide feedback on this story.

Thank you to everyone in my local literary community, especially the friends I've made from Silent Book Club and the Sugar and Spice book club.

To all my author friends, I could not do this without you.

And finally, I want to thank my lovely husband. From listening to me talk about my stories, to encouraging my writing sessions, you're always there for me. I love you.

About the Author

Courtney Corlew lives in the Midwest with her husband, Ryan, and their two kids. When she's not writing, she's reading (like everyone else) and spending time in coffee shops and bookstores around the city. She looks forward to writing many more stories filled with dreams, love, and friendship. To stay up to date, follow her on Instagram @courtneycorlewauthor or visit her website www.courtneycorlewauthor.com.

www.ingramcontent.com/pod-product-compliance
Lightning Source LLC
Chambersburg PA
CBHW032010310726
48972CB00002B/347